THE STAR CHAMBER VOL-I

By

WILLIAM HARRISON AINSWORTH

The Star Chamber Vol-I
By William Harrison Ainsworth

Copyright © 2023

All Rights reserved.
No part of this publication may be reproduced, stored in a retrieval system, or transmitted in any form or by any means, electronic, mechanical, photocopying or Otherwise, without the written permission of the publisher.

The author/editor asserts the moral right to be identified as the author/editor of this work.

ISBN: 978-93-57273-20-6

Published by

DOUBLE 9 BOOKS
2/13-B, Ansari Road, Daryaganj
New Delhi – 110002
info@double9books.com
www.double9books.com
Tel. 011-40042856

This book is under public domain

HarperCollins *Publishers* India

At HarperCollins India, we believe in telling the best stories and finding the widest readership for our books in every format possible. We started publishing in 1992; a great deal has changed since then, but what has remained constant is the passion with which our authors write their books, the love with which readers receive them, and the sheer joy and excitement that we as publishers feel in being a part of the publishing process.

Over the years, we've had the pleasure of publishing some of the finest writing from the subcontinent and around the world, including several award-winning titles and some of the biggest bestsellers in India's publishing history. But nothing has meant more to us than the fact that millions of people have read the books we published, and that somewhere, a book of ours might have made a difference.

As we look to the future, we go back to that one word— a word which has been a driving force for us all these years.

Read.

About the Author

D<small>R</small> T.P. Deshpande is a former associate professor and head of department, Hindi and Postgraduate Research Centre, Pratibha Niketan College, Nanded. He completed his M.S. (Education) from S.P. College, Pune, and postgraduation from Poona University. He received his doctorate from Marathwada University, Aurangabad.

After retirement in 2003, he studied astrophysics and the Vedas under the guidance of Dr V. R. Parnerkar, his Divine Guru.

He is the author of textbooks on language and literature for undergraduate and postgraduate. He mentors students of Hindi literature and philosophy as a research guide. He has also completed Minor and Major Research Projects of University Grants Commission, New Delhi.

He is the member of Indian Philosophical Congress, Asian Philosophical Congress and World Congress of Philosophy (WCP) and actively participated in its conferences.

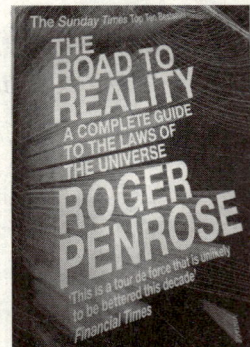

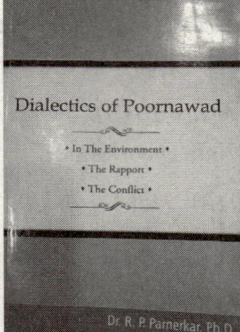

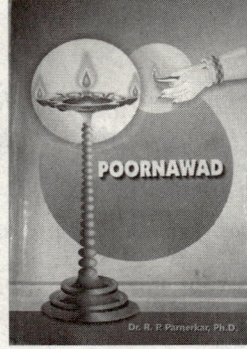

Penrose, Roger (2005). The Road to Reality, London: Vintage Books.

Radhakrishna, S. (2014). The Principal Upanishads. Noida: HarperCollins Publishers India.

Raju, P.T. (2007). Introduction to Comparative Philosophy. Delhi: Motilal Banarasidass Publishers.

Ranade, R.D. (1986). A Constructive Survey of Upanishadic Philosophy. Mumbai: Bhartiya Vidya Bhavan.

Russel, Bertrand (2010). History of Western Philosophy. London: George Allen and Unwin Ltd.

Venkataramiah, Munagala (2010). Talks with Sri Ramana Maharshi. Tiruvannamalai: Sri Ramanasramam.

Verma, Meera Devi (2012). Hinduism and Christianity. Ranchi: Ashish Publications.

Woods, Alan and Grant, Ted (2014). Reason in Revolt: Marxist Philosophy and Modern Science. New Delhi: Aakar Books.

Walsch, Neale Donald (1995). Conversations with God. London: Hodder & Stoughton.

Yogananda, Sri Sri Paramahansa (1998). Man's Eternal Quest and Other Talks. New Delhi: Oxford and IBH Publishing Co. Pvt. Ltd.

Yogananda, Sri Sri Paramahansa (2011). Journey to Self-Realization. Kolkata: Yogoda Satsanga Society of India.

Durant, Will (2006). The Story of Philosophy. New York City, NY: Pocket Books.

Durant, Will (2015). The Case for India. Mumbai: Strand Book Stall.

Kumthekar, Uday (2007). Samkhya Darshan (Marathi). Pune: Prasad Prakashan.

Kumthekar, Uday (2007). Uttar Mimansa (Marathi). Pune: Prasad Prakashan.

Kumthekar, Uday (2007). Yog Darshan (Marathi). Pune: Prasad Prakashan.

Kumthekar, Uday, Gangakhedkar, Kishor, and Deshpande, T.P. (2016). 'Summary Presentation'. First International Poornavad Philosophy Conference. Nanded: Aditya Publications.

Kumthekar, Uday (2007). Vaisheshik Darshan (Marathi). Pune: Prasad Prakashan.

Malhotra, Rajiv (2016). Indra's Net: Defending Hinduism's Philosophical Unity. Noida: HarperCollins Publishers India.

Masih, Y. (2010). A Comparative Study of Religions. Delhi: Motilal Banarasidass Publishers.

Masih, Y. (2010). Introduction to Religious Philosophy. Delhi: Motilal Banarasidass Publishers.

Parnerkar, Gunesh (2015). Proceedings of Round Table on Poornavad Philosophy. XXIII World Congress of Philosophy-2013, Athens. Nanded: Aditya Publications.

Parnerkar, R.P. (2002). Poornavad. Pune: Vimal Prakashan.

Parnerkar, R.P. (2009). Humanism. Pune: Vimal Prakashan.

Parnerkar, R.P. (2010). Dialectics of Poornavad. Pune: Vimal Prakashan.

Parnerkar, R.P. (2010). Parichay (Marathi). Pune: Vimal Prakashan.

Parnerkar, R.P. (2010). Prasadik Owibaddha Sagun Charitra (Marathi). Pune: Vimal Prakashan.

Parnerkar, R.P. (2010). Saarth Abhinav Abhang. Pune: Vimal Prakashan.

Parnerkar, V.R. (2011). Poornavad Prabodh (Marathi). Pune: Vimal Prakashan.

Parnerkar, V.R. (2016). Poornavad: Reinterpretation of Indian Philosophy. New Delhi: New B.B.C. Publishers.

Bibliography

Belsare, S. K. (2017). *Dnyaneshwari – Nirupan, Vol. 9.* Mumbai: Raykar R.G.

Blavatsky, H.P. (2001). *Gems of the East.* Rochester, UK: Grange Books, PLC.

Blavatsky, Madame (2016). *A Spiritual Adventure in India.* Walnut, CA: Mt. San Antonio College, Philosophy Group.

Capra, Fritjof (2010). *The Tao of Physics.* Colorado: Shambhala Publications.

Chopra, Anu (2019). *Altituainis: Seekers, Sinners & Secrets.* Ahmedabad; Multipen Publishers.

Engels, Frederick (1974). *Dialectics of Nature.* Moscow: Progress Publishers.

Holger, Kersten (2001). *Jesus Lived in India.* New Delhi: Penguin Books India.

Ferguson, Naill (2012). *Civilization.* London: Penguin Books.

Ingle, S.G. (2009). *A Way to Heart of the Rigveda.* Baltimore, MD: Publish America.

Joshi, Tarkateerth Laxman Shastri (2001). *Development of Indian Culture: Vedas to Gandhi.* Translated by S.R. Nene. Mumbai: Lokvangmaya Gruha.

Kamtikar, Anagha Ajit (2012). *Vardhishnu,* Pune: Vimal Prakashan.

Kumthekar, Uday (2007). *Nayay Darshan (Marathi).* Pune: Prasad Prakashan.

Kumthekar, Uday (2007). *Purva Mimansa (Marathi).* Pune: Prasad Prakashan.

ABOUT THE AUTHOR

A 19th-century English historian and author, William Harrison Ainsworth studied law and worked in the publishing industry along with journalism and literature. William Harrison Ainsworth wrote more than 39 novels on various topics. William Harrison was educated at Manchester Grammar School. Some of his best and most well-known novels are The Tower of London (1840), Windsor Castle (1843), The Lancashire Witches (1848), and Old St. Paul's (1841). He was a well-trained lawyer, but he was uninterested in the profession, so he gave up and decided to devote himself to the world of writing. Ainsworth's first success as a writer came with his work "Rookwood" in 1834, and he last appeared in the year 1881.

CONTENTS

CHAPTER I.
THE THREE CRANES IN THE VINTRY. 7

CHAPTER II.
SIR GILES MOMPESSON AND HIS PARTNER. 14

CHAPTER III.
THE FRENCH ORDINARY. 20

CHAPTER IV.
A STAR-CHAMBER VICTIM. 26

CHAPTER V.
JOCELYN MOUNCHENSEY. 31

CHAPTER VI.
PROVOCATION. 35

CHAPTER VII.
HOW LORD ROOS OBTAINED SIR FRANCIS MITCHELL'S
SIGNATURE. 40

CHAPTER VIII.
OF LUPO VULP, CAPTAIN BLUDDER, CLEMENT LANYERE,
AND SIR GILES'S OTHER MYRMIDONS. 44

CHAPTER IX.
THE LETTERS-PATENT. 48

CHAPTER X.
THE 'PRENTICES AND THEIR LEADER. 61

CHAPTER XI.
JOHN WOLFE. 66

CHAPTER XII.
THE ARREST AND THE RESCUE... 71

CHAPTER XIII.
HOW JOCELYN MOUNCHENSEY ENCOUNTERED A MASKED
HORSEMAN ON STAMFORD HILL. 80

CHAPTER XIV.
 THE MAY-QUEEN AND THE PURITAN'S DAUGHTER. 90
CHAPTER XV.
 HUGH CALVELEY. 99
CHAPTER XVI.
 OF THE SIGN GIVEN BY THE PURITAN TO THE
 ASSEMBLAGE........ 102
CHAPTER XVII.
 A RASH PROMISE 108
CHAPTER XVIII.
 HOW THE PROMISE WAS CANCELLED. 113
CHAPTER XIX.
 THEOBALDS' PALACE.. 119
CHAPTER XX.
 KING JAMES THE FIRST. 131
CHAPTER XXI.
 CONSEQUENCES OF THE PURITAN'S WARNING. 140
CHAPTER XXII.
 WIFE AND MOTHER-IN-LAW. 149
CHAPTER XXIII.
 THE TRESS OF HAIR... 158
CHAPTER XXIV.
 THE FOUNTAIN COURT. 168
CHAPTER XXV.
 SIR THOMAS LAKE.. 171
CHAPTER XXVI.
 THE FORGED CONFESSION.. 178
CHAPTER XXVII.
 THE PURITAN'S PRISON.. 187
CHAPTER XXVIII.
 THE SECRET. 191
CHAPTER XXIX.
 LUKE HATTON.. 196

CHAPTER I.
THE THREE CRANES IN THE VINTRY.

Adjoining the Vintry Wharf, and at the corner of a narrow lane communicating with Thames Street, there stood, in the early part of the Seventeenth Century, a tavern called the Three Cranes. This old and renowned place of entertainment had then been in existence more than two hundred years, though under other designations. In the reign of Richard II., when it was first established, it was styled the Painted Tavern, from the circumstance of its outer walls being fancifully coloured and adorned with Bacchanalian devices. But these decorations went out of fashion in time, and the tavern, somewhat changing its external features, though preserving all its internal comforts and accommodation, assumed the name of the Three Crowns, under which title it continued until the accession of Elizabeth, when it became (by a slight modification) the Three Cranes; and so remained in the days of her successor, and, indeed, long afterwards.

Not that the last-adopted denomination had any reference, as might be supposed, to the three huge wooden instruments on the wharf, employed with ropes and pulleys to unload the lighters and other vessels that brought up butts and hogsheads of wine from the larger craft below Bridge, and constantly thronged the banks; though, no doubt, they indirectly suggested it. The Three Cranes depicted on the large signboard, suspended in front of the tavern, were long-necked, long-beaked birds, each with a golden fish in its bill.

But under whatever designation it might be known—Crown or Crane—the tavern had always maintained a high reputation for excellence of wine: and this is the less surprising when we take into account its close proximity to the vast vaults and cellars of the Vintry, where the choicest produce of Gascony, Bordeaux, and other wine-

growing districts, was deposited; some of which we may reasonably conclude would find its way to its tables. Good wine, it may be incidentally remarked, was cheap enough when the Three Cranes was first opened, the delicate juice of the Gascoign grape being then vended, at fourpence the gallon, and Rhenish at sixpence! Prices, however, had risen considerably at the period of which we propose to treat; but the tavern was as well-reputed and well-frequented as ever: even more so, for it had considerably advanced in estimation since it came into the hands of a certain enterprising French skipper, Prosper Bonaventure by name, who intrusted its management to his active and pretty little wife Dameris, while he himself prosecuted his trading voyages between the Garonne and the Thames. And very well Madame Bonaventure fulfilled the duties of hostess, as will be seen.

Now, as the skipper was a very sharp fellow, and perfectly understood his business—practically anticipating the Transatlantic axiom of buying at the cheapest market and selling at the dearest—he soon contrived to grow rich. He did more: he pleased his customers at the Three Cranes. Taking care to select his wines judiciously, and having good opportunities, he managed to obtain possession of some delicious vintages, which, could not be matched elsewhere; and, with this nectar at his command, the fortune of his house was made. All the town gallants flocked to the Three Cranes to dine at the admirable French ordinary newly established there, and crush a flask or so of the exquisite Bordeaux, about which, and its delicate flavour and bouquet, all the connoisseurs in claret were raving. From, midday, therefore, till late in the afternoon, there were nearly as many gay barges and wherries as lighters lying off the Vintry Wharf; and sometimes, when accommodation was wanting, the little craft were moored along the shore all the way from Queenhithe to the Steelyard; at which latter place the Catherine Wheel was almost as much noted for racy Rhenish and high-dried neat's tongues, as our tavern was for fine Bordeaux and well-seasoned pâtés.

Not the least, however, of the attractions of the Three Cranes, was the hostess herself. A lively little brunette was Madame Bonaventure, still young, or, at all events, very far from being old; with extremely fine teeth, which she was fond of displaying, and a remarkably neat ankle, which she felt no inclination to hide beneath the sweep of her round circling farthingale. Her figure was quite that of a miniature

Venus; and as, like most of her country-women, she understood the art of dress to admiration, she set off her person to the best advantage; always attiring herself in a style, and in colours, that suited her, and never indulging in an unwarrantable extravagance of ruff, or absurd and unbecoming length of peaked boddice. As to the stuffs she wore, they were certainly above her station, for no Court dame could boast of richer silks than those in which the pretty Dameris appeared on fête days; and this was accounted for by reason that the good skipper seldom returned from a trip to France without bringing his wife a piece of silk, brocade, or velvet from Lyons; or some little matter from Paris, such as a ruff, cuff, partlet, bandlet, or fillet. Thus the last French mode might be seen at the Three Crowns, displayed by the hostess, as well as the last French entremet at its table; since, among other important accessories to the well-doing of the house, Madame Bonaventure kept a chef de cuisine—one of her compatriots—of such superlative skill, that in later times he must infallibly have been distinguished as a cordon bleu.

But not having yet completed our description of the charming Bordelaise we must add that she possessed a rich southern complexion, fine sparkling black eyes, shaded by long dark eye-lashes, and over-arched by jetty brows, and that her raven hair was combed back and gathered in a large roll over her smooth forehead, which had the five points of beauty complete. Over this she wore a prettily-conceived coif, with a frontlet. A well-starched, well-plaited ruff encompossed her throat. Her upper lip was darkened, but in the slightest degree, by down like the softest silk; and this peculiarity (a peculiarity it would be in an Englishwoman, though frequently observable in the beauties of the South of France) lent additional piquancy and zest to her charms in the eyes of her numerous adorers. Her ankles we have said were trim; and it may be added that they were oftener displayed in an embroidered French velvet shoe than in one of Spanish leather; while in walking out she increased her stature "by the altitude of a chopine."

Captain Bonaventure was by no means jealous; and even if he had been, it would have mattered little, since he was so constantly away. Fancying, therefore, she had some of the privileges of a widow, our lively Dameris flirted a good deal with the gayest and handsomest of the galliards frequenting her house. But she knew where to stop;

no licence or indecorum was ever permitted at the Three Cranes; and that is saying a great deal in favour of the hostess, when the dissolute character of the age is taken into consideration. Besides this, Cyprien, a stout well-favoured young Gascon, who filled the posts of drawer and chamberlain, together with two or three other trencher-scrapers, who served at table, and waited on the guests, were generally sufficient to clear the house of any troublesome roysterers. Thus the reputation of the Three Cranes was unblemished, in spite of the liveliness and coquetry of its mistress; and in spite, also, of the malicious tongues of rival tavern-keepers, which were loud against it. A pretty woman is sure to have enemies and calumniators, and Madame Bonaventure had more than enow; but she thought very little about them.

There was one point, however, on which it behoved her to be careful: and extremely careful she was, — not leaving a single loop-hole for censure or attack. This was the question of religion. On first taking the house, Madame Bonaventure gave it out that she and the skipper were Huguenots, descended from families who had suffered much persecution during the time of the League, for staunch adherence to their faith; and the statement was generally credited, though there were some who professed to doubt it. Certain it was, our hostess did not wear any cross, beads, or other outward symbol of Papacy. And though this might count for little, it was never discovered that she attended mass in secret. Her movements were watched, but without anything coming to light that had reference to religious observances of any kind. Those who tried to trace her, found that her visits were mostly paid to Paris Garden, the Rose, and the Globe (where our immortal bard's plays were then being performed), or some other place of amusement; and if she did go on the river at times, it was merely upon a party of pleasure, accompanied by gay gallants in velvet cloaks and silken doublets, and by light-hearted dames like herself, and not by notorious plotters or sour priests. Still, as many Bordeaux merchants frequented the house, as well as traders from the Hanse towns, and other foreigners, it was looked upon by the suspicious as a hotbed of Romish heresy and treason. Moreover, these maligners affirmed that English recusants, as well as seminary priests from abroad, had been harboured there, and clandestinely spirited away from the pursuit of justice by the skipper; but the charges were never substantiated, and could, therefore, only proceed from envy

and malice. Whatever Madame Bonaventure's religious opinions might be, she kept her own council so well that no one ever found them out.

But evil days were at hand. Hitherto, all had been smiling and prosperous. The prospect now began to darken.

Within the last twelve months a strange and unlooked for interference had taken place with our hostess's profits, which she had viewed, at first, without much anxiety, because she did not clearly comprehend its scope; but latterly, as its formidable character became revealed, it began to fill her with uneasiness. The calamity, as she naturally enough regarded it, arose in the following manner. The present was an age of monopolies and patents, granted by a crown ever eager to obtain money under any pretext, however unjustifiable and iniquitous, provided it was plausibly coloured; and these vexatious privileges were purchased by greedy and unscrupulous persons for the purpose of turning them into instruments of extortion and wrong. Though various branches of trade and industry groaned under the oppression inflicted upon them, there were no means of redress. The patentees enjoyed perfect immunity, grinding them down as they pleased, farming out whole districts, and dividing the spoil. Their miserable victims dared scarcely murmur; having ever the terrible court of Star-Chamber before them, which their persecutors could command, and which punished libellers—as they would be accounted, if they gave utterance to their wrongs, and charged their oppressors with mis-doing,—with fine, branding, and the pillory. Many were handled in this sort, and held up in terrorem to the others. Hence it came to pass, that the Star-Chamber, from the fearful nature of its machinery; its extraordinary powers; the notorious corruption and venality of its officers; the peculiarity of its practice, which always favoured the plaintiff; and the severity with which it punished any libelling or slanderous words uttered against the king's representative (as the patentees were considered), or any conspiracy or false accusation brought against them; it came to pass, we say, that this terrible court became as much dreaded in Protestant England as the Inquisition in Catholic Spain. The punishments inflicted by the Star-Chamber were, as we learn from a legal authority, and a counsel in the court, "fine, imprisonment, loss of ears, or nailing to the pillory, slitting the nose, branding the forehead, whipping of late days,

wearing of papers in public places, or any punishment but death." And John Chamberlain, Esq., writing to Sir Dudley Carlton, about the same period, observes, that "The world is now much terrified with the Star-Chamber, there being not so little an offence against any proclamation, but is liable and subject to the censure of that court. And for proclamations and patents, they are become so ordinary that there is no end; every day bringing forth some new project or other. As, within these two days, here is one come forth for tobacco, wholly engrossed by Sir Thomas Roe and his partners, which, if they can keep and maintain against the general clamour, will be a great commodity; unless, peradventure, indignation, rather than all other reasons, may bring that filthy weed out of use." [What, would be the effect of such a patent now-a-days? Would it, at all, restrict the use of the "filthy weed?"] "In truth," proceeds Chamberlain, "the world doth even groan under the burthen of these perpetual patents, which are become so frequent, that whereas at the king's coming in there were complaints of some eight or nine monopolies then in being, they are now said to be multiplied to as many scores."

From the foregoing citation, from a private letter of the time, the state of public feeling may be gathered, and the alarm occasioned in all classes by these oppressions perfectly understood.

Amongst those who had obtained the largest share of spoil were two persons destined to occupy a prominent position in our history. They were Sir Giles Mompesson and Sir Francis Mitchell,—both names held in general dread and detestation, though no man ventured to speak ill of them openly, since they were as implacable in their animosities, as usurious and griping in their demands; and many an ear had been lost, many a nose slit, many a back scourged at the cart's tail, because the unfortunate owners had stigmatized them according to their deserts. Thus they enjoyed a complete immunity of wrong; and, with the terrible court of Star-Chamber to defend them and to punish their enemies, they set all opposition at defiance.

Insatiable as unscrupulous, this avaricious pair were ever on the alert to devise new means of exaction and plunder, and amongst the latest and most productive of their inventions were three patents, which they had obtained through the instrumentality of Sir Edward Villiers (half-brother of the ruling favourite, the Marquess of Buckingham)—and for due consideration-money, of course,—for

the licensing of ale-houses the inspection of inns and hostelries, and the exclusive manufacture of gold and silver thread. It is with the two former of these that we have now to deal; inasmuch as it was their mischievous operation that affected Madame Bonaventure so prejudicially; and this we shall more fully explain, as it will serve to show the working of a frightful system of extortion and injustice happily no longer in existence.

By the sweeping powers conferred upon them by their patents, the whole of the inns of the metropolis were brought under the control of the two extortioners, who levied such imposts as they pleased. The withdrawal of a license, or the total suppression of a tavern, on the plea of its being a riotous and disorderly house, immediately followed the refusal of any demand, however excessive; and most persons preferred the remote possibility of ruin, with the chance of averting it by ready submission, to the positive certainty of losing both substance and liberty by resistance.

Fearful was the havoc occasioned by these licensed depredators, yet no one dared to check them—no one ventured to repine. They had the name of law to justify their proceedings, and all its authority to uphold them. Compromises were attempted in some instances, but they were found unavailing. Easily evaded by persons who never intended to be bound by them, they only added keenness to the original provocation, without offering a remedy for it. The two bloodsuckers, it was clear, would not desist from draining the life-current from the veins of their victims while a drop remained. And they were well served in their iniquitous task,—for the plain reason that they paid their agents, well. Partners they had none; none, at least, who cared to acknowledge themselves as such. But the subordinate officers of the law (and indeed some high in office, it was hinted), the sheriff's followers, bailiffs, tipstaves, and others, were all in their pay; besides a host of myrmidons,—base, sordid knaves, who scrupled not at false-swearing, cozenage, or any sort of rascality, even forgery of legal documents, if required.

No wonder poor Madame Bonaventure, finding she had got into the clutches of these harpies, began to tremble for the result.

CHAPTER II.
SIR GILES MOMPESSON
AND HIS PARTNER.

Madame Bonaventure had already paid considerable sums to the two extortioners, but she resisted their last application; in consequence of which she received a monition from Sir Giles Mompesson, to the effect that, in a month's time, her license would be withdrawn, and her house shut up, unless, in the interim, she consented to make amends to himself and his co-patentee, Sir Francis Mitchell, by payment of the sum in question, together with a further sum, equal to it in amount, by way of forfeit; thus doubling the original demand.

Our pretty hostess, it would seem, had placed herself in an awkward predicament by her temerity. Sir Giles was not a man to threaten idly, as all who had incurred his displeasure experienced to their cost. His plan was to make himself feared; and he was inexorable, as fate itself, to a creditor. He ever exacted the full penalty of his bond. In this instance, according to his own notion, he had acted with great leniency; and certainly, judged by his customary mode of proceeding in such cases, he had shown some little indulgence. In this line of conduct he had been mainly influenced by his partner, who, not being insensible to the attractions of the fair hostess, hoped to win her favour by a show of consideration. But though Madame Bonaventure was willing enough, for her own purposes, to encourage Sir Francis Mitchell's attentions (she detested him in her secret heart), she by no means relied upon him for security. A more powerful friend was held in reserve, whom she meant to produce at the last moment; and, consequently, she was not so ill at ease as she otherwise would have been, though by no means free from misgiving.

Sir Giles Mompesson was a terrible enemy, and seldom thwarted in his purpose. That she knew. But no man was more keenly alive to

his own interest than he; and she persuaded herself he would find it to his advantage not to molest her: in which case she was safe. Of Sir Francis Mitchell she had less apprehension; for, though equally mischievous and malevolent with his partner, he was far feebler of purpose, and for the most part governed by him. Besides, she felt she had the amorous knight in her toils, and could easily manage him if he were alone.

So the case stood with respect to our pretty hostess; but, before proceeding further, it may be well to give a more complete description of the two birds of prey by whom she was threatened with beak and talon.

The master-spirit of the twain was undoubtedly Sir Giles Mompesson. Quick in conception of villainy, he was equally daring in execution. How he had risen to his present bad eminence no one precisely knew; because, with the craft and subtlety that distinguished him, he laid his schemes so deeply, and covered his proceedings with so thick a veil, that they had been rarely detected. Report, however, spoke of him as a usurer of the vilest kind, who wrung exorbitant interest from needy borrowers, — who advanced money to expectant heirs, with the intention of plundering them of their inheritance, — and who resorted to every trick and malpractice permitted by the law to benefit himself at his neighbour's expense. These were bad enough, but even graver accusations were made against him. It was whispered that he had obtained fraudulent possession of deeds and family papers, which had enabled him to wrest estates from their rightful owners; and some did not scruple to add to these charges that he had forged documents to carry out his nefarious designs. Be this as it may, from comparative poverty he speedily rose to wealth; and, as his means increased, so his avaricious schemes were multiplied and extended. His earlier days were passed in complete obscurity, none but the neediest spendthrift or the most desperate gambler knowing where he dwelt, and every one who found him out in his wretched abode near the Marshalsea had reason to regret his visit. Now he was well enough known by many a courtly prodigal, and his large mansion near Fleet Bridge (it was said of him that he always chose the neigbourhood of a prison for his dwelling) was resorted to by the town gallants whose necessities or extravagance compelled them to obtain supplies at exorbitant interest. Lavish in his expenditure on

occasions, Sir Giles was habitually so greedy and penurious, that he begrudged every tester he expended. He wished to keep up a show of hospitality without cost, and secretly pleased himself by thinking that he made his guests pay for his entertainments, and even for his establishment. His servants complained of being half-starved, though he was constantly at war with them for their wastefulness and riot. He made, however, a great display of attendants, inasmuch as he had a whole retinue of myrmidons at his beck and call; and these, as before observed, were well paid. They were the crows that followed the vultures, and picked the bones of the spoil when their ravening masters had been fully glutted.

In the court of Star-Chamber, as already remarked, Sir Giles Mompesson found an instrument in every way fitted to his purposes; and he worked it with terrible effect, as will be shown hereafter. With him it was at once a weapon to destroy, and a shield to protect. This court claimed "a superlative power not only to take causes from other courts and punish them there, but also to punish offences secondarily, when other courts have punished them." Taking advantage of this privilege, when a suit was commenced against him elsewhere, Sir Giles contrived to remove it to the Star-Chamber, where, being omnipotent with clerks and counsel, he was sure of success, — the complaints being so warily contrived, the examinations so adroitly framed, and the interrogatories so numerous and perplexing, that the defendant, or delinquent, as he was indifferently styled, was certain to be baffled and defeated. "The sentences of this court," it has been said by one intimately acquainted with its practice, and very favourably inclined to it, "strike to the root of men's reputations, and many times of their estates;" and, again, it was a rule with it, that the prosecutor "was ever intended to be favoured." Knowing this as well as the high legal authority from whom we have quoted, Sir Giles ever placed himself in the favoured position, and, with the aid of this iniquitous tribunal, blasted many a fair reputation, and consigned many a victim of its injustice to the Fleet, there to rot till he paid him the utmost of his demands, or paid the debt of nature.

In an age less corrupt and venal than that under consideration, such a career could not have long continued without check. But in the time of James the First, from the neediness of the monarch himself, and the rapacity of his minions and courtiers and their satellites, —

each striving to enrich himself, no matter how—a thousand abuses, both of right and justice, were tolerated or connived at, crime stalking abroad unpunished. The Star-Chamber itself served the king as, in a less degree, it served Sir Giles Mompesson, and others of the same stamp, as a means of increasing his revenue; half the fines mulcted from those who incurred its censure or its punishments being awarded to the crown. Thus nice inquiries were rarely made, unless a public example was needed, when the wrongdoer was compelled to disgorge his plunder. But this was never done till the pear was fully ripe. Sir Giles, however, had no apprehensions of any such result in his case. Like a sly fox, or rather like a crafty wolf, he was too confident in his own cunning and resources to fear being caught in such a trap.

His title was purchased, and he reaped his reward in the consequence it gave him. Sir Francis Mitchell acted likewise; and it was about this time that the connection between the worthy pair commenced. Hitherto they had been in opposition, and though very different in temperament and in modes of proceeding, they had one aim in common; and recognizing great merit in each other, coupled with a power of mutual assistance, they agreed to act in concert. Sir Francis was as cautious and timid as Sir Giles was daring and inflexible: the one being the best contriver of a scheme, and the other the fittest to carry it out. Sir Francis trembled at his own devices and their possible consequences: Sir Giles adopted his schemes, if promising, and laughed at the difficulties and dangers that beset them. The one was the head; the other the arm. Not that Sir Giles lacked the ability to weave as subtle a web of deceit as his partner; but each took his line. It saved time. The plan of licensing and inspecting taverns and hotels had originated with Sir Francis, and very profitable it proved. But Sir Giles carried it out much further than his partner had proposed, or thought prudent.

And they were as different in personal appearance, as in mental qualities and disposition. Mompesson was the dashing eagle; Mitchell the sorry kite. Sir Francis was weakly, emaciated in frame; much given to sensual indulgence; and his body conformed to his timorous organization. His shrunken shanks scarcely sufficed to support him; his back was bent; his eyes blear; his head bald; and his chin, which was continually wagging, clothed with a scanty yellow beard, shaped like a stiletto, while his sandy moustachios were curled upward. He

was dressed in the extremity of the fashion, and affected the air of a young court gallant. His doublet, hose, and mantle were ever of the gayest and most fanciful hues, and of the richest stuffs; he wore a diamond brooch in his beaver, and sashes, tied like garters, round his thin legs, which were utterly destitute of calf. Preposterously large roses covered his shoes; his ruff was a "treble-quadruple-dedalion;" his gloves richly embroidered; a large crimson satin purse hung from his girdle; and he was scented with powders and pulvilios. This withered coxcomb affected the mincing gait of a young man; and though rather an object of derision than admiration with the fair sex, persuaded himself they were all captivated by him. The vast sums he so unjustly acquired did not long remain in his possession, but were dispersed in ministering to his follies and depravity. Timorous he was by nature, as we have said, but cruel and unrelenting in proportion to his cowardice; and where an injury could be securely inflicted, or a prostrate foe struck with impunity, he never hesitated for a moment. Sir Giles himself was scarcely so malignant and implacable.

A strong contrast to this dastardly debauchee was offered by the bolder villain. Sir Giles Mompesson was a very handsome man, with a striking physiognomy, but dark and sinister in expression. His eyes were black, singularly piercing, and flashed with the fiercest fire when kindled by passion. A finely-formed aquiline nose gave a hawk-like character to his face; his hair was coal-black (though he was no longer young), and hung in long ringlets over his neck and shoulders. He wore the handsomely cut beard and moustache subsequently depicted in the portraits of Vandyke, which suited the stern gravity of his countenance. Rich, though sober in his attire, he always affected a dark colour, being generally habited in a doublet of black quilted silk, Venetian hose, and a murrey-coloured velvet mantle. His conical hat was ornamented with a single black ostrich feather; and he carried a long rapier by his side, in the use of which he was singularly skilful; being one of Vincentio Saviolo's best pupils. Sir Giles was a little above the middle height, with a well proportioned athletic figure; and his strength and address were such, that there seemed good reason for his boast when he declared, as he often did, "that he feared no man living, in fair fight, no, nor any two men."

Sir Giles had none of the weaknesses of his partner. Temperate in his living, he had never been known to commit an excess at table;

nor were the blandishments or lures of the fair sex ever successfully spread for him. If his arm was of iron, his heart seemed of adamant, utterly impenetrable by any gentle emotion. It was affirmed, and believed, that he had never shed a tear. His sole passion appeared to be the accumulation of wealth; unattended by the desire to spend it. He bestowed no gifts. He had no family, no kinsmen, whom he cared to acknowledge. He stood alone—a hard, grasping man: a bond-slave of Mammon.

When it pleased him, Sir Giles Mompesson could play the courtier, and fawn and gloze like the rest. A consummate hypocrite, he easily assumed any part he might be called upon to enact; but the tone natural to him was one of insolent domination and bitter raillery. He sneered at all things human and divine; and there was mockery in his laughter, as well as venom in his jests. His manner, however, was not without a certain cold and grave dignity; and he clothed himself, like his purposes, in inscrutable reserve, on occasions requiring it. So ominous was his presence, that many persons got out of his way, fearing to come in contact with him, or give him offence; and the broad walk at Paul's was sometimes cleared as he took his way along it, followed by his band of tipstaves.

If this were the case with persons who had no immediate ground of apprehension from him, how much terror his sombre figure must have inspired, when presented, as it was, to Madame Bonaventure, with the aspect of a merciless creditor, armed with full power to enforce his claims, and resolved not to abate a jot of them, will be revealed to the reader in our next chapter.

CHAPTER III.
THE FRENCH ORDINARY.

The month allowed by the notice expired, and Madame Bonaventure's day of reckoning arrived.

No arrangement had been attempted in the interim, though abundant opportunities of doing so were afforded her, as Sir Francis Mitchell visited the Three Cranes almost daily. She appeared to treat the matter very lightly, always putting it off when mentioned; and even towards the last seemed quite unconcerned, as if entertaining no fear of the result. Apparently, everything went on just as usual, and no one would have supposed, from Madame Bonaventure's manner, that she was aware of the possibility of a mine being sprung beneath her feet. Perhaps she fancied she had countermined her opponents, and so felt secure. Her indifference puzzled Sir Francis, who knew not whether to attribute it to insensibility or over-confidence. He was curious to see how she would conduct herself when the crisis came; and for that purpose repaired to the tavern, about dinner-time, on the appointed day.

The hostess received him very graciously, trifled and jested with him as was her custom, and looked all blandishments and smiles to him and everybody else, as if nothing could possibly happen to disturb her serenity. Sir Francis was more perplexed than ever. With the levity and heedlessness of a Frenchwoman, she must have forgotten all about the claim. What if he should venture to remind her of it? Better not. The application would come soon enough. He was glad it devolved upon his partner, and not on himself, to proceed to extremities with so charming a person. He really could not do it. And yet all the while he chuckled internally as he thought of the terrible dilemma in which she would be speedily caught, and how completely it would place her at his mercy. She must come to terms then. And

Sir Francis rubbed his skinny hands gleefully at the thought. On her part, Madame Bonaventure guessed what was passing in his breast, and secretly enjoyed the idea of checkmating him. With a captivating smile she left him to attend to her numerous guests.

And very numerous they were on that day. More so than usual. Sir Francis, who had brought a boat from Westminster, where he dwelt, experienced some difficulty in landing at the stairs, invested as they were with barges, wherries and watermen, all of whom had evidently brought customers to the Three Cranes. Besides these, there were two or three gilded pinnaces lying off the wharf, with oarsmen in rich liveries, evidently belonging to persons of rank.

The benches and little tables in front of the tavern were occupied by foreign merchants and traders, discussing their affairs over a stoop of Bordeaux. Others, similarly employed, sat at the open casements in the rooms above; each story projecting so much beyond the other that the old building, crowned with its fanciful gables and heavy chimneys, looked top-heavy, and as if it would roll over into the Thames some day. Others, again, were seated over their wine in the pleasant little chamber built over the porch, which, advancing considerably beyond the door, afforded a delightful prospect, from its lantern-like windows, of the river, now sparkling with sunshine (it was a bright May day), and covered with craft, extending on the one hand to Baynard's Castle, and on the other to the most picturesque object to be found then, or since, in London—the ancient Bridge, with its towers, gateways, lofty superstructures, and narrow arches through which the current dashed swiftly; and, of course, commanding a complete view of the opposite bank, beginning with Saint Saviour's fine old church, Winchester House, the walks, gardens, and play-houses, and ending with the fine groves of timber skirting Lambeth Marshes. Others repaired to the smooth and well-kept bowling alley in the narrow court at the back of the house, where there was a mulberry tree two centuries older than the tavern itself—to recreate themselves with the healthful pastime there afforded, and indulge at the same time in a few whiffs of tobacco, which, notwithstanding the king's fulminations against it, had already made its way among the people.

The ordinary was held in the principal room in the house; which was well enough adapted for the purpose, being lofty and spacious, and lighted by an oriel window at the upper end. Over the high

carved chimney-piece were the arms of the Vintners' Company, with a Bacchus for the crest. The ceiling was moulded, and the wainscots of oak; against the latter several paintings were hung. One of these represented the Massacre of St. Bartholomew, and another the triumphal entry of Henri IV. into rebellious Paris. Besides these, there were portraits of the reigning monarch, James the First; the Marquis of Buckingham, his favourite; and the youthful Louis XIII., king of France. A long table generally ran down the centre of the room; but on this occasion there was a raised cross-table at the upper end, with a traverse, or curtain, partially drawn before it, proclaiming the presence of important guests. Here the napery was finer, and the drinking-vessels handsomer, than those used at the lower board. A grand banquet seemed taking place. Long-necked flasks were placed in coolers, and the buffets were covered with flagons and glasses. The table groaned beneath the number and variety of dishes set upon it. In addition to the customary yeomen-waiters, there were a host of serving-men in rich and varied liveries, but these attended exclusively on their lords at the raised table, behind the traverse.

As Sir Francis was ushered into the eating-room, he was quite taken aback by the unusually magnificent display, and felt greatly surprised that no hint of the banquet had been given him, on his arrival, by the hostess. The feast had already commenced; and all the yeomen-waiters and trencher-scrapers were too busily occupied to attend to him. Cyprien, who marshalled the dishes at the lower table, did not deign to notice him, and was deaf to his demand for a place. It seemed probable he would not obtain one at all; and he was about to retire, much disconcerted, when a young man somewhat plainly habited, and who seemed a stranger to all present, very good-naturedly made room for him. In this way he was squeezed in.

Sir Francis then cast a look round to ascertain who were present; but he was so inconveniently situated, and the crowd of serving-men was so great at the upper table, that he could only imperfectly distinguish those seated at it; besides which, most of the guests were hidden by the traverse. Such, however, as he could make out were richly attired in doublets of silk and satin, while their rich velvet mantles, plumed and jewelled caps, and long rapiers, were carried by their servants.

Two or three turned round to look at him as he sat down; and amongst these he remarked Sir Edward Villiers, whose presence was far from agreeable to him,—for though Sir Edward was secretly connected with him and Sir Giles, and took tithe of their spoliations, he disowned them in public, and would assuredly not countenance any open display of their rapacious proceedings.

Another personage whom he recognised, from his obesity, the peculiarity of his long flowing periwig, and his black velvet Parisian pourpoint, which contrasted forcibly with the glittering habiliments of his companions, was Doctor Mayerne-Turquet, the celebrated French professor of medicine, then so high in favour with James, that, having been loaded with honours and dignities, he had been recently named the King's first physician. Doctor Mayerne's abilities were so distinguished, that his Protestant faith alone, prevented him from occupying the same eminent position in the court of France that he did in that of England. The doctor's presence at the banquet was unpropitious; it was natural he should befriend a countrywoman and a Huguenot like himself, and, possessing the royal ear, he might make such representations as he pleased to the King of what should occur. Sir Francis hoped he would be gone before Sir Giles appeared.

But there was yet a third person, who gave the usurious knight more uneasiness than the other two. This was a handsome young man, with fair hair and delicate features, whose slight elegant figure was arrayed in a crimson-satin doublet, slashed with white, and hose of the same colours and fabric. The young nobleman in question, whose handsome features and prematurely-wasted frame bore the impress of cynicism and debauchery, was Lord Roos, then recently entrapped into marriage with the daughter of Sir Thomas Lake, Secretary of State: a marriage productive of the usual consequences of such imprudent arrangements—neglect on the one side, unhappiness on the other. Lord Roos was Sir Francis's sworn enemy. Like many other such gay moths, he had been severely singed by fluttering into the dazzling lights held up to him, when he wanted money, by the two usurers; and he had often vowed revenge against them for the manner in which they had fleeced him. Sir Francis did not usually give any great heed to his threats, being too much accustomed to reproaches and menaces from his victims to feel alarm or compunction; but just now the case was different, and he could not help fearing the vindictive

young lord might seize the opportunity of serving him an ill turn,— if, indeed, he had not come there expressly for the purpose, which seemed probable, from the fierce and disdainful glances he cast at him.

An angry murmur pervaded the upper table on Sir Francis's appearance; and something was said which, though he could not gather its precise import did not sound agreeably to his ears. He felt he had unwittingly brought his head near a hornet's nest, and might esteem himself lucky if he escaped without stinging. However, there was no retreating now; for though his fear counselled flight, very shame restrained him.

The repast was varied and abundant, consisting of all kinds of fricassees, collops and rashers, boiled salmon from the Thames, trout and pike from the same river, boiled pea-chickens, and turkey-poults, and florentines of puff paste, calves-foot pies, and set custards. Between each guest a boiled salad was placed, which was nothing more than what we should term a dish of vegetables, except that the vegetables were somewhat differently prepared; cinnamon, ginger, and sugar being added to the pulped carrots, besides a handful of currants, vinegar, and butter. A similar plan was adopted with the salads of burrage, chicory, marigold leaves, bugloss, asparagus, rocket, and alexanders, and many other plants discontinued in modern cookery, but then much esteemed; oil and vinegar being used with some, and spices with all; while each dish was garnished with slices of hard-boiled eggs. A jowl of sturgeon was carried to the upper table, where there was also a baked swan, and a roasted bustard, flanked by two stately venison pasties. This was only the first service; and two others followed, consisting of a fawn, with a pudding inside it, a grand salad, hot olive pies, baked neats' tongues, fried calves' tongues, baked Italian puddings, a farced leg of lamb in the French fashion, orangeado pie, buttered crabs, anchovies, and a plentiful supply of little made dishes, and quelquechoses, scattered over the table. With such a profusion of good things, it may appear surprising that Sir Francis should find very little to eat; but the attendants all seemed in league against him, and whenever he set his eye upon a dish, it was sure to be placed out of reach. Sir Francis was a great epicure, and the Thames salmon looked delicious; but he would have failed in obtaining a slice of it, if his neighbour (the young man who had made

room for him) had not given him the well-filled trencher intended for himself. In the same way he secured the wing of a boiled capon, larded with preserved lemons, the sauce of which was exquisite, as he well knew, from experience. Cyprien, however, took care he should get none of the turkey poults, or the florentines, but whipped off both dishes from under his very nose; and a like fate would have attended a lumbar pie but for the interference of his good-natured neighbour, who again came to his aid, and rescued it from the clutches of the saucy Gascon, just as it was being borne away.

CHAPTER IV.
A STAR-CHAMBER VICTIM.

His hunger being somewhat stayed, Sir Francis now found leisure to consider the young man who had so greatly befriended him, and, as a means of promoting conversation between them, began by filling his glass from a flask of excellent Bordeaux, of which, in spite of Cyprien's efforts to prevent him, he had contrived to gain possession. The young man acknowledged his courtesy with a smile, praised the wine, and expressed his astonishment at the wonderful variety and excellence of the repast, for which he said he was quite unprepared. It was not Sir Francis's way to feel or express much interest in strangers, and he disliked young men, especially when they were handsome, as was the case with his new acquaintance; but there was something in the youth that riveted his attention.

From the plainness of his attire, and a certain not unpleasing rusticity of air, Sir Francis comprehended at once that he was fresh from the country; but he also felt satisfied, from his bearing and deportment, that he was a gentleman: a term not quite so vaguely applied then, as it is now-a-days. The youth had a fine frank countenance, remarkable for manly beauty and intelligence, and a figure perfectly proportioned and athletic. Sir Francis set him down as well skilled in all exercises; vaulting, leaping, riding, and tossing the pike; nor was he mistaken. He also concluded him to be fond of country sports; and he was right in the supposition. He further imagined the young man had come to town to better his fortune, and seek a place at Court; and he was not far wrong in the notion. As the wily knight scanned the handsome features of his companion, his clean-made limbs, and symmetrical figure, he thought that success must infallibly attend the production of such a fair youth at a Court where personal advantages were the first consideration.

"A likely gallant," he reflected, "to take the fancy of the king; and if I aid him with means to purchase rich attire, and procure him a presentation, he may not prove ungrateful. But of that I shall take good security. I know what gratitude is. He must be introduced to my Lady Suffolk. She will know how to treat him. In the first place, he must cast his country slough. That ill-made doublet of green cloth must be exchanged for one of velvet slashed in the Venetian style like mine own, with hose stuffed and bombasted according to the mode. A silk stocking will bring out the nice proportions of his leg; though, as I am a true gentleman, the youth has so well formed a limb that even his own villainous yarn coverings cannot disfigure it. His hair is of a good brown colour, which the king affects much, and seems to curl naturally; but it wants trimming to the mode, for he is rough as a young colt fresh from pasture; and though he hath not much beard on his chin or upper lip, yet what he hath becomes him well, and will become him better, when properly clipped and twisted. Altogether he is as goodly a youth as one would desire to see. What if he should supplant Buckingham, as Buckingham supplanted Somerset? Let the proud Marquis look to himself! We may work his overthrow yet. And now to question him."

After replenishing his glass, Sir Francis addressed himself in his blandest accents, and with his most insidious manner, to his youthful neighbour:—

"For a stranger to town, as I conclude you to be, young Sir," he said, "you have made rather a lucky hit in coming hither to-day, since you have not only got a better dinner than I (a constant frequenter of this French ordinary) ever saw served here—(though the attendance is abominable, as you must have remarked—that rascally Cyprien deserves the bastinado,); but your civility and good manners have introduced you to one, who may, without presumption, affirm that he hath the will, and, it may be, the ability to serve you; if you will only point out to him the way."

"Nay, worthy Sir, you are too kind," the young man modestly replied; "I have done nothing to merit your good opinion, though I am happy to have gained it. I rejoice that accident has so far befriended me as to bring me here on this festive occasion; and I rejoice yet more that it has brought me acquainted with a worthy gentleman like yourself, to whom my rustic manners prove not to be displeasing. I have too

few friends to neglect any that chance may offer; and as I must carve my own way in the world, and fight for a position in it, I gladly accept any hand that may be stretched out to help me in the struggle."

"Just as I would have it," Sir Francis thought, "The very man I took him for. As I am a true gentleman, mine shall not be wanting, my good youth," he added aloud, with apparent cordiality, and affecting to regard the other with great interest; "and when I learn the particular direction in which you intend to shape your course, I shall be the better able to advise and guide you. There are many ways to fortune."

"Mine should be the shortest if I had any choice," the young man rejoined with a smile.

"Right, quite right," the crafty knight returned. "All men would take that road if they could find it. But with some the shortest road would not be the safest. In your case I think it might be different. You have a sufficiently good mien, and a sufficiently good figure, to serve you in lieu of other advantages."

"Your fair speech would put me in conceit with myself, worthy Sir," the young man rejoined with a well-pleased air; "were I not too conscious of my own demerits, not to impute what you say of me to good nature, or to flattery."

"There you wrong me, my good young friend—on my credit, you do. Were I to resort to adulation, I must strain the points of compliment to find phrases that should come up to my opinion of your good looks; and as to my friendly disposition towards you, I have already said that your attentions have won it, so that mere good nature does not prompt my words. I speak of you, as I think. May I, without appearing too inquisitive, ask from what part of the country you come?"

"I am from Norfolk, worthy Sir," the young man answered, "where my life has been spent among a set of men wild and uncouth, and fond of the chase as the Sherwood archers we read of in the ballads. I am the son of a broken gentleman; the lord of a ruined house; with one old servant left me out of fifty kept by my father, and with scarce a hundred acres that I can still call my own, out of the thousands swept away from me. Still I hunt in my father's woods; kill my father's deer; and fish in my father's lakes; since no one molests

me. And I keep up the little church near the old tumble-down hall, in which are the tombs of my ancestors, and where my father lies buried; and the tenantry come there yet on Sundays, though I am no longer their master; and my father's old chaplain, Sir Oliver, still preaches there, though my father's son can no longer maintain him."

"A sad change, truly," Sir Francis said, in a tone of sympathy, and with a look of well-feigned concern; "and attributable, I much fear, to riot and profusion on the part of your father, who so beggared his son."

"Not so, Sir," the young man gravely replied; "my father was a most honourable man, and would have injured no one, much less the son on whom he doated. Neither was he profuse; but lived bountifully and well, as a country gentleman, with a large estate, should live. The cause of his ruin was that he came within the clutches of that devouring monster, which, like the insatiate dragon of Rhodes, has swallowed up the substance of so many families, that our land is threatened with desolation. My father was ruined by that court, which, with a mockery of justice, robs men of their name, their fame, their lands, and goods; which perverts the course of law, and saps the principles of equity; which favours the knave, and oppresses the honest man; which promotes and supports extortion and plunder; which reverses righteous judgments, and asserts its own unrighteous supremacy, which, by means of its commissioners, spreads its hundred arms over the whole realm, to pillage and destroy—so that no one, however distant, can keep out of its reach, or escape its supervision; and which, if it be not uprooted, will, in the end, overthrow the kingdom. Need I say my father was ruined by the Star-Chamber?"

"Hush! hush! my good young Sir," Sir Francis cried, having vainly endeavoured to interrupt his companion's angry denunciation. "Pray heaven your words have reached no other ears than mine! To speak of the Star-Chamber as you have spoken is worse than treason. Many a man has lost his ears, and been branded on the brow, for half you have uttered."

"Is free speech denied in this free country?" the young man cried in astonishment. "Must one suffer grievous wrong, and not complain?"

"Certes, you must not contemn the Star-Chamber, or you will incur its censure," Sir Francis replied in a low tone. "No court in England is so jealous of its prerogatives, nor so severe in punishment of its maligners. It will not have its proceedings canvassed, or its judgments questioned."

"For the plain reason, that it knows they will not bear investigation or discussion. Such is the practice of all arbitrary and despotic rule. But will Englishmen submit to such tyranny?"

"Again, let me counsel you to put a bridle on your tongue, young Sir. Such matters are not to be talked of at public tables—scarcely in private. It is well you have addressed yourself to one who will not betray you. The Star-Chamber hath its spies everywhere. Meddle not with it, as you value liberty. Light provocation arouses its anger; and once aroused, its wrath is all-consuming."

CHAPTER V.
JOCELYN MOUNCHENSEY.

Notwithstanding the risk incurred, the young man, whose feelings were evidently deeply interested, seemed disposed to pursue the dangerous theme; but perceiving one of their opposite neighbours glancing at them, Sir Francis checked him; and filling his glass essayed to change the conversation, by inquiring how long he had been in town, and where he lodged?

"I only arrived in London yesterday," was the reply; "yet I have been here long enough to make me loth to return to the woods and moors of Norfolk. As to my lodging, it is without the city walls, near St. Botolph's Church, and within a bow shot of Aldgate: a pleasant situation enough, looking towards the Spital Fields and the open country. I would fain have got me others in the Strand, or near Charing Cross, if my scanty means would have allowed me. Chance, as I have said, brought me here to-day. Strolling forth early to view the sights of town, I crossed London Bridge, the magnificence of which amazed me; and, proceeding along the Bankside, entered Paris Garden, of which I had heard much, and where I was greatly pleased, both with the mastiffs kept there, and the formidable animals they have to encounter; and, methought, I should like to bait mine enemies with those savage dogs, instead of the bear. Returning to the opposite shore in a wherry, the waterman landed me at this wharf, and so highly commended the Three Cranes, as affording the best French ordinary and the best French wine in London, that seeing many gentlefolk flocking towards it, which seemed to confirm his statement, I came in with them, and have reason to be satisfied with my entertainment, never having dined so sumptuously before, and, certes, never having tasted wine so delicious."

"Let me fill your glass again. As I am a true gentleman, it will not hurt you; a singular merit of pure Bordeaux being that you may drink it with impunity; and the like cannot be said of your sophisticated sack. We will crush another flask. Ho! drawer—Cyprien, I say! More wine—and of the best Bordeaux. The best, I say."

And for a wonder the order was obeyed, and the flask set before him.

"You have been at the Bankside you say, young Sir? On my credit, you must cross the river again and visit the theatres—the Globe or the Rose. Our great actor, Dick Burbadge, plays Othello to-day, and, I warrant me, he will delight you. A little man is Dick, but he hath a mighty soul. There is none other like him, whether it be Nat Field or Ned Alleyn. Our famous Shakespeare is fortunate, I trow, in having him to play his great characters. You must see Burbadge, likewise, in the mad Prince of Denmark,—the part was written for him, and fits him exactly. See him also in gentle and love-sick Romeo, in tyrannous and murderous Macbeth, and in crookback Richard; in all of which, though different, our Dick is equally good. He hath some other parts of almost equal merit,—as Malevole, in the 'Malcontent;' Frankford, in the 'Woman Killed with Kindness;' Brachiano, in Webster's 'White Devil;' and Vendice, in Cyril Tournour's 'Revenger's Tragedy.'"

"I know not what may be the nature of that last-named play," the young man rather sternly remarked; "but if the character of Vendice at all bears out its name, it would suit me. I am an avenger."

"Forbear your wrongs awhile, I pray you, and drown your resentment in a cup of wine. As I am a true gentleman! a better bottle than the first! Nay, taste it. On my credit, it is perfect nectar. I pledge you in a brimmer; wishing Success may attend you, and Confusion await your Enemies! May you speedily regain your Rights!"

"I drink that toast most heartily, worthy Sir," the young man exclaimed, raising his beaded flagon on high. "Confusion to my Enemies—Restoration to my Rights!"

And he drained the goblet to its last drop.

"By this time he must be in a fit mood for my purpose," Sir Francis thought, as he watched him narrowly. "Harkye, my good young friend," he said, lowering his tone, "I would not be overheard in what I have to say. You were speaking just now of the shortest

way to fortune. I will point it out to you. To him, who is bold enough to take it, and who hath the requisites for the venture, the shortest way is to be found at Court. Where think you most of those gallants, of whom you may catch a glimpse through the traverse, derive their revenues?—As I am a true gentleman!—from the royal coffers. Not many years ago, with all of them; not many months ago, with some; those brilliant and titled coxcombs were adventurers like yourself, having barely a Jacobus in their purses, and scarce credit for board and lodging with their respective landladies. Now you see how nobly they feast, and how richly they bedeck themselves. On my credit! the like good fortune may attend you; and haply, when I dine at an ordinary a year hence, I may perceive you at the upper table, with a curtain before you to keep off the meaner company, and your serving-man at your back, holding your velvet mantle and cap, like the best of your fellow nobles."

"Heaven grant it may be so!" the young man exclaimed, with a sigh. "You hold a dazzling picture before me; but I have little expectation of realizing it."

"It will be your own fault if you do not," the tempter rejoined. "You are equally well-favoured with the handsomest of them; and it was by good looks alone that the whole party rose to their present eminence. Why not pursue the same course; with the same certainty of success? You have courage enough to undertake it, I presume?"

"If courage alone were wanting, I have that," the young man replied;—"but I am wholly unknown in town. How then shall I accomplish an introduction at Court, when I know not even its humblest attendant?"

"I have already said you were lucky in meeting with me," Sir Francis replied; "and I find you were luckier than I supposed, when I told you so; for I knew not then towards what bent your desires tended, nor in what way I could help you; but now, finding out the boldness of your flight, and the high game you aim at, I am able to offer you effectual assistance, and give you an earnest of a prosperous issue. Through my means you shall be presented to the king, and in such sort that the presentation shall not be idly made. It will rest then with yourself to play your cards dexterously, and to follow up a winning game. Doubtless, you will have many adversaries, who will trip up your heels if they can, and throw every obstacle in your way;

but if you possess the strong arm I fancy you do, and daring to second it, you have nothing to fear. As I am a true gentleman! you shall have good counsel, and a friend in secret to back you."

"To whom am I indebted for this most gracious and unlooked-for offer?" the young man asked, his breast heaving, and his eye flashing with excitement.

"To one you may perchance have heard of," the knight answered, "as the subject of some misrepresentation; how justly applied, you yourself will be able to determine from my present conduct. I am Sir Francis Mitchell."

At the mention of this name the young man started, and a deep angry flush overspread his face and brow.

Perceiving the effect produced, the wily knight hastened to remove it.

"My name, I see, awakens unpleasant associations in your breast," he said; "and your look shows you have been influenced by the calumnies of my enemies. I do not blame you. Men can only be judged of by report; and those I have had dealings with have reported ill enough of me. But they have spoken falsely. I have done no more than any other person would do. I have obtained the best interest I could for my money; and my losses have been almost equal to my gains. Folks are ready enough to tell all they can against you; but slow to mention aught they conceive to be in your favour. They stigmatize me as a usurer; but they forget to add, I am ever the friend of those in need. They use me, and abuse me. That is the way of the world. Wherefore, then, should I complain? I am no worse off than my neighbours. And the proof that I can be disinterested is the way in which I have acted towards you, a perfect stranger, and who have no other recommendation to my good offices than your gracious mien and gentle manners."

"I cannot accept your proffered aid, Sir Francis," the young man replied, in an altered tone, and with great sternness. "And you will understand why I cannot, when I announce myself to you as Jocelyn Mounchensey."

It was now the knight's turn to start, change colour, and tremble.

CHAPTER VI.
PROVOCATION.

A momentary pause ensued, during which Mounchensey regarded the knight so fiercely, that the latter began to entertain apprehensions for his personal safety, and meditated a precipitate retreat. Yet he did not dare to move, lest the action should bring upon him the hurt he wished to avoid. Thus he remained, like a bird fascinated by the rattlesnake, until the young man, whose power of speech seemed taken from him by passion, went on, in a tone of deep and concentrated rage, that communicated a hissing sound to his words.

"Yes, I am Jocelyn Mounchensey," he said, "the son of him whom your arts and those of your partner in iniquity, Sir Giles Mompesson, brought to destruction; the son of him whom you despoiled of a good name and large estates, and cast into a loathsome prison, to languish and to die: I am the son of that murdered man. I am he whom you have robbed of his inheritance; whose proud escutcheon you have tarnished; whose family you have reduced to beggary and utter ruin."

"But Sir Jocelyn, my worthy friend," the knight faltered, "have patience, I pray of you. If you consider yourself aggrieved, I am willing to make reparation—ample reparation. You know what were my intentions towards you, before I had the slightest notion who you might be. (If I had but been aware of it, he thought, I would have taken care to keep at a respectful distance from him.) I will do more than I promised. I will lend you any sums of money you may require; and on your personal security. Your bare word shall suffice. No bonds—no written obligations of any kind. Does that sound like usury? As I am a true gentleman! I am most unfairly judged. I am not the extortioner men describe me. You shall find me your friend," he added in a low earnest tone. "I will re-establish your fortune; give you

a new title, higher and prouder than that which you have lost; and, if you will follow my counsel, you shall supplant the haughty favourite himself. You shall stand where Buckingham now stands. Hear reason, good Sir Jocelyn. Hear reason, I entreat you."

"I will hear nothing further," Jocelyn rejoined. "Were you to talk till Doomsday, you could not alter my feelings towards you a jot. My chief errand in coming to London was to call you and Sir Giles Mompesson to strict account."

"And we will answer any charges you may bring against us readily—most readily, Sir Jocelyn. All was done in fairness—according to law. The Star-Chamber will uphold us."

"Tut! you think to terrify me with that bugbear; but I am not so easily frightened. We have met for the first time by chance, but our next meeting shall be by appointment."

"When and where you please, Sir Jocelyn," the knight replied; "but recollect the duello is forbidden, and, though I would not willingly disappoint you in your desire to cut my throat, I should be sorry to think you might be hanged for it afterwards. Come, Sir Jocelyn, lay aside this idle passion, and look to your true interests, which lie not in quarrelling with me, but in our reconciliation. I can help you effectually, as I have shown; and, as I am a true gentleman, I will help you. Give me your hand, and let us be friends!"

"Never!" Jocelyn exclaimed, withdrawing from him, "never shall the hand of a Mounchensey grasp yours in friendship! I would sooner mine rotted off! I am your mortal foe. My father's death has to be avenged."

"Provoke him not, my good young Sir," interposed an elderly man, next him, in a long furred gown, with hanging sleeves, and a flat cap on his head, who had heard what was now passing. "You know not the mischief he may do you."

"I laugh at his malice, and defy him," Jocelyn cried—"he shall not sit one moment longer beside me. Out, knave! out!" he added, seizing Sir Francis by the wing of his doublet, and forcibly thrusting him from his seat. "You are not fit company for honest men. Ho! varlets, to the door with him! Throw him into the kennel."

"You shall rue this, villain!—you shall rue it bitterly," Sir Francis cried, shaking his clenched hands at him. "Your father perished like

a dog in the Fleet, and you shall perish there likewise. You have put yourself wholly in my power, and I will make a fearful example of you. You have dared to utter scandalous and contemptuous language against the great and high court of Star-Chamber, before the decrees of which, all men bow; impugning its justice and denying its authority; and you shall feel the full weight of its displeasure. I call upon these worthy gentlemen to testify against you."

"We have heard nothing, and can testify nothing," several voices cried.

"But you, Sir, who were next him, you must have heard him?" Sir Francis said, addressing the elderly man in the furred gown.

"Not I!" rejoined the person appealed to; "I gave no heed to what was said."

"But I did, Sir Francis," squeaked a little whey-faced man, in a large ruff and tight-laced yellow doublet, from the opposite side of the table; "I heard him most audaciously vilipend the high court of Star-Chamber and its councils; and I will bear testimony against him when called upon."

"Your name, good Sir, your name?" Sir Francis demanded, taking out his tablets.

"Set me down as Thopas Trednock, tailor, at the sign of the Pressing Iron, in Cornhill," the whey-faced man replied, in his shrill tones, amid the derisive laughter of the assemblage.

"Thopas Trednock, tailor—good!" the knight repeated, as he wrote the name down. "You will be an excellent witness, Master Trednock. Fare you well for the present, Master Jocelyn Mounchensey, for I now mind well your father was degraded from the honour of knighthood. As I am a true gentleman! you may be sure of committal to the Fleet."

As may be supposed, the scuffle which had taken place, attracted the attention of those in its immediate vicinity; and when the cause of it became known, as it presently did throughout both tables, great indignation was expressed against Sir Francis, who was censured on all hands, jeered and flouted, as he moved to the door. So great was the clamour, and so opprobrious were the epithets and terms applied to him, that the knight was eager to make his escape; but he met Cyprien in his way; and the droll young Gascon, holding a dish-cover

in one hand, by way of buckler, and a long carving-knife in the other, in place of a sword, opposed his egress.

"Let me pass, knave," Sir Francis cried in alarm.

"By your leave, no," returned Cyprien, encouraged by the laughter and plaudits of the company. "You have come hither uninvited, and must stay till you have permission to depart. Having partaken of the banquet, you must, perforce, tarry for the rerebanquet. The sweets and cates have yet to come, Sir Francis."

"What mean you, sirrah?" the knight demanded, in increased trepidation.

"Your presence is necessary at a little entertainment I have provided to follow the dinner, sweet Sir Francis," Madame Bonaventure cried, advancing towards him; "and as you have a principal part in it, I can by no means spare you."

"No one can spare you, sweet Sir Francis," several voices chimed in, derisively. "You must remain with us a little longer."

"But I will not stay. I will not be detained. There is some conspiracy a-foot against me. I will indict you all for it, if you hinder me in going forth," the knight vociferated, in accents of mingled rage and terror. "Stop me at your peril, thou saucy Gascon knave."

"Cornes du diable!—no more a knave than yourself, gros usurier!" Cyprien cried.

"Laissez-lui, Cyprien," Madame Bonaventure interposed;—"the courteous knight will yield to my entreaties, and stay of his own free will."

"I have business that calls me hence. I must go," Sir Francis said, endeavouring to push by them.

"Let the door be closed," an authoritative voice cried from the head of the table.

The order was instantly obeyed. Two serving-men stationed themselves before the place of exit, and Sir Francis found himself a prisoner.

The roof rang with the laughter and gibes of the guests.

"This is a frolic, gentleman, I perceive. You are resolved to make me your sport—ha! ha!" Sir Francis said, trying to disguise his uneasiness under an appearance of levity—"But you will not carry the jest too

far. You will not maltreat me. My partner, Sir Giles Mompesson, will be here anon, and will requite any outrage committed upon me."

"Sir Giles is impatiently expected by us," a spruce coxcomb near him replied. "Madame Bonaventure had prepared us for his coming. We will give him the welcome he deserves."

"Ah! traitress! then it was all planned," Sir Francis thought;—"and, blind owl that I am, I have fallen into the snare."

But the poor knight was nearly at his wit's end with fright, when he saw Lord Roos quit his place at the upper table and approach him.

CHAPTER VII.
HOW LORD ROOS OBTAINED SIR FRANCIS MITCHELL'S SIGNATURE.

"What, my prince of usurers!" exclaimed Lord Roos, in a mocking tone; "my worthy money-lender, who never takes more than cent. per cent., and art ill content with less; who never exacts more than the penalty of thy bond,—unless more may be got; who never drives a hard bargain with a needy man—by thine own account; who never persecutes a debtor—as the prisons shall vouch for thee; who art just in all thy transactions—as every man who hath had dealings with thee will affirm; and who knows not how to lie, to cheat, to cozen—as some usurers do."

"You are pleasant, my lord," Sir Francis replied.

"I mean to be so," Lord Roos said; "for I esteem thee for thy rare qualities. I know not thy peer for cunning and knavery. Thy mischievous schemes are so well-conceived that they prove thee to have an absolute genius for villany. Scruples thou hast none; and considerations and feelings which might move men less obdurate than thyself, have no influence over thee. To ruin a man is with thee mere pastime; and groans of the oppressed are music in thine ears."

"Aha! a good jest. You were always merry with me, my lord."

"Yes, when I borrowed money from thee—but not when I had to repay it twice over. I laughed not then; but was foolish enough to threaten to take thy life. My anger is past now. But we must drink together—a rousing toast."

"At your lordship's pleasure," Sir Francis replied.

"Cyprien! a flask of wine, and thy largest goblet," Lord Roos cried. "'Tis well! Now pour the whole into the flagon. Do me reason in this cup, Sir Francis?"

"What! in this mighty cup, my lord?" the knight replied. "Nay, 'tis too much, I swear. If I become drunken, the sin will lie at your door."

"Off with it! without more ado. And let the toast be what thou practisest—'Pillage and Extortion!'"

"I cannot drink that toast, my lord. 'Twill choke me."

"'Sdeath! villain, but thou shalt, or thou shalt never taste wine more. Down with it, man! And now your signature to this paper?"

"My signature!" Sir Francis cried, reeling from the effect of the wine he had swallowed. "Nay, my good lord; I can sign nothing that I have not read. What is it?"

"A blank sheet," Lord Roos rejoined. "I will fill it up afterwards."

"Then, my lord, I refuse—that is, I decline—that is, I had rather not, if your lordship pleases."

"But my lordship pleases otherwise. Give him pen and ink, and set him near the table."

This was done; and Sir Francis regarded the paper with swimming eyes.

"Now, your name,—written near the bottom of the sheet," Lord Roos cried.

"'Tis done under com—compulsion; and I pro—protest against it."

"Sign, I say," the young nobleman exclaimed, rapping the table peremptorily.

On this, Sir Francis wrote his name in the place indicated.

"Enough!" Lord Roos cried, snatching up the paper. "This is all I want. Now set him on the table, that his partner may have him in full view when he arrives. 'Twill give him a foretaste of what he may himself expect."

"What mean you, ruff—ruffians? 'Tis an indignity to which I shall not submit," cried Sir Francis, who was now, however, too far gone to offer any resistance.

A leathern girdle was found, with which he was fastened to the chair, so as to prevent him slipping from it; and in this state he was hoisted upon the table, and set with his face to the door; looking the

very picture of inebriety, with his head drooping on one side, his arms dangling uselessly down, and his thin legs stretched idly out. After making some incoherent objections to this treatment, he became altogether silent, and seemed to fall asleep. His elevation was received with shouts of laughter from the whole company.

The incident had not taken place many minutes, and a round had scarcely been drunk by the guests, when a loud and peremptory summons was heard at the door. The noise roused even the poor drunkard in the chair, who, lifting up his head, stared about him with vacant eyes.

"Let the door be opened," the same authoritative voice exclaimed, which had before ordered its closure.

The mandate was obeyed; and, amidst profound silence, which suddenly succeeded the clashing of glasses, and expressions of hilarity, Sir Giles Mompesson entered, with his body-guard of myrmidons behind him.

Habited in black, as was his custom, with a velvet mantle on his shoulder, and a long rapier by his side, he came forward with a measured step and assured demeanour. Though he must necessarily have been surprised by the assemblage he found—so much more numerous and splendid than he could have anticipated—he betrayed no signs whatever of embarrassment. Nor, though his quick eye instantly detected Sir Francis, and he guessed at once why the poor knight had been so scandalously treated, did he exhibit any signs of displeasure, or take the slightest notice of the circumstance; reserving this point for consideration, when his first business should be settled. An additional frown might have darkened his countenance; but it was so stern and sombre, without it, that no perceptible change could be discerned; unless it might be in the lightning glances he cast around, as if seeking some one he might call to account presently for the insult. But no one seemed willing to reply to the challenge. Though bold enough before he came, and boastful of what they would do, they all looked awed by his presence, and averted their gaze from him. There was, indeed, something so formidable in the man, that to shun a quarrel with him was more a matter of prudence than an act of cowardice; and on the present occasion, no one liked to be first to provoke him; trusting to his neighbour to commence the attack, or awaiting the general outbreak.

There was one exception, however, and that was Jocelyn Mounchensey, who, so far from desiring to shun Sir Giles's searching regards, courted them; and as the knight's eagle eye ranged round the table and fell upon him, the young man (notwithstanding the efforts of his pacific neighbour in the furred cloak to restrain him) suddenly rose up, and throwing all the scorn and defiance he could muster into his countenance, returned Mompesson's glance with one equally fierce and menacing.

A bitter smile curled Sir Giles's lip at this reply to his challenge, and he regarded the young man fixedly, as if to grave his features upon his memory. Perhaps they brought Mounchensey's father to mind, for Sir Giles withdrew his gaze for a moment to reflect, and then looked again at Jocelyn with fresh curiosity. If he had any doubts as to whom he beheld, they were removed by Sir Francis, who managed to hiccup forth —

"'Tis he, Sir Giles — 'tis Jocelyn Mounchensey."

"I thought as much," Sir Giles muttered. "A moment, young man," he cried, waving his hand imperiously to his antagonist. "Your turn will come presently."

And without bestowing further notice on Jocelyn, who resisted all his neighbour's entreaties to him to sit down, Sir Giles advanced towards the middle chamber, where he paused, and took off his cap, having hitherto remained covered.

In this position, he looked like a grand inquisitor attended by his familiars.

CHAPTER VIII.
OF LUPO VULP, CAPTAIN BLUDDER, CLEMENT LANYERE, AND SIR GILES'S OTHER MYRMIDONS.

Close behind Sir Giles, and a little in advance of the rest of the myrmidons, stood Lupo Vulp, the scrivener.

Lupo Vulp was the confidential adviser of our two extortioners, to whom they referred all their nefarious projects. He it was who prepared their bonds and contracts, and placed out their ill-gotten gains at exorbitant usance. Lupo Vulp was in all respects worthy of his employers, being just as wily and unscrupulous as they were, while, at the same time, he was rather better versed in legal tricks and stratagems, so that he could give them apt counsel in any emergency. A countenance more replete with cunning and knavery than that of Lupo Vulp, it would be difficult to discover. A sardonic smile hovered perpetually about his mouth, which was garnished with ranges of the keenest and whitest teeth. His features were sharp; his eyes small, set wide apart, of a light gray colour, and with all the slyness of a fox lurking within their furtive glances. Indeed, his general resemblance to that astute animal must have struck a physiognomist. His head was shaped like that of a fox, and his hair and beard were of a reddish-tawny hue. His manner was stealthy, cowering, suspicious, as if he feared a blow from every hand. Yet Lupo Vulp could show his teeth and snap on occasions. He was attired in a close-fitting doublet of russety-brown, round yellow hose, and long stockings of the same hue. A short brown mantle and a fox-skin cap completed his costume.

The leader of the troop was Captain Bludder, a huge Alsatian bully, with fiercely-twisted moustachios, and fiery-red beard cut like a spade. He wore a steeple-crowned hat with a brooch in it, a buff jerkin and boots, and a sword and buckler dangled from his waist. Besides

these, he had a couple of petronels stuck in his girdle. The captain drank like a fish, and swaggered and swore like twenty troopers.

The rear of the band was formed by the tipstaves—stout fellows with hooks at the end of their poles, intended to capture a fugitive, or hale him along when caught. With these were some others armed with brown-bills. No uniformity prevailed in the accoutrements of the party, each man arraying himself as he listed. Some wore old leather jerkins and steel skirts; some, peascod doublets of Elizabeth's time, and trunk-hose that had covered many a limb besides their own; others, slops and galligaskins; while the poorer sort were robed in rusty gowns of tuft-mockado or taffeta, once guarded with velvet or lined with skins, but now tattered and threadbare. Their caps and bonnets were as varied as their apparel,—some being high-crowned, some trencher-shaped, and some few wide in the leaf and looped at the side. Moreover, there was every variety of villainous aspect; the savage scowl of the desperado, the cunning leer of the trickster, and the sordid look of the mean knave. Several of them betrayed, by the marks of infamy branded on their faces, or by the loss of ears, that they had passed through the hands of the public executioner.

Amongst these there was one with a visage more frightfully mutilated than those of his comrades; the nose having been slit, and subsequently sewed together again, but so clumsily that the severed parts had only imperfectly united, communicating a strange, distorted, and forbidding look to the physiognomy. Clement Lanyere, the owner of this gashed and ghastly face, who was also reft of his ears, and branded on the cheek, had suffered infamy and degradation, owing to the licence he had given his tongue in respect to the Star-Chamber. Prosecuted in that court by Sir Giles Mompesson, as a notorious libeller and scandaller of the judges and first personages of the realm, he was found guilty, and sentenced accordingly. The court showed little leniency to such offenders; but it was a matter of grace that his clamorous tongue was not torn out likewise, in addition to the punishment actually inflicted. A heavy fine and imprisonment accompanied the corporal penalties. Thus utterly ruined and degraded, and a mark for the finger of scorn to point at, Clement Lanyere, whose prospects had once been fair enough, as his features had been prepossessing, became soured and malevolent, embittered against the world, and at war with society. He turned promoter, or, in

modern parlance, informer; lodging complaints, seeking out causes for prosecutions, and bringing people into trouble in order to obtain part of the forfeits they incurred for his pains. Strange to say, he attached himself to Sir Giles Mompesson,—the cause of all his misfortunes,—and became one of the most active and useful of his followers. It was thought no good could come of this alliance, and that the promoter only bided his time to turn upon his master, against whom it was only natural he should nourish secret vengeance. But, if it were so, Sir Giles seemed to entertain no apprehensions of him, probably thinking he could crush him whenever he pleased. Either way the event was long deferred. Clement Lanyere, to all appearance, continued to serve his master zealously and well; and Sir Giles gave no sign whatever of distrust, but, on the contrary, treated him with increased confidence. The promoter was attired wholly in black—cloak, cap, doublet, and hose were of sable. And as, owing to the emoluments springing from his vile calling, his means were far greater than those of his comrades; so his habiliments were better. When wrapped in his mantle, with his mutilated countenance covered with a mask which he generally wore, the informer might have passed for a cavalier; so tall and well formed was his figure, and so bold his deportment. The dangerous service he was employed upon, which exposed him to insult and injury, required him to be well armed; and he took care to be so.

Two or three of Sir Giles's myrmidons, having been selected for particular description, the designations of some others must suffice—such as Staring Hugh, a rascal of unmatched effrontery; the Gib Cat and Cutting Dick, dissolute rogues from the Pickt-hatch in Turnbull Street, near Clerkenwell; old Tom Wootton, once a notorious harbourer of "masterless men," at his house at Smart's Quay, but now a sheriffs officer; and, perhaps, it ought to be mentioned, that there were some half-dozen swash-bucklers and sharpers from Alsatia, under the command of Captain Bludder, who was held responsible for their good conduct.

Such was Sir Giles's body-guard.

On his entrance, it may be remarked, the curtain in front of the raised table was more closely drawn, so as completely to conceal the guests. But their importance might be inferred from the serving-men, in rich liveries, standing before the traverse.

Profound silence reigned throughout the assemblage.

Having uncovered, as before mentioned, and made a formal reverence to the company, Sir Giles spoke as follows:—

"I crave your pardon, worthy Sirs," he said, in a distinct and resolute voice, "for this intrusion, and regret to be the means of marring your festivity. I came hither wholly unprepared to find such an assemblage. Yet, though I would willingly have chosen a more fitting opportunity for my visit, and would postpone, if I could, to another occasion, the unpleasant duty I have to fulfil; the matter is urgent, and will not admit of delay. You will hold me excused, therefore, if I proceed with it, regardless of your presence; and I am well assured no let or interruption will be offered me, seeing I act with the royal licence and authority, of which I am the unworthy representative."

"Truly, your conduct requires explanation," Jocelyn Mounchensey cried, in a mocking tone. "If I had not been here in London, I should have judged, from your appearance, and that of your attendants, that a band of desperate marauders had broken in upon us, and that we must draw our swords to defend our lives, and save the house from pillage. But after what you have said, I conclude you to be the sheriff, come with your followers to execute some writ of attachment; and therefore, however annoying the presence of such a functionary may be,—however ill-timed may be your visit, and unmannerly your deportment,—we are bound not to molest you."

Provocation like this was rarely addressed to Sir Giles; and the choler occasioned by it was increased by the laughter and cheers of the company. Nevertheless he constrained his anger, replying in a stern, scornful tone—

"I would not counsel you to molest me, young man. The mistake you have committed in regard to myself may be pardoned in one of your evident inexperience; who, fresh from the boorish society of the country, finds himself, for the first time, amongst well-bred gentlemen. Of all here present you are probably the sole person ignorant that I am Sir Giles Mompesson. But it is scarcely likely that they should be aware, as I chance to be, that the clownish insolent who has dared to wag his tongue against me, is the son of a Star-Chamber delinquent."

CHAPTER IX.
THE LETTERS-PATENT.

A slight reaction in Sir Giles's favour was produced by his speech, but Jocelyn quite regained his position with the company when he exclaimed—

"My father was misjudged. His prosecutor was a villain, and his sentence iniquitous."

"You have uttered your own condemnation, Jocelyn Mounchensey," Sir Giles cried, with a savage laugh. "Know, to your confusion, that the High Court of Star-Chamber is so tender of upholding the honour of its sentences, that it ever punishes such as speak against them with the greatest severity. You have uttered your scandals openly."

"Imprudent young man, you have, indeed, placed yourself in fearful jeopardy," a gentleman near him observed to Jocelyn. "Escape, if you can. You are lost, if you remain here."

But instead of following the friendly advice, Jocelyn would have assaulted Sir Giles, if he had not been forcibly withheld by the gentleman.

The knight was not slow to follow up the advantage he had gained.

"Stand forward, Clement Lanyere," he exclaimed, authoritatively.

The promoter instantly advanced.

"Look at this man," Sir Giles continued, addressing Jocelyn; "and you will perceive how those who malign the Star-Chamber are treated. This disfigured countenance was once as free from seam or scar as your own; and yet, for an offence lighter than yours, it hath been stamped, as you see, with indelible infamy. Answer, Clement Lanyere,—and answer according to your conscience,—Was the

sentence just of the high and honourable court by which you were tried?"

"It was just," the promoter replied, a deep flush dyeing his ghastly visage.

"And lenient?"

"Most lenient. For it left my foul tongue the power of speech it now enjoys."

"By whom were you prosecuted in the Star-Chamber?"

"By him I now serve."

"That is, by myself. Do you bear me malice for what I did?"

"I have never said so. On the contrary, Sir Giles, I have always declared I owe you a deep debt."

"Which you strive to pay?"

"Which I will pay."

"You hear what this man says, Mounchensey?" Sir Giles cried. "You have been guilty of the same offence as he. Why should you not be similarly punished?"

"If I were so punished, I would stab my prosecutor to the heart," Jocelyn replied.

At this rejoinder, Lanyere, who had hitherto kept his eyes on the ground, suddenly raised them, with a look of singular expression at the speaker.

"Humph!" Sir Giles ejaculated. "I must proceed to extremities with him, I find. Keep strict watch upon him, Lanyere; and follow him if he goes forth. Trace him to his lair. Now to business. Give me the letters-patent, Lupo," he added, turning to the scrivener, as Lanyere retired. "These Letters-Patent," continued Sir Giles, taking two parchment scrolls with large seals pendent from them from Lupo Vulp, and displaying them to the assemblage, "these Royal Letters," he repeated in his steady, stern tones, and glancing round with a look of half-defiance, "passed under the great seal, and bearing the king's sign-manual, as ye see, gentlemen, constitute the authority on which I act. They accord to me and my co-patentee, Sir Francis Mitchell, absolute and uncontrolled power and discretion in granting and refusing licenses to all tavern-keepers and hostel-keepers throughout London. They give us full power to enter and inspect all taverns and

hostels, at any time that may seem fit to us; to prevent any unlawful games being used therein; and to see that good order and rule be maintained. They also render it compulsory upon all ale-house-keepers, tavern-keepers, and inn-keepers throughout London, to enter into their own recognizances with us against the non-observance of our rules and regulations for their governance and maintenance, and to find two sureties: and in case of the forfeiture of such recognizances by any act of the parties, coming within the scope of our authority, it is provided that one moiety of the sum forfeited be paid to the Crown, and the other moiety to us. Lend me your ears yet further, I pray ye, gentlemen. These Royal Letters empower us to inflict certain fines and penalties upon all such as offend against our authority, or resist our claims; and they enable us to apprehend and commit to prison such offenders without further warrant than the letters themselves contain. In brief, gentlemen," he continued in a peremptory tone, as if insisting upon attention, "you will observe, that the absolute control of all houses of entertainment, where exciseable liquors are vended, is delegated to us by his most gracious Majesty, King James. To which end ample powers have been given us by his Majesty, who has armed us with the strong arm of the law. Will it please ye to inspect the letters, gentlemen?" holding them forth. "You will find that his Majesty hath thus written;—'*In cujus rei testimonium has Literas nostras fieri fecimus patentes. Teste Meipso, apud Westm. 10 die Maij, Anno Regni nostri,*' &c. Then follows the royal signature. None of ye, I presume, will question its authenticity?"

A deep silence succeeded, in the midst of which Jocelyn Mounchensey broke forth:—

"I, for one, question it," he cried. "I will never believe that a king, who, like our gracious sovereign, has the welfare of his subjects at heart, would sanction the oppression and injustice which those warrants, if entrusted to unscrupulous hands, must inevitably accomplish. I therefore mistrust the genuineness of the signature. If not forged, it has been obtained by fraud or misrepresentation."

Some murmurs of applause followed this bold speech; but the gentleman who had previously counselled the young man again interposed, and whispered these words in his ear:—

"Your rash vehemence will undo you, if you take not heed. Beyond question, Sir Giles hath the king's sanction for what he does,

and to censure him as you have done is to censure the Crown, which is next to treason. Be ruled by me, my good young Sir, and meddle no more in the matter."

Sir Giles, who had some difficulty in controlling his choler, now spoke: —

"You have cast an imputation upon me, Jocelyn Mounchensey," he cried with concentrated fury, "which you shall be compelled to retract as publicly as you have made it. To insult an officer of the Crown, in the discharge of his duty, is to insult the Crown itself, as you will find. In the King's name, I command you to hold your peace, or, in the King's name, I will instantly arrest you; and I forbid any one to give you aid. I will not be troubled thus. Appointed by his Majesty to a certain office, I exercise it as much for the benefit of the Royal Exchequer, as for my own personal advantage. I have his Majesty's full approval of what I do, and I need nothing more. I am accountable to no man—save the King," addressing this menace as much to the rest of the company as to Jocelyn. "But I came not here to render explanation, but to act. What, ho! Madame Bonaventure! Where are ye, Madame? Oh! you are here!"

"Bon jour, sweet Sir Giles," the landlady said, making him a profound obeisance. "What is your pleasure with me, Sir? And to what am I to attribute the honour of this visit?"

"Tut! Madame. You know well enough what brings me hither, and thus attended," he replied. "I come in pursuance of a notice, served upon you a month ago. You will not deny having received it, since the officer who placed it in your hands is here present." And he indicated Clement Lanyere.

"Au contraire, Sir Giles," Madame Bonaventure replied. "I readily admit the receipt of a written message from you, which, though scarcely intelligible to my poor comprehension, did not seem as agreeably worded as a billet-doux. Mais, ma foi! I attached little importance to it. I did not suppose it possible—nor do I suppose it possible now"—with a captivating smile, which was totally lost upon Sir Giles—"that you could adopt such rigorous measures against me."

"My measures may appear rigorous, Madame," Sir Giles coldly replied; "but I am warranted in taking them. Nay, I am compelled to take them. Not having made the satisfaction required by the notice,

you have deprived yourself of the protection I was willing to afford you. I am now merely your judge. The penalties incurred by your neglect are these: Your licence was suspended a month ago; the notice expressly stating that it would be withdrawn, unless certain conditions were fulfilled. Consequently, as ever since that time you have been vending exciseable liquors without lawful permission, you have incurred a fine of one hundred marks a day, making a total of three thousand marks now due and owing from you, partly to his Majesty, and partly to his Majesty's representatives. This sum I now demand."

"Ah! Dieu! three thousand marks!" Madame Bonaventure screamed. "What robbery is this!—what barbarity! 'T is ruin—utter ruin! I may as well close my house altogether, and return to my own fair country. As I am an honest woman, Sir Giles, I cannot pay it. So it is quite useless on your part to make any such demand."

"You profess inability to pay, Madame," Sir Giles rejoined. "I cannot believe you; having some knowledge of your means. Nevertheless, I will acquaint you with a rule of law applicable to the contingency you put. 'Quod non habet in cere, luet in corpore' is a decree of the Star-Chamber; meaning, for I do not expect you to understand Latin, that he who cannot pay in purse shall pay in person. Aware of the alternative, you will make your choice. And you may thank me that I have not adjudged you at once—as I have the power—to three months within the Wood Street Compter."

"Ah, Sir Giles! what an atrocious idea. You are worse than a savage to talk of such a loathsome prison to me. Ah! mon Dieu! what is to happen to me! would I were back again in my lovely Bordeaux!"

"You will have an opportunity of revisiting that fine city, Madame; for you will no longer be able to carry on your calling here."

"Ciel! Sir Giles! what mean you?"

"I mean, Madame, that you are disabled from keeping any tavern for the space of three years."

Madame Bonaventure clasped her hands together, and screamed aloud.

"In pity, Sir Giles!—In pity!" she cried.

The inexorable knight shook his head. The low murmurs of indignation among the company which had been gradually gathering

force during the foregoing dialogue, now became clamorous. "A most scandalous proceeding!" exclaimed one. "Deprive us of our best French ordinary!" cried another. "Infamous extortioner!" shouted a third. "We'll not permit such injustice. Let us take the law into our own hands, and settle the question!" shouted a fourth. "Ay, down with the knight!" added a fifth.

But Sir Giles continued perfectly unmoved by the tempest raging around, and laughed to scorn these menaces, contenting himself with signing to Captain Bludder to be in readiness.

"A truce to this, gentlemen;" he at length thundered forth; "the King's warrant must be respected."

Again Madame Bonaventure besought his pity, but in vain. She took hold of his arm, and feigned to kneel to him; but he shook her coldly off.

"You are a very charming woman, no doubt, Madame," he said sarcastically; "and some men might find you irresistible; but I am not made of such yielding stuff, and you may spare yourself further trouble, for all your powers of persuasion will fail with me. I renew my demand—and for the last time. Do not compel me to resort to extremities with you. It would grieve me," he added with a bitter smile, "to drag so pretty a woman through the public streets, like a common debtor, to the Compter."

"Grace! grace! Sir Giles," cried Madame Bonaventure. Then seeing him remain inflexible, she added, in an altered tone, "I will never submit with life to such an indignity—never!"

"We'll all protect you, Madame," cried the assemblage with one voice—"Let him lay hands upon you, and he shall see."

Sir Giles glanced at his myrmidons. They stepped quickly towards him in a body. At the same time Jocelyn Mounchensey, whom no efforts of the friendly gentleman could now restrain, sprang forward, and, drawing his sword, was just in time to place himself before Madame Bonaventure, as she drew hastily back.

"Have no fear, Madame, you are safe with me," the young man said, glancing fiercely at the knight and his troop.

The greatest confusion now reigned throughout the room. Other swords were drawn, and several of the guests mounted upon the benches to overlook the scene. Cyprien, and the rest of the drawers

and tradesmen ranged themselves behind their mistress, prepared to resist any attempt on the part of the myrmidons to seize her. The curtain at the head of the room was partly drawn aside, showing that the distinguished persons at the upper table were equally excited.

"Gentlemen," Sir Giles said, still maintaining perfect calmness in the midst of the tumult, "a word with you ere it be too late. I don't address myself to you, Jocelyn Mounchensey, for you are undeserving of any friendly consideration—but to all others I would counsel forbearance and non-resistance. Deliver up that woman to me."

"I will die upon the spot sooner than you shall be surrendered," said Jocelyn, encouraging the hostess, who clung to his disengaged arm.

"Oh! merci! grand merci, mon beau gentilhomme!" she exclaimed.

"Am I to understand then, that you mean to impede me in the lawful execution of my purposes, gentlemen?" Sir Giles demanded.

"We mean to prevent an unlawful arrest," several voices rejoined.

"Be it so," the knight said; "I wash my hands of the consequences." Then turning to his followers, he added—"Officers, at all hazards, attach the person of Dameris Bonaventure, and convey her to the Compter. At the same time, arrest the young man-beside her—Jocelyn Mounchensey,—who has uttered treasonable language against our sovereign lord the King. I will tell you how to dispose of him anon. Do my bidding at once."

But ere the order could be obeyed, the authoritative voice which had previously been heard from the upper table exclaimed—"Hold!"

Sir Giles paused; looked irresolute for a minute; and then checked his myrmidons with a wave of the hand.

"Who is it stays the law?" he said, with the glare of a tiger from whom a bone has been snatched.

"One you must needs obey, Sir Giles," replied Lord Roos, coming towards him from the upper table. "You have unconsciously played a part in a comedy—and played it very well, too—but it is time to bring the piece to an end. We are fast verging on the confines of tragedy."

"I do not understand you, my lord," Sir Giles returned, gravely. "I discern nothing comic in the matter; though much of serious import."

"You do not perceive the comedy, because it has been part of our scheme to keep you in the dark, Sir Giles."

"So there is a scheme, then, a-foot here, my lord?—ha!"

"A little merry plot; nothing more, Sir Giles—in the working of which your worthy co-patentee, Sir Francis Mitchell, has materially assisted."

"Ha!" exclaimed Sir Giles, glancing at his partner, who still occupied his elevated position upon the table—"I presume, then, I have to thank you, my lord, for the indignity offered to my friend?"

"As you please, Sir Giles," Lord Roos returned carelessly. "You call it an indignity; but in my opinion the best thing to be done with a man whose head so swims with wine that his legs refuse to support him, is to tie him in a chair. He may else sacrifice his dignity by rolling under the table. But let this pass for the nonce. Before Sir Francis was wholly overcome, he was good enough to give me his signature. You saw him do it, gentlemen?" he added, appealing to the company.

"Yes—yes!—we saw him write it!" was the general reply.

"And to what end was this done, my lord?" Sir Giles demanded, sternly.

"To enable me," replied the imperturbable young nobleman, "to draw out a receipt in full of your joint claims against Madame Bonaventure. I have done it, Sir Giles; and here it is. And I have taken care to grant a renewal of her licence from the date of your notice; so that no penalties or fines can attach to her for neglect. Take it, Madame Bonaventure," he continued, handing her the paper. "It is your full acquittance."

"And think you, my lord, that this shallow artifice—to give it no harsher term—will avail you any thing?" Sir Giles cried scornfully. "I set it aside at once."

"Your pardon, Sir Giles; you will do no such thing."

"And who will hinder me?—You, my lord?"

"Even I, Sir Giles. Proceed at your peril."

The young nobleman's assurance staggered his opponent.

"He must have some one to uphold him, or he would not be thus confident," he thought. "Whose was the voice I heard? It sounded like—No matter! 'Tis needful to be cautious."

"You do not, then, hold yourself bound by the acts of your partner, Sir Giles?" Lord Roos said.

"I deny this to be his act," the knight replied.

"Better question him at once on the subject," Lord Roos said. "Set him free, Cyprien."

The Gascon did as he was bidden, and with the aid of his fellow drawers, helped Sir Francis from the table. To the surprise of the company, the knight then managed to stagger forward unassisted, and would have embraced Sir Giles, if the latter had not thrust him off in disgust, with some violence.

"What folly is this, Sir Francis?" Sir Giles cried angrily. "You have forgotten yourself strangely, you have taken leave of your senses, methinks!"

"Not a whit of it, Sir Giles — not a whit. I never was more my own master than I am at present, as I will prove to you."

"Prove it, then, by explaining how you came to sign that paper. You could not mean to run counter to me?"

"But I did," Sir Francis rejoined, highly offended. "I meant to run counter to you in signing it, and I mean it now."

"'Sdeath! you besotted fool, you are playing into their hands!"

"Besotted fool in your teeth, Sir Giles. I am as sober as yourself. My hand has been put to that paper, and what it contains I stand by."

"You design, then, to acquit Madame Bonaventure? Consider what you say?"

"No need for consideration; I have always designed it."

"Ten thousand thanks, Sir Francis!" the hostess cried. "I knew I had an excellent friend in you."

The enamoured knight seized the hand she extended towards him, but in the attempt to kiss it fell to the ground, amid the laughter of the company.

"Are you satisfied now, Sir Giles?" asked Lord Roos.

"I am satisfied that Sir Francis has been duped," he replied, "and that when his brain is free from the fumes of wine, he will bitterly regret his folly. But even his discharge will be insufficient. Though it

may bind me, it will not bind the Crown, which will yet enforce its claims."

"That, Sir Giles, I leave competent authority to decide," Lord Roos replied, retiring.

And as he withdrew, the curtains before the upper table were entirely withdrawn, disclosing the whole of the brilliant assemblage, and at the head of them one person far more brilliant and distinguished than the rest.

"Buckingham!" Sir Giles exclaimed. "I thought I knew the voice."

It was, indeed, the King's omnipotent favourite. Magnificently attired, the Marquis of Buckingham as far outshone his companions in splendour of habiliments as he did in stateliness of carriage and beauty of person. Rising from the table, and donning his plumed hat, looped with diamonds, with a gesture worthy of a monarch, while all the rest remained uncovered, as if in recognition of his superior dignity, he descended to where Sir Giles Mompesson was standing. It need scarcely be said that Jocelyn Mounchensey had never seen the superb favourite before; but he did not require to be told whom he beheld, so perfectly did Buckingham realize the descriptions given of him. A little above the ordinary height, with a figure of the most perfect symmetry, and features as aristocratic and haughty as handsome, it was impossible to conceive a prouder or a nobler-looking personage than the marquis. His costume was splendid, consisting of a doublet of white cut velvet, roped with pearls, which fitted him to admiration. Over his shoulders he wore a mantle of watchet-coloured velvet; his neck was encircled by a falling band; and silken hose of the same colour as the doublet completed his costume. His deportment was singularly dignified; but his manner might have conciliated more if it had been less imperious and disdainful.

Sir Giles made a profound obeisance as Buckingham advanced towards him. His salutation was haughtily returned.

"I have heard something of your mode of proceeding with the keepers of taverns and hostels, Sir Giles," the proud marquis said; "but this is the first occasion on which I have seen it put in practice,—and I am free to confess that you deal not over gently with them, if the present may be considered a specimen of your ordinary conduct. Those letters-patent were not confided to you by his Majesty to

distress his subjects, for your own particular advantage and profit, but to benefit the community by keeping such places of entertainment in better order than heretofore. I fear you have somewhat abused your warrant, Sir Giles."

"If to devote myself, heart and soul, to his Majesty's service, and to enrich his Majesty's exchequer be to abuse my warrant, I have done so, my lord Marquis,—but not otherwise. I have ever vindicated the dignity and authority of the Crown. You have just heard that, though my own just claims have been defeated by the inadvertence of my co-patentee, I have advanced those of the King."

"The King relinquishes all claims in the present case," Buckingham replied. "His gracious Majesty gave me full discretion in the matter, and I act as I know he himself would have acted."

And waving his hand to signify that he would listen to no remonstrances, the Marquis turned to Madame Bonaventure, who instantly prostrated herself before him, as she would have done before royalty itself, warmly thanking him for his protection.

"You must thank my Lord Roos, and not me, Madame," Buckingham graciously replied, raising her as he spoke. "It was at his lordship's instance I came here. He takes a warm interest in you, Madame."

"I shall ever be beholden to his lordship, I am sure," Madame Bonaventure said, casting down her eyes and blushing, or feigning to blush, "as well as to you, Monseigneur."

"My Lord Roos avouched," pursued Buckingham, "that at the Three Cranes I should find the prettiest hostess and the best wine in London; and on my faith as a gentleman! I must say he was wrong in neither particular. Brighter eyes I have never beheld—rarer claret I have never drunk."

"Oh, Monseigneur! you quite overwhelm me. My poor house can scarcely hope to be honoured a second time with such a presence; but should it so chance"—

"You will give me as good welcome as you have done to-day. No lack of inducement to repeat the visit. Sir Giles Mompesson!"

"My lord Marquis."

"I lay my commands upon you, good Sir Giles, that no further molestation be offered to Madame Bonaventure, but that you give a good report of her house. Withdraw your followers without delay."

"Your commands shall be obeyed, my lord Marquis," Sir Giles rejoined; "but before I go I have an arrest to make. That young man," pointing to Jocelyn, "has been talking treason."

"It is false, my lord Marquis," Jocelyn replied. "His Majesty hath not a more loyal subject than myself. I would cut out my tongue rather than speak against him. I have said the King is ill served in such officers as Giles Mompesson and Sir Francis Mitchell, and I abide by my words. They can reflect no dishonour on his Majesty."

"Save that they seem to imply a belief on your part that his Majesty has chosen his officers badly," Buckingham said, regarding the young man fixedly.

"Not so, my lord Marquis, These men may have been favourably represented to his Majesty, who no doubt has been kept in ignorance of their iniquitous proceedings."

"What are you driving at, Sir?" Buckingham cried, almost fiercely.

"I mean, my lord Marquis, that these persons may be the creatures of some powerful noble, whose interest it is to throw a cloak over their malpractices."

"'Fore heaven! some covert insult would seem to be intended," exclaimed Buckingham. "Who is this young man, Sir Giles?"

"He is named Jocelyn Mounchensey, my lord Marquis; and is the son of an old Norfolk knight baronet, who, you may remember, was arraigned before the Court of Star-Chamber, heavily fined, and imprisoned."

"I do remember the case, and the share you and Sir Francis had in it, Sir Giles," Buckingham rejoined.

"I am right glad to hear that, my lord," said Jocelyn. "You will not then wonder that I avow myself their mortal enemy."

"We laugh to scorn these idle vapourings," said Sir Giles; "and were it permitted," he added, touching his sword, "I myself would find an easy way to silence them. But the froward youth, whose brains seem crazed with his fancied wrongs, is not content with railing against us, but must needs lift up his voice against all constituted

authority. He hath spoken contemptuously of the Star-Chamber,— and that, my lord Marquis, as you well know, is an offence, which cannot be passed over."

"I am sorry for it," Buckingham rejoined; "but if he will retract what he has said, and express compunction, with promise of amendment in future, I will exert my influence to have him held harmless."

"I will never retract what I have said against that iniquitous tribunal," Jocelyn rejoined firmly. "I will rather die a martyr, as my father did, in the cause of truth."

"Your kindness is altogether thrown away upon him, my lord," Sir Giles said, with secret satisfaction.

"So I perceive," Buckingham rejoined. "Our business is over," he added, to the nobles and gallants around him; "so we may to our barges. You, my lord," he added to Lord Roos, "will doubtless tarry to receive the thanks of our pretty hostess."

And graciously saluting Madame Bonaventure, he quitted the tavern accompanied by a large train, and entering his barge amid the acclamations of the spectators, was rowed towards Whitehall.

CHAPTER X.
THE 'PRENTICES AND THEIR LEADER.

While the Marquis of Buckingham and his suite were moving towards the wharf, amid the acclamations of the crowd (for in the early part of his brilliant career the haughty favourite was extremely popular with the multitude, probably owing to the princely largesses he was in the habit of distributing among them), a very different reception awaited those who succeeded him. The hurrahs and other vociferations of delight and enthusiasm were changed into groans, hootings, and discordant yells, when Sir Francis Mitchell came in sight, supported between two stout myrmidons, and scarcely able to maintain his perpendicular as he was borne by them towards the wherry in waiting for him near the stairs. Though the knight was escorted by Captain Bludder and his Alsatian bullies, several of the crowd did not seem disposed to confine themselves to jeers and derisive shouts, but menaced him with some rough usage. Planting themselves in his path, they shook their fists in his face, with other gestures of defiance and indignity, and could only be removed by force. Captain Bludder and his roaring blades assumed their fiercest looks, swore their loudest oaths, twisted their shaggy moustaches, and tapped their rapier-hilts; but they prudently forbore to draw their weapons, well knowing that the proceeding would be a signal for a brawl, and that the cry of "Clubs!" would be instantly raised.

Amongst the foremost of those who thus obstructed Sir Francis and his party was a young man with a lithe active figure, bright black eyes, full of liveliness and malice, an olive complexion, and a gipsy-like cast of countenance. Attired in a tight-fitting brown frieze jerkin with stone buttons, and purple hose, his head was covered with a montero cap, with a cock's feather stuck in it. He was armed neither with sword nor dagger, but carried a large cudgel or club, the well-

known and formidable weapon, of the London 'prentices, in the use of which, whether as a quarterstaff or missile, they were remarkably expert. Even a skilful swordsman stood but poor chance with them. Besides this saucy-looking personage, who was addressed as Dick Taverner by his comrades, there were many others, who, to judge from their habiliments and their cudgels, belonged to the same fraternity as himself; that is to say, they were apprentices to grocers, drapers, haberdashers, skinners, ironmongers, vintners, or other respectable artificers or tradesfolk.

Now Dick Taverner had an especial grudge against our two extortioners, for though he himself, being 'prentice to a bookseller in Paul's Churchyard, had little concern with them, he was the son of an inn-keeper — Simon Taverner, of the Emperor's Head, Garlick Hill — who had been recently mined by their exactions, his licence taken from him, and his house closed: enough to provoke a less mettlesome spark than Dick, who had vowed to revenge the parental injuries on the first opportunity. The occasion now seemed to present itself, and it was not to be lost. Chancing to be playing at bowls in the alley behind the Three Cranes with some of his comrades on the day in question, Dick learnt from Cyprien what was going forward, and the party resolved to have their share in the sport. If needful, they promised the drawer to rescue his mistress from the clutches of her antagonists, and to drive them from the premises. But their services in this respect were not required. They next decided on giving Sir Francis Mitchell a sound ducking in the Thames.

Their measures were quickly and warily taken. Issuing from an arched doorway at the side of the tavern, they stationed some of their number near it, while the main party posted themselves at the principal entrance in front. Scouts were planted inside, to communicate with Cyprien, and messengers were despatched to cry "Clubs!" and summon the neighbouring 'prentices from Queenhithe, Thames Street, Trinity Lane, Old Fish Street, and Dowgate Hill; so that fresh auxiliaries were constantly arriving. Buckingham, with the young nobles and gallants, were, of course, allowed to pass free, and were loudly cheered; but the 'prentices soon ascertained from their scouts that Sir Francis was coming forth, and made ready for him.

Utterly unconscious of his danger, the inebriate knight replied to the gibes, scoffs, and menaces addressed to him, by snapping his

fingers in his opponents' faces, and irritating them in their turn; but if he was insensible of the risk he ran, those around him were not, and his two supporters endeavoured to hurry him forward. Violently resisting their efforts, he tried to shake them off, and more than once stood stock-still, until compelled to go on. Arrived at the stairhead, he next refused to embark, and a scene of violent altercation ensued between him and his attendants. Many boats were moored off the shore, with a couple of barges close at hand; and the watermen and oarsmen standing up in their craft, listened to what was going forward with much apparent amusement.

Hastily descending the steps, Captain Bludder placed himself near the wherry intended for the knight, and called to the others to make short work of it and bring him down. At this juncture the word was given by Dick Taverner, who acted as leader, and in less than two minutes, Sir Francis was transferred from the hands of his myrmidons to those of the 'prentices. To accomplish this, a vigorous application of cudgels was required, and some broken pates were the consequence of resistance; but the attack was perfectly successful; the myrmidons and Alsatians were routed, and the 'prentices remained masters of the field, and captors of a prisoner. Stupefied with rage and astonishment, Captain Bludder looked on; at one moment thinking of drawing his sword, and joining the fray; but the next, perceiving that his men were evidently worsted, he decided upon making off; and with this view he was about to jump into the wherry, when his purpose was prevented by Dick Taverner, and a few others of the most active of his companions, who dashed down the steps to where he stood. The captain had already got one foot in the wherry, and the watermen, equally alarmed with himself, were trying to push off, when the invaders came up, and, springing into the boat, took possession of the oars, sending Bludder floundering into the Thames, where he sunk up to the shoulders, and stuck fast in the mud, roaring piteously for help.

Scarcely were the 'prentices seated, than Sir Francis Mitchell was brought down to them, and the poor knight, beginning to comprehend the jeopardy in which he was placed, roared for help as lustily as the half-drowned Alsatian captain, and quite as ineffectually. The latter was left to shift for himself, but the former was rowed out some twenty or thirty yards from the shore, where, a stout cord being fastened to

his girdle, he was plunged head-foremost into the river; and after being thrice drawn up, and as often submerged again, he was dragged on board, and left to shiver and shake in his dripping habiliments in the stern of the boat. The bath had completely sobered him, and he bitterly bemoaned himself, declaring that if he did not catch his death of cold he should be plagued with cramps and rheumatism during the rest of his days. He did not dare to utter any threats against his persecutors, but he internally vowed to be revenged upon them — cost what it might. The 'prentices laughed at his complaints, and Dick Taverner told him — "that as he liked not cold water, he should have spared them their ale and wine; but, as he had meddled with their liquors, and with those who sold them, they had given him a taste of a different beverage, which they should provide, free of cost, for all those who interfered with their enjoyments, and the rights of the public." Dick added, "that his last sousing was in requital for the stoppage of the Emperor's Head, and that, with his own free will, he would have left him under the water, with a stone round his neck."

This measure of retributive justice accomplished, the 'prentices and their leader made for the stairs, where they landed, after telling the watermen to row their fare to the point nearest his lodgings; an order which was seconded by Sir Francis himself, who was apprehensive of further outrage. Neither would he tarry to take in Captain Bludder, though earnestly implored to do so by that personage, who, having in his struggles sunk deeper into the oozy bed, could now only just keep his bearded chin and mouth above the level of the tide. Taking compassion upon him, Dick Taverner threw him an oar, and, instantly grasping it, the Alsatian was in this way dragged ashore; presenting a very woful spectacle. his nether limbs being covered with slime, while the moisture poured from his garments, as it would from the coat of a water-spaniel. His hat had floated down the stream, and he had left one boot sticking in the mud, while his buff jerkin, saturated with wet, clung to his skin like a damp glove.

Leaving him to wring his cloak and dry his habiliments in the best way he could, the leader of the 'prentices collected together his forces, and, disposing them in something like military array, placed himself at their head, and marched towards the tavern, where they set up a great shout. Hitherto they had met with no interruption whatever. On the contrary, the watermen, bargemen, and others,

had cheered them on in their work of mischief; and the crowd on shore appeared rather friendly to them than otherwise. Flushed with success, the riotous youths seemed well disposed to carry their work of retribution to extremities, and to inflict some punishment upon Sir Giles proportionate to his enormities. Having ascertained, from their scouts, that no one connected with the usurious knight had come forth, they felt quite secure of their prey, and were organising a plan of attack, when intelligence was brought by a scout that a great disturbance was going on inside, in consequence of a young gentleman having been arrested by Sir Giles and his crew, and that their presence was instantly required by Madame Bonaventure.

On hearing this, Dick Taverner shouted—"To the rescue! to the rescue!" and rushed into the house, followed by the 'prentices, who loudly echoed his cries.

"Par ici, Messieurs! Par ici!—this way, this way!" vociferated Cyprien, who met them in the passage—"the bowling-alley—there they are!"

But the Gascon's directions were scarcely needed. The clashing of swords would have served to guide the 'prentices to the scene of conflict.

CHAPTER XI.
JOHN WOLFE.

When Jocelyn Mounchensey called for his reckoning, Madame Bonaventure took him aside, showing, by her looks, that she had something important to communicate to him, and began by telling him he was heartily welcome to all he had partaken of at her ordinary, adding that she considered herself very greatly his debtor for the gallantry and zeal he had displayed in her behalf.

"Not that I was in any real peril, my fair young Sir," she continued, "though I feigned to be so, for I have powerful protectors, as you perceive; and indeed this was all a preconcerted scheme between my Lord Roos and his noble friends to turn the tables on the two extortioners. But that does not lessen my gratitude to you; and I shall try to prove it. You are in more danger than, perchance, you wot of; and I feel quite sure Sir Giles means to carry his threat into execution, and to cause your arrest."

Seeing him smile disdainfully, as if he had no apprehensions, she added, somewhat quickly—"What will your bravery avail against so many, mon beau gentilhomme? Mon Dieu! nothing. No! no! I must get you assistance. Luckily I have some friends at hand, the 'prentices—grands et forts gaillards, avec des estocs;—Cyprien has told me they are here. Most certainly they will take your part. So, Sir Giles shall not carry you off, after all."

Jocelyn's lips again curled with the same disdainful smile as before.

"Ah! vous etes trop temeraire!" Madame Bonaventure cried, tapping his arm. "Sit down here for awhile. I will give you the signal when you may depart with safety. Do not attempt to stir till then. You understand?"

Jocelyn did not understand very clearly; but without making any observation to the contrary, he took the seat pointed out to him. The position was well-chosen, inasmuch as it enabled him to command the movements of the foe, and offered him a retreat through a side-door, close at hand; though he was naturally quite ignorant whither the outlet might conduct him.

While this was passing, Sir Giles was engaged in giving directions respecting his partner, whose inebriate condition greatly scandalized him; and it was in pursuance of his orders that Sir Francis was transported to the wharf where the misadventure before related befel him. Never for a moment did Sir Giles' watchful eye quit Jocelyn, upon whom he was ready to pounce like a tiger, if the young man made any movement to depart; and he only waited till the tavern should be clear of company to effect the seizure.

Meanwhile another person approached the young man. This was the friendly stranger in the furred gown and flat cap, who had sat next him at dinner, and who, it appeared, was not willing to abandon him in his difficulties. Addressing him with much kindness, the worthy personage informed him that he was a bookseller, named John Wolfe, and carried on business at the sign of the Bible and Crown in Paul's Churchyard, where he should be glad to see the young man, whenever he was free to call upon him.

"But I cannot disguise from you, Master Jocelyn Mounchensey — for your dispute with Sir Francis Mitchell has acquainted me with your name," John Wolfe said — "that your rashness has placed you in imminent peril; so that there is but little chance for the present of my showing you the hospitality and kindness I desire. Sir Giles seems to hover over you as a rapacious vulture might do before making his swoop. Heaven shield you from his talons! And now, my good young Sir, accept one piece of caution from me, which my years and kindly feelings towards you entitle me to make. An you 'scape this danger, as I trust you may, let it be a lesson to you to put a guard upon your tongue, and not suffer it to out-run your judgment. You are much too rash and impetuous, and by your folly (nay, do not quarrel with me, my young friend — I can give no milder appellation to your conduct) have placed yourself in the power of your enemies. Not only have you provoked Sir Francis Mitchell, whose malice is more easily aroused than appeased, but you have defied Sir Giles Mompesson,

who is equally implacable in his enmities; and as if two such enemies were not enough, you must needs make a third, yet more dangerous than either."

"How so, good Master Wolfe?" Jocelyn cried. "To whom do you refer?"

"To whom should I refer, Master Jocelyn." Wolfe rejoined, "but to my lord of Buckingham, whom you wantonly insulted? For the latter indiscretion there can be no excuse, whatever there may be for the former; and it was simple madness to affront a nobleman of his exalted rank, second only in authority to the King himself."

"But how have I offended the Marquis?" demanded Jocelyn, surprised.

"Is it possible you can have spoken at random, and without knowledge of the force of your own words?" John Wolfe rejoined, looking hard at him. "It may be so, for you are plainly ignorant of the world. Well, then," he added, lowering his tone, "when you said that these two abominable extortioners were the creatures of some great man, who glozed over their villainous practices to the King, and gave a better account of them than they deserve, you were nearer the truth than you imagined; but it could hardly be agreeable to the Marquis to be told this to his face, since it is notorious to all (except to yourself) that he is the man."

"Heavens!" exclaimed Jocelyn, "I now see the error I have committed."

"A grave error indeed," rejoined Wolfe, shaking his head, "and most difficult to be repaired — for the plea of ignorance, though it may suffice with me, will scarcely avail you with the Marquis. Indeed, it can never be urged, since he disowns any connection with these men; and it is suspected that his half-brother, Sir Edward Villiers, goes between them in all their secret transactions. Of this, however, I know nothing personally, and only tell you what I have heard. But if it were not almost treasonable to say it, I might add, that his Majesty is far too careless of the means whereby his exchequer is enriched, and his favourites gratified; and, at all events, suffers himself to be too easily imposed upon. Hence all these patents and monopolies under which we groan. The favourites must have money; and as the King has little to give them, they raise as much as they please on the credit

of his name. Thus everything is sold; places, posts, titles, all have their price—bribery and corruption reign everywhere. The lord-keeper pays a pension to the Marquis—so doth the attorney-general—and simony is openly practised; for the Bishop of Salisbury paid him £3,500 for his bishopric. But this is not the worst of it. Is it not terrible to think of a proud nobleman, clothed almost with supreme authority, being secretly leagued with sordid wretches, whose practices he openly discountenances and contemns, and receiving share of their spoil? Is it not yet more terrible to reflect that the royal coffers are in some degree supplied by similar means?"

"'Tis enough to drive an honest man distracted," Jocelyn said, "and you cannot wonder at my indignation, though you may blame my want of caution. I have said nothing half so strong as you have just uttered, Master Wolfe."

"Ah! but, my good young Sir, I do not publicly proclaim my opinions as you do. My lord of Buckingham's name must no more be called in question than his Majesty's. To associate the Marquis's name with those of his known instruments were to give him mortal offence. Even to hint at such a connection is sufficient to provoke his displeasure! But enough of this. My purpose is not to lecture you, but to befriend you. Tell me frankly, my good young Sir—and be not offended with the offer—will my purse be useful to you? If so, 'tis freely at your service; and it may help you in your present emergency—for though there is not enough in it to bribe the master to forego his purpose against you, there is amply sufficient to procure your liberation, privily, from the men."

"I thank you heartily, good Master Wolfe, and believe me, I am not withheld by false pride from accepting your offer," Jocelyn replied; "but I must trust to my own arm to maintain my liberty, and to my own address to regain it, if I be taken. Again, I thank you, Sir."

"I grieve that I cannot lend you other aid," John Wolfe replied, looking compassionately at him; "but my peaceful avocations do not permit me to take any part in personal conflicts, and I am loath to be mixed up in such disturbances. Nevertheless, I do not like to stand by, and see outrage done."

"Concern yourself no more about me, worthy Sir," interrupted Jocelyn. "Perhaps I shall not be molested, and if I should be, I am

well able to take care of myself. Let those who assail me bear the consequences."

But John Wolfe still lingered. "If some of my apprentices were only here," he said, "and especially that riotous rogue, Dick Taverner, something might be done to help you effectually.—Ha! what is that uproar?" as a tumultuous noise, mixed with the cries of "Clubs!—Clubs!" was heard without, coming from the direction of the wharf. "As I live! the 'prentices are out, and engaged in some mischievous work, and it will be strange if Dick Taverner be not among them. I will see what they are about." And as he spoke he hurried to the oriel window which looked out upon the wharf, exclaiming—"Ay, ay,—'t is as I thought. Dick is among them, and at their head. 'Fore heaven! they are attacking those ruffianly braggarts from Whitefriars, and are laying about them lustily with their cudgels. Ha! what is this I see? The Alsatians and the myrmidons are routed, and the brave lads have captured Sir Francis Mitchell. What are they about to do with him? I must go forth and see."

His purpose, however, was prevented by a sudden movement on the part of Sir Giles and his attendants. They came in the direction of Jocelyn Mounchensey, with the evident intention of seizing the young man. Jocelyn instantly sprang to his feet, drew his sword, and put himself in a posture of defence. The myrmidons prepared to beat down the young man's blade with their halberds, and secure him, when Jocelyn's cloak was plucked from behind, and he heard Madame Bonaventure's voice exclaim—"Come this way!—follow me instantly!"

Thus enjoined, he dashed through the door, which was instantly fastened, as soon as he had made good his retreat.

CHAPTER XII.
THE ARREST AND THE RESCUE.

Lupo Vulp had endeavoured to dissuade Sir Giles from putting his design of arresting Jocelyn into immediate execution; alleging the great risk he would incur, as well from the resolute character of the young man himself, who was certain to offer determined resistance, as from the temper of the company, which, being decidedly adverse to any such step, might occasion a disturbance that would probably result in the prisoner's rescue.

"In any case, Sir Giles," said the wily scrivener, "let me counsel you to tarry till the greater part of the guests be gone, and the assemblage outside dispersed; for I noted many turbulent 'prentices among the mob, who are sure to be troublesome."

"Since the young man shows no present disposition to quit the house," Sir Giles replied, looking askance at Jocelyn, who just then had moved to another part of the room with Madame Bonaventure, "there is no urgency; and it may be prudent to pause a few moments, as you suggest, good Lupo. But I will not suffer him to depart. I perceive, from her gestures and glances, that our tricksy hostess is plotting some scheme with him. Plot away, fair mistress; you must have more cunning than I give you credit for, if you outwit me a second time in the same day. I can guess what she proposes. You note that side door near them, Lupo? She is advising the youth's flight that way; and he, like a hair-brained fool, will not listen to the suggestion. But it will be well to watch the outlet. Hark ye, Lanyere," he added to the promoter, "take three men with you, and go round quickly to the passage with which yon door communicates. Station yourselves near the outlet; and if Mounchensey comes forth, arrest him instantly. You see the door I mean? About it, quick!"

And Lanyere instantly departed with three of the myrmidons.

"I would this arrest could be lawfully effected, Sir Giles," said Lupo Vulp, "by a serjeant-at-arms or pursuivant. There would then be no risk. Again I venture to counsel you to proceed regularly. No great delay would be occasioned, if your worship went to Westminster, and made a complaint against the young man before the Council. In that case a messenger of the Court would be despatched to attach his person; and even if he should quit the house in the meanwhile, Lanyere will keep on his track. That were the surest course. As to the manner of proceeding, I conclude it will be by Ore tenus. It is not likely that this youth's headstrong temper, coupled with his fantastic notions of honour, will permit him to deny your worship's accusation, and therefore his confession being written down, and subscribed by himself, will be exhibited against him when he is brought to the bar of the Star-Chamber, and he will be judged ex ore suo. Your worship will make quick work of it."

"Cum confitente reo citius est agendum" replied Sir Giles. "No one knows better than thou, good Lupo, how promptly and effectually the court of Star-Chamber will vindicate its authority, and how severely it will punish those who derogate from its dignity. No part of the sentence shall be remitted with my consent. This insolent youth shall suffer to the same extent as Lanyere. Pilloried, branded, mutilated, degraded, he shall serve as a warning to my enemies."

"Your worship can scarce make him more of a scarecrow than you have made of Lanyere," Lupo remarked with a grin. "But do you decide on applying in the first instance to the Council?"

"No," Sir Giles replied, "I will not lose sight of him. He shall not have a chance of escape. Marked you not, Lupo, how the rash fool committed himself with Buckingham? And think you the proud Marquis would hold me blameless, if, by accident, he should get off scot-free, after such an outrage? But see! the room is well-nigh cleared. Only a few loiterers remain. The time is come."

And he was about to order the attack, when the disturbance outside reached his ears, and checked him for a moment. Sir Giles was considering what could be the cause of the tumult, and hesitating whether to go forth and support Sir Francis, in case he stood in need of assistance, when the discomfited myrmidons rushed into the room. A few words sufficed to explain what had occurred, and indeed the bloody visages of some of the men showed how roughly they had

been handled. Though greatly exasperated, Sir Giles was determined not to be baulked of his prey; and fearing Jocelyn might escape in the confusion, which an attack upon the 'prentices would occasion, he gave the word for his instant seizure, and rushed towards him, as before related. How he was baffled has already been told. His wrath knew no bounds when the young man disappeared. He hurled himself furiously against the door, but it resisted all his efforts to burst it open. Suddenly the bolt was withdrawn, and Clement Lanyere and his men stood before him.

"Have you secured him?" Sir Giles demanded, trying to descry the fugitive among them. "Death and fiends! you have not let him escape?"

"No one has passed us, except Madame Bonaventure," the promoter replied. "She was wholly unattended, and came in this direction. We were stationed within yon anti-chamber, which appears to be the sole means of communication with this passage, and we ought therefore to have intercepted the young man when he came forth."

"You were not wont to be thus short-sighted, Lanyere. There must be some other mode of exit, which you have failed to discover," Sir Giles cried furiously. "Ha! here it is!" he exclaimed, dashing aside a piece of tapestry that seemed merely hung against the wall, but in reality concealed a short flight of steps. "Purblind dolts that you are, not to find this out. You shall answer for your negligence hereafter, if we take him not."

And, accompanied by the troop, he hurried down the steps, which brought him to a lower room, communicating on one hand with a small court, and, on the other, with the kitchen and offices attached to the tavern. Directing Lanyere to search the latter, Sir Giles rushed into the court, and uttered a shout of savage joy on perceiving Jocelyn, sword in hand, scaling a wall which separated the court from the bowling-green.

Some difficulty, it appeared, had occurred to the hostess in forcing open a private door in the yard leading to the green, which being rarely used (for the principal entrance was situated elsewhere), its fastenings were rusty, and refused to act. This delay favoured the

pursuers; and on hearing their approach, Jocelyn strove to effect his retreat in the manner described.

But Sir Giles was further served, though unintentionally, by Madame Bonaventure, who succeeded in drawing back the rusty bolt at the very moment he came up; and no impediment now existing, the knight thrust her rudely aside, and sprang through the doorway just as Jocelyn leaped from the wall.

Disregarding Sir Giles's summons to surrender, the young man hurried on till he reached the middle of the bowling-green, where, finding flight impossible, as there was no apparent outlet at the further end of the garden, while it was certain that the tipstaves would pluck him from the wall with their hooks if he attempted to clamber over it, he turned, and stood upon his defence.

Willing to have the credit of disarming him unaided, and confident in his own superior strength and skill, Sir Giles signed to his myrmidons to stand back, while he alone advanced towards the young man. A turn in his strong wrist would, he imagined, suffice to accomplish his purpose. But he found out his error the moment he engaged with his opponent. In dexterity and force the latter was fully his match, while in nimbleness of body Jocelyn surpassed him. The deadly glances thrown at him by the young man showed that the animosity of the latter would only be satisfied with blood. Changing his purpose, therefore, Sir Giles, in place of attempting to cross his antagonist's sword, rapidly disengaged his point, and delivered a stoccata, or in modern terms of fence, a thrust in carte, over the arm, which was instantly parried. For some minutes the conflict continued without material success on either side. Holding his rapier short, with the point towards his adversary's face, Jocelyn retreated a few paces at first, but then, charging in turn, speedily won back his ground. Stoccatas, imbroccatas, drittas, mandrittas, and riversas were exchanged between them in a manner that delighted the myrmidons, most of whom were amateurs of sword-play. Infuriated by the unexpected resistance he encountered, Sir Giles, at length, resolved to terminate the fight; and, finding his antagonist constantly upon some sure ward, endeavoured to reach him with a half incartata; but instantly shifting his body with marvellous dexterity, Jocelyn struck down the other's blade, and replied with a straight thrust, which must infallibly have taken effect, if his rapier had not been beaten

from his grasp by Clement Lanyere at the very moment it touched his adversary's breast. At the same time the young man's arms were grasped from behind by two of the myrmidons, and he lay at his enemy's disposal.

Sir Giles, however, sheathed his rapier, saying, with a grim smile, "that he did not mean to deprive himself of the satisfaction of seeing his foe stand in the pillory, and submit to the sworn torturer's knife;" adding, "it was somewhat strange that one who could guard his body so well, should keep such indifferent watch over his tongue."

Jocelyn made no reply to the sarcasm, and the knight was preparing to depart with his followers, when a loud and tumultuous uproar proclaimed the approach of the apprentices. The posse of victorious youths made their way to the bowling-green by the principal entrance, situated, as before mentioned, at a different point from the door by which the others had gained it. More apprehensive of losing his prisoner, than concerned for his personal safety (for though the aggressive party greatly exceeded his own in numbers, he knew well how to deal with them, being accustomed to such encounters), Sir Giles gave some orders respecting Jocelyn to Clement Lanyere, and then prepared to resist the onslaught, by causing his band to form a solid square; those armed with bills and staves being placed in the foremost ranks. This disposition being quickly made, he drew his sword, and in a loud authoritative tone commanded the apprentices to stand back. Such was the effect produced by his voice, and the terrors of his countenance, which seldom failed to strike awe into beholders, that the intending rescuers came to a halt, and showed some hesitation in engaging him.

"What means this disturbance?" thundered Sir Giles; "and why do you offer to molest me in the execution of my duty? Know you not that assemblages like yours are unlawful, and that you are liable to severe punishment, unless you immediately disperse yourselves, and peaceably depart to your own habitations? About your business, I say, and trouble me no longer! But first, I command you to deliver up your ringleaders, and especially those who, as I am told, have perpetrated the gross outrage and violence upon the person of Sir Francis Mitchell. An example shall be made of them."

"You waste your breath, Sir Giles, and your big words will avail you nothing with us," Dick Taverner replied. "Now hear me in return.

We, the bold and loyal 'prentices of London, who serve our masters and our masters' master, the king's highness, well and truly, will not allow an unlawful arrest to be made by you or by any other man. And we command you peaceably to deliver up your prisoner to us; or, by the rood! we will take him forcibly from your hands!"

"Out, insolent fellow!" cried Sir Giles; "thou wilt alter thy tune when thou art scourged at the cart's-tail."

"You must catch me first, Sir Giles," replied Dick; "and two words will go to that. We have read Sir Francis Mitchell a lesson he is not likely to forget; and we will read you one, an you provoke us. We have a few old scores to wipe off."

"Ay, marry! have we," cried an embroiderer's apprentice; "these extortioners have ruined my master's trade by their gold-and-silver-thread monopoly."

"Hundreds of worthy men have been thrown out of employment by their practices," said a vintner's 'prentice. "We sell not half the wine we used to do. And no wonder! seeing two-thirds of the inns in London are shut up."

"The brewers will be all ruined," said a burly 'prentice, with a wooden shovel over his shoulder; "since every day a fresh ale-house is closed; and no new licences are granted. Murrain seize all such monopolists! They are worse than the fly in hops, or smut in barley."

"Ay, plague take 'em!" exclaimed Dick Taverner. "They are as bad as the locusts of Egypt. When they have devoured the substance of one set of tradesfolk they will commence upon that of another. No one is safe from them. It will be your turn next, Master Mercer. Yours after him, Master Ironmonger, however hard of digestion may be your wares. You will come third, Master Fishmonger. You fourth, Master Grocer. And when they are surfeited with spiceries and fish, they will fall upon you, tooth and nail, Master Goldsmith."

"I trow not," cried the apprentice last appealed to. "Our masters are too rich and too powerful to submit to such usage."

"The very reason they will undergo it," replied Dick. "Their riches are only a temptation to plunder. I repeat, no man is safe from

these extortioners. Since the law will not give us redress, and put them down, we must take the law into our own hands. They shall have Club Law."

"Ay, ay—'Prentices' law—Club law!" chorussed the others.

"Sir Giles will make a Star-Chamber matter of it. He will have us up before the Council," laughed the goldsmith's 'prentice.

"He will buy a monopoly of cudgels to deprive us of their use," cried a bowyer.

"We will bestow that patent upon him gratis," quoth Dick, making his staff whistle round his head.

"The prisoner!—gentlemen 'prentices—do not forget him!" cried Cyprien, who, with two other serving-men and the cook, had joined the assailing party. "Madame Bonaventure implores you to effect his rescue."

"And so we will, my jovial Gascon," replied Dick. "Come, Sir Giles! are we to have the young gentleman from you by force or free-will?"

"You shall have him in neither way, sirrah," the knight rejoined. "You, yourself, shall bear him company in the Fleet. Upon them, my men, and make for the door!"

And as the command was given, he and his troop made a sudden dash upon the 'prentices, who, unable to stand against the bills levelled against their breasts, gave way. Still, the gallant youths were by no means routed. Instantly closing upon their opponents, and being quite as nimble of foot as they, they contrived to cut off their retreat from the garden; and a sharp conflict took place between the parties, as they came to close quarters near the entrance. Three of the myrmidons were felled by Dick Taverner's cudgel; and at last, watching his opportunity, with both hands he launched a bowl which he had picked up at Sir Giles's head. If the missile had taken effect, the fight would have been over; but the knight avoided the blow by stooping down, and the bowl, passing over him, hit Lupo Vulp full in the stomach, and brought him to the ground deprived of

breath. Meanwhile, Sir Giles, springing quickly forward, pinned the apprentice against the wall with his rapier's point.

"I have thee at last, knave," he cried, seizing Dick by the collar, and delivering him to the custody of the myrmidons nearest him—"I told thee thou should'st visit the Fleet. And so thou shalt."

Notwithstanding the capture of their leader, the 'prentices fought manfully, and it still appeared doubtful whether Sir Giles would be able to effect a retreat after all, embarrassed as he now was with two prisoners. Under these circumstances he made a sign to Clement Lanyere to withdraw with Jocelyn through the other door, ordering the two myrmidons who had charge of Dick Taverner to follow him with their captive.

It was no easy task to carry out the order; but the promoter managed to accomplish it. Single-handed he drove back all who opposed his progress, while the two prisoners were borne towards the door by the men having them in custody.

Hitherto Jocelyn had made no attempt at self-liberation; awaiting, probably, the result of the 'prentices' efforts in his behalf, or some more favourable opportunity than had hitherto presented itself. On reaching the little court the time for exertion seemed to be come. Shaking off the myrmidons who pinioned him, and seizing a bill from one of them, he instantly stretched the fellow at his feet, and drove off his comrade. This done, he lent immediate assistance to Dick Taverner, setting him free, and arming him with as much promptitude as he had used to effect his own deliverance.

While thus engaged, he received no interruption from Clement Lanyere, though, if he had chosen, the promoter might no doubt have effectually opposed him. But Lanyere either was, or feigned to be, engaged with some skirmishers at the door; and it was only when both the prisoners had got free, that he rushed towards them, loudly reprehending the men for their carelessness. But if they were to blame, he was no less so, for he showed little address in following the fugitives, and managed to take a wrong turn in the passage, which led both him and the myrmidons astray, so that the prisoners got clear off.

How Jocelyn and Dick Taverner contrived to reach the Vintry Wharf, neither of them very distinctly knew,—such was the hurried

manner in which they passed through the tavern; but there they were, precisely at the moment that Sir Giles Mompesson, having fought his way through all opposition, issued from the porch at the head of his band.

Quite satisfied with his previous encounter with the redoubtable knight, and anxious to escape before his evasion should be discovered, Dick beckoned to his companion, and, making all the haste they could to the stairs, they both jumped into the nearest wherry, when the apprentice ordered the two watermen within it to row for their lives to London-bridge.

CHAPTER XIII.
HOW JOCELYN MOUNCHENSEY ENCOUNTERED A MASKED HORSEMAN ON STAMFORD HILL.

Two days after the events last recorded, a horseman, followed at a respectful distance by a mounted attendant, took his way up Stamford Hill. He was young, and of singularly prepossessing appearance, with a countenance full of fire and spirit, and blooming with health, and it was easy to see that his life had been passed in the country, and in constant manly exercise; for though he managed his horse — a powerful bay charger — to perfection, there was nothing of the town gallant, or of the soldier, about him. His doublet and cloak were of a plain dark material, and had seen service; but they well became his fine symmetrical figure, as did the buff boots defending his well-made, vigorous limbs. Better seat in saddle, or lighter hand with bridle, no man could possess than he; and his noble steed, which like himself was full of courage and ardour, responded to all his movements, and obeyed the slightest indication of his will. His arms were rapier and dagger; and his broad-leaved hat, ornamented with a black feather, covered the luxuriant brown locks that fell in long ringlets over his shoulders. So débonnair was the young horseman in deportment, so graceful in figure, and so comely in looks, that he had excited no little admiration as he rode forth at an early hour that morning from Bishopgate Street, and passing under the wide portal in the old city walls, speeded towards the then rural district of Shoreditch, leaving Old Bedlam and its saddening associations on the right, and Finsbury Fields, with its gardens, dog-houses, and windmills, on the left. At the end of Bishopgate-Street-Without a considerable crowd was collected round a party of comely young milkmaids, who were

executing a lively and characteristic dance to the accompaniment of a bagpipe and fiddle. Instead of carrying pails as was their wont, these milkmaids, who were all very neatly attired, bore on their heads a pile of silver plate, borrowed for the occasion, arranged like a pyramid, and adorned with ribands and flowers. In this way they visited all their customers and danced before their doors. A pretty usage then observed in the environs of the metropolis in the month of May. The merry milkmaids set up a joyous shout as the youth rode by; and many a bright eye followed his gallant figure till it disappeared. At the Conduit beyond Shoreditch, a pack of young girls, who were drawing water, suspended their task to look after him; and so did every buxom country lass he encountered, whether seated in tilted cart, or on a pillion behind her sturdy sire. To each salutation addressed to him the young man cordially replied, in a voice blithe as his looks; and in some cases, where the greeting was given by an elderly personage, or a cap was respectfully doffed to him, he uncovered his own proud head, and displayed his handsome features yet more fully.

So much for the master: now for the man. In his own opinion, at least—for he was by no means deficient in self-conceit—the latter came in for an equal share of admiration; and certes, if impudence could help him to win it, he lacked not the recommendation. Staring most of the girls out of countenance, he leered at some of them so offensively, that their male companions shook their fists or whips at him, and sometimes launched a stone at his head. Equally free was he in the use of his tongue; and his jests were so scurrilous and so little relished by those to whom they were addressed, that it was, perhaps, well for him, in some instances, that the speed at which he rode soon carried him out of harm's reach. The knave was not ill-favoured; being young, supple of limb, olive-complexioned, black-eyed, saucy, roguish-looking, with a turned-up nose, and extremely white teeth. He wore no livery, and indeed his attire was rather that of a citizen's apprentice than such as beseemed a gentleman's lacquey. He was well mounted on a stout sorrel horse; but though the animal was tractable enough, and easy in its paces, he experienced considerable difficulty in maintaining his seat on its back.

In this way, Jocelyn Mounchensey and Dick Taverner (for the reader will have had no difficulty in recognising the pair) arrived at

Stamford Hill; and the former, drawing in the rein, proceeded slowly up the gentle ascent.

It was one of those delicious spring mornings, when all nature seems to rejoice; when the newly-opened leaves are greenest and freshest; when the lark springs blithest from the verdant mead, and soars nearest heaven; when a thousand other feathered choristers warble forth their notes in copse and hedge: when the rooks caw mellowly near their nests in the lofty trees; when gentle showers, having fallen overnight, have kindly prepared the earth for the morrow's genial warmth and sunshine; when that sunshine, each moment, calls some new object into life and beauty; when all you look upon is pleasant to the eye, all you listen to is delightful to the ear; — in short, it was one of those exquisite mornings, only to be met with in the merry month of May, and only to be experienced in full perfection in Merry England.

Arrived at the summit of the hill, commanding such extensively charming views, Jocelyn halted and looked back with wonder at the vast and populous city he had just quitted, now spread out before him in all its splendour and beauty. In his eyes it seemed already overgrown, though it had not attained a tithe of its present proportions; but he could only judge according to his opportunity, and was unable to foresee its future magnitude. But if London has waxed in size, wealth, and population during the last two centuries and a-half, it has lost nearly all the peculiar features of beauty which distinguished it up to that time, and made it so attractive to Jocelyn's eyes. The diversified and picturesque architecture of its ancient habitations, as yet undisturbed by the innovations of the Italian and Dutch schools, and brought to full perfection in the latter part of the reign of Elizabeth, gave the whole city a characteristic and fanciful appearance. Old towers, old belfries, old crosses, slender spires innumerable, rose up amid a world of quaint gables and angular roofs. Story above story sprang those curious dwellings; irregular yet homogeneous; dear to the painter's and the poet's eye; elaborate in ornament; grotesque in design; well suited to the climate, and admirably adapted to the wants and comforts of the inhabitants; picturesque like the age itself, like its costume, its manners, its literature. All these characteristic beauties and peculiarities are now utterly gone. All the old picturesque habitations have been devoured by fire, and a New City has risen in their stead; —

not to compare with the Old City, though—and conveying no notion whatever of it—any more than you or I, worthy reader, in our formal, and, I grieve to say it, ill-contrived attire, resemble the picturesque-looking denizens of London, clad in doublet, mantle, and hose, in the time of James the First.

Another advantage in those days must not be forgotten. The canopy of smoke overhanging the vast Modern Babel, and oftentimes obscuring even the light of the sun itself, did not dim the beauties of the Ancient City,—sea coal being but little used in comparison with wood, of which there was then abundance, as at this time in the capital of France. Thus the atmosphere was clearer and lighter, and served as a finer medium to reveal objects which would now be lost at a quarter the distance.

Fair, sparkling, and clearly defined, then, rose up Old London before Jocelyn's gaze. Girded round with gray walls, defended by battlements, and approached by lofty gates, four of which—to wit, Cripplegate, Moorgate, Bishopgate, and Aldgate—were visible from where he stood; it riveted attention from its immense congregation of roofs, spires, pinnacles, and vanes, all glittering in the sunshine; while in the midst of all, and pre-eminent above all, towered one gigantic pile—the glorious Gothic cathedral. Far on the east, and beyond the city walls, though surrounded by its own mural defences, was seen the frowning Tower of London—part fortress and part prison—a structure never viewed in those days without terror, being the scene of so many passing tragedies. Looking westward, and rapidly surveying the gardens and pleasant suburban villages lying on the north of the Strand, the young man's gaze settled for a moment on Charing Cross—the elaborately-carved memorial to his Queen, Eleanor, erected by Edward I.—and then ranging over the palace of Whitehall and its two gates, Westminster Abbey—more beautiful without its towers than with them—it became fixed upon Westminster Hall; for there, in one of its chambers, the ceiling of which was adorned with gilded stars, were held the councils of that terrible tribunal which had robbed him of his inheritance, and now threatened him with deprivation of liberty, and mutilation of person. A shudder crossed him as he thought of the Star-Chamber, and he turned his gaze elsewhere, trying to bring the whole glorious city within his ken.

A splendid view, indeed! Well might King James himself exclaim when standing, not many years previously, on the very spot where Jocelyn now stood, and looking upon London for the first time since his accession to the throne of England — well might he exclaim in rapturous accents, as he gazed on the magnificence of his capital — "At last the richest jewel in a monarch's crown is mine!"

After satiating himself with this, to him, novel and wonderful prospect, Jocelyn began to bestow his attention on objects closer at hand, and examined the landscapes on either side of the eminence, which, without offering any features of extraordinary beauty, were generally pleasing, and exercised a soothing influence upon his mind. At that time Stamford Hill was crowned with a grove of trees, and its eastern declivity was overgrown with brushwood. The whole country, on the Essex side, was more or less marshy, until Epping Forest, some three miles off, was reached. Through a swampy vale on the left, the river Lea, so dear to the angler, took its slow and silent course; while through a green valley on the right, flowed the New River, then only just opened. Pointing out the latter channel to Jocelyn, Dick Taverner, who had now come up, informed him that he was present at the completion of that important undertaking. And a famous sight it was, the apprentice said. The Lord Mayor of London, the Aldermen, and the Recorder were all present in their robes and gowns to watch the floodgate opened, which was to pour the stream that had run from Amwell Head into the great cistern near Islington. And this was done amidst deafening cheers and the thunder of ordnance.

"A proud day it was for Sir Hugh Myddleton," Dick added; "and some reward for his perseverance through difficulties and disappointments."

"It is to be hoped the good gentleman has obtained more substantial reward than that," Jocelyn replied. "He has conferred an inestimable boon upon his fellow-citizens, and is entitled to their gratitude for it."

"As to gratitude on the part of the citizens, I can't say much for that, Sir. And it is not every man that meets with his desserts, or we know where our friends Sir Giles Mompesson and Sir Francis Mitchell would be. The good cits are content to drink the pure water of the New River, without bestowing a thought on him who has brought it to their doors. Meantime, the work has well-nigh beggared Sir Hugh

Myddleton, and he is likely to obtain little recompense beyond what the consciousness of his own beneficent act will afford him."

"But will not the King requite him?" Jocelyn asked.

"The King has requited him with a title," Dick returned. "A title, however, which may be purchased at a less price than good Sir Hugh has paid for it, now-a-days. But it must be owned, to our sovereign's credit, that he did far more than the citizens of London would do; since when they refused to assist Master Myddleton (as he then was) in his most useful work, King James undertook, and bound himself by indenture under the great seal, to pay half the expenses. Without this, it would probably never have been accomplished."

"I trust it may be profitable to Sir Hugh in the end," Jocelyn said; "and if not, he will reap his reward hereafter."

"It is not unlikely we may encounter him, as he now dwells near Edmonton, and is frequently on the road," Dick said; "and if so, I will point him out to you, I have some slight acquaintance with him, having often served him in my master's shop in Paul's Churchyard. Talking of Edmonton, with your permission, Sir, we will break our fast at the Bell, (1) where I am known, and where you will be well served. The host is a jovial fellow and trusty, and may give us information which will be useful before we proceed on our perilous expedition to Theobalds."

"I care not how soon we arrive there," Jocelyn cried; "for the morning has so quickened my appetite, that the bare idea of thy host's good cheer makes all delay in attacking it unsupportable."

"I am entirely of your opinion, Sir," Dick said, smacking his lips. "At the Bell at Edmonton we are sure of fresh fish from the Lea, fresh eggs from the farm-yard, and stout ale from the cellar; and if these three things do not constitute a good breakfast, I know not what others do. So let us be jogging onwards. We have barely two miles to ride. Five minutes to Tottenham; ten to Edmonton; 'tis done!"

It was not, however, accomplished quite so soon as Dick anticipated. Ere fifty yards were traversed, they were brought to a stop by an unlooked-for incident.

Suddenly emerging from a thick covert of wood, which had concealed him from view, a horseman planted himself directly in their path; ordering them in a loud, authoritative voice, to stand; and

enforcing attention to the injunction by levelling a caliver at Jocelyn's head.

The appearance of this personage was as mysterious as formidable. The upper part of his features was concealed by a black mask. His habiliments were sable; and the colour of his powerful steed was sable likewise. Boots, cap, cloak, and feather, were all of the same dusky hue. His frame was strongly built, and besides the caliver he was armed with sword and poniard. Altogether, he constituted an unpleasant obstacle in the way.

Dick Taverner was not able to render much assistance on the occasion. The suddenness with which the masked horseman burst forth upon them scared his horse; and the animal becoming unmanageable, began to rear, and finally threw its rider to the ground—luckily without doing him much damage.

Meanwhile the horseman, lowering his caliver, thus addressed Jocelyn, who, taking him for a robber, was prepared to resist the attack.

"You are mistaken in me, Master Jocelyn Mounchensey," he said; "I have no design upon your purse. I call upon you to surrender yourself my prisoner."

"Never, with life," the young man replied. "In spite of your disguise, I recognise you as one of Sir Giles Mompesson's myrmidons; and you may conclude from our former encounter, whether my resistance will be determined or not."

"You had not escaped on that occasion, but for my connivance, Master Jocelyn," the man in the mask rejoined. "Now, hear me. I am willing to befriend you on certain conditions; and, to prove my sincerity, I engage you shall go free if you accept them."

"I do not feel disposed to make any terms with you," Jocelyn said sternly; "and as to my freedom of departure, I will take care that it is not hindered."

"I hold a warrant from the Star-Chamber for your arrest," said the man in the mask; "and you will vainly offer resistance if I choose to execute it. Let this be well understood before I proceed. And now to show you the extent of my information concerning you, and that I am fully aware of your proceedings, I will relate to you what you have done since you fled with that froward apprentice, whose tricks will

assuredly bring him to Bridewell, from the Three Cranes. You were landed at London Bridge, and went thence with your companion to the Rose at Newington Butts, where you lay that night, and remained concealed, as you fancied, during the whole of the next day. I say, you fancied your retreat was unknown, because I was aware of it, and could have seized you had I been so disposed. The next night you removed to the Crown in Bishopgate Street, and as you did not care to return to your lodgings near Saint Botolph's Church without Aldgate, you privily despatched Dick Taverner to bring your horses from the Falcon in Gracechurch Street, where you had left them, with the foolhardy intention of setting forth this morning to Theobalds, to try and obtain an interview of the King."

"You have spoken the truth," Jocelyn replied in amazement; "but if you designed to arrest me, and could have done so, why did you defer your purpose?"

"Question me not on that point. Some day or other I may satisfy you. Not now. Enough that I have conceived a regard for you, and will not harm you, unless compelled to do so by self-defence. Nay more, I will serve you. You must not go to Theobalds. 'Tis a mad scheme, conceived by a hot brain, and will bring destruction upon you. If you persist in it, I must follow you thither, and prevent greater mischief."

"Follow me, then, if you list," Jocelyn cried; "for go I shall. But be assured I will liberate myself from you if I can."

"Go, hot-headed boy," the man in the mask rejoined, but he then added quickly; "yet no!—I will not deliver you thus to the power of your enemies, without a further effort to save you. Since you are resolved to go to Theobalds you must have a protector—a protector able to shield you even from Buckingham, whose enmity you have reason to dread. There is only one person who can do this, and that is Count Gondomar, the Spanish lieger-ambassador. Luckily, he is with the King now. In place of making any idle attempts to obtain an interview of his Majesty, or forcing yourself unauthorised on the royal presence, which will end in your arrest by the Knight Marshall, seek out Count Gondomar, and deliver this token to him. Tell him your story; and do what he bids you."

And as he spoke the man in the mask held forth a ring, which Jocelyn took.

"I intended to make certain conditions with you," the mysterious personage pursued, "for the service I should render you, but you have thwarted my plans by your obstinacy, and I must reserve them to our next meeting. For we shall meet again, and that ere long; and then when you tender your thanks for what I have now done, I will tell you how to requite the obligation."

"I swear to requite it if I can—and as you desire," Jocelyn cried, struck by the other's manner.

"Enough!" the masked personage rejoined. "I am satisfied. Proceed on your way, and may good fortune attend you! Your destiny is in your own hands. Obey Count Gondomar's behests, and he will aid you effectually."

And without a word more, the man in the mask struck spurs into his horse's sides, and dashed down the hill, at a headlong pace, in the direction of London.

Jocelyn looked after him, and had not recovered from his surprise at the singular interview that had taken place when he disappeared.

By this time, Dick Taverner having regained his feet, limped towards him, leading his horse.

"It must be the Fiend in person," quoth the apprentice, contriving to regain the saddle. "I trust you have made no compact with him, Sir."

"Not a sinful one I hope," Jocelyn replied, glancing at the ring.

And they proceeded on their way towards Tottenham, and were presently saluted by the merry ringing of bells, proclaiming some village festival.

NOTE 1: Lest we should be charged with an anachronism, we may mention that the Bell at Edmonton, immortalized in the story of John Gilpin, was in good repute in the days we treat of, as will appear from the following extract from John Savile's Tractate entitled, King James, his Entertainment at Theobald's, with his Welcome to London. Having described the vast concourse of people that flocked forth to greet their new Sovereign on his approach to the metropolis, honest John says—"After our breakfast at Edmonton at the sign of the Bell, we took occasion to note how many would come down in the next hour, so coming up into a chamber next to the street, where we might both best see, and likewise take notice of all passengers, we called for

an hour-glass, and after we had disposed of ourselves who should take the number of the horse, and who the foot, we turned the hour-glass, which before it was half run out, we could not possibly truly number them, they came so exceedingly fast; but there we broke off, and made our account of 309 horses, and 137 footmen, which course continued that day from four o'clock in the morning till three o'clock in the afternoon, and the day before also, as the host of the house told us, without intermission." Besides establishing the existence of the renowned Bell at this period, the foregoing passage is curious in other respects.

CHAPTER XIV.
THE MAY-QUEEN AND THE PURITAN'S DAUGHTER.

Popular sports and pastimes were wisely encouraged by James the First, whose great consideration for the enjoyments of the humbler classes of his subjects cannot be too highly commended; and since the main purpose of this history is to point out some of the abuses prevalent during his reign, it is but fair that at least one of the redeeming features should be mentioned. It has ever been the practice of sour-spirited sectarianism to discountenance recreations of any kind, however harmless, on the Sabbath; and several flagrant instances of this sort of interference, on the part of the puritanical preachers and their disciples, having come before James during his progress through the northern counties of England, and especially Lancashire, he caused, on his return to London, his famous Declaration concerning Lawful Sports on Sundays and holidays to be promulgated; wherein a severe rebuke was administered to the Puritans and precisians, and the cause of the people espoused in terms, which, while most creditable to the monarch, are not altogether inapplicable to other times besides those in which they were delivered. "Whereas," says King James, in his Manifesto, "We did justly rebuke some Puritans and precise people, and took order that the like unlawful carriage should not be used by any of them hereafter, in the prohibiting and unlawful punishing of our good people for using their lawful recreations and honest exercises upon Sundays and other holidays, after the afternoon sermon or service: we now find that two sorts of people wherewith that country is much infested (we mean Papists and Puritans) have maliciously traduced those our just and honourable proceedings. And therefore we have thought good hereby to clear and make our pleasure to be manifested to all our good people in those parts." And he sums up

his arguments, in favour of the license granted, as follows: — "For when shall the common people have leave to exercise, if not upon the Sundays and holidays, seeing they must apply their labour, and win their living in all working days?" Truly, an unanswerable proposition.

At the same time that these provisions for rational recreation were made, all unlawful games were prohibited. Conformity was strictly enjoined on the part of the Puritans themselves; and disobedience was rendered punishable by expatriation, as in the case of recusants generally. Such was the tenor of the royal mandate addressed to the bishop of each diocese and to all inferior clergy throughout the kingdom. Arbitrary it might be, but it was excellent in intention; for stubborn-necked personages had to be dealt with, with whom milder measures would have proved ineffectual. As it was, violent opposition was raised against the decree, and the Puritanical preachers wore loud in its condemnation, and as far as was consistent with safety, vehement in their attacks upon its royal author.

The boon, however, was accepted by the majority of the people in the spirit in which it was offered, and the licence afforded them was but little abused. Perfect success, indeed, must have attended the benign measure, had it not been for the efforts of the Puritanical and Popish parties, who made common cause against it, and strove by every means to counteract its beneficial influence: the first because in the austerity of their faith they would not have the Sabbath in the slightest degree profaned, even by innocent enjoyment; the second, not because they cared about the fancied desecration of the Lord's day, but because they would have no other religion enjoy the same privileges as their own. Thus sectarianism and intolerance went for once hand in hand, and openly or covertly, as they found occasion, did their best to make the people dissatisfied with the benefit accorded them, trying to persuade them its acceptance would prejudice their eternal welfare.

Such arguments, however, had no great weight with the masses, who could not be brought to see any heinous or deadly sin in lawful recreation or exercises after divine service, always provided the service itself were in no respect neglected; and so the King's decree prevailed over all sectarian opposition, and was fully carried out. The merry month of May became really a season of enjoyment, and was kept as a kind of floral festival in every village throughout the

land. May-games, Whitsun-ales, Morrice-dances, were renewed as in bygone times; and all robust and healthful sports, as leaping, vaulting, and archery, were not only permitted on Sundays by the authorities, but enjoined.

These preliminary remarks are made for the better understanding of what is to follow.

We have already stated that long before Jocelyn and his companion reached Tottenham, they were made aware by the ringing of bells from its old ivy-grown church tower, and by other joyful sounds, that some festival was taking place there; and the nature of the festival was at once revealed, as they entered the long straggling street, then, as now, constituting the chief part of the pretty little village, and beheld a large assemblage of country folk, in holiday attire, wending their way towards the green for the purpose of setting up a May-pole upon it, and making the welkin ring with their gladsome shouts.

All the youths and maidens of Tottenham and its vicinity, it appeared, had risen before daybreak that morning, and sallied forth into the woods to cut green boughs, and gather wild—flowers, for the ceremonial. At the same time they selected and hewed down a tall, straight tree—the tallest and straightest they could find; and, stripping off its branches, placed it on a wain, and dragged it to the village with the help of an immense team of oxen, numbering as many as forty yoke. Each ox had a garland of flowers fastened to the tip of its horns; and the tall spar itself was twined round with ropes of daffodils, blue-bells, cowslips, primroses, and other early flowers, while its summit was surmounted with a floral crown, and festooned with garlands, various-coloured ribands, kerchiefs, and streamers. The foremost yokes of oxen had bells hung round their necks, which they shook as they moved along, adding their blithe melody to the general hilarious sounds.

When the festive throng reached the village, all its inhabitants—male and female, old and young—rushed forth to greet them; and such as were able to leave their dwellings for a short while joined in the procession, at the head of which, of course, was borne the May-pole. After it, came a band of young men, armed with the necessary implements for planting the shaft in the ground; and after them a troop of maidens, bearing bundles of rushes. Next came the minstrels, playing merrily on tabor, fife, sacbut, rebec, and tambourine. Then

followed the Queen of the May, walking by herself,—a rustic beauty, hight Gillian Greenford,—fancifully and prettily arrayed for the occasion, and attended, at a little distance, by Robin Hood, Maid Marian, Friar Tuck, the Hobby-horse, and a band of morrice-dancers. Then came the crowd, pellmell, laughing, shouting, and huzzaing,— most of the young men and women bearing green branches of birch and other trees in their hands.

The spot selected for the May-pole was a piece of green sward in the centre of the village, surrounded by picturesque habitations, and having, on one side of it, the ancient Cross. The latter, however, was but the remnant of the antique structure, the cross having been robbed of its upper angular bar, and otherwise mutilated, at the time of the Reformation, and it was now nothing more than a high wooden pillar, partly cased with lead to protect it from the weather, and supported by four great spurs.

Arrived at the green, the wain was brought to a halt; the crowd forming a vast circle round it, so as not to interfere with the proceedings. The pole was then taken out, reared aloft, and so much activity was displayed, so many eager hands assisted, that in an inconceivably short space of time it was firmly planted in the ground; whence it shot up like the central mast of a man-of-war, far overtopping the roofs of the adjoining houses, and looking very gay indeed, with its floral crown a-top, and its kerchiefs and streamers fluttering in the breeze.

Loud and reiterated shouts broke from the assemblage on the satisfactory completion of the ceremony, the church bells pealed merrily, and the minstrels played their most enlivening strains. The rushes were strewn on the ground at the foot of the May-pole, and arbours were formed, with marvellous celerity, in different parts of the green, with the branches of the trees. At the same time, the ancient Cross was decorated with boughs and garlands. The whole scene offered as pretty and cheerful a sight as could be desired; but there was one beholder, as will presently appear, who viewed it in a different light.

It now came to the Queen of the May's turn to advance to the pole, and stationing herself beneath it, the morrice-dancers and the rest of the mummers formed a ring round her, and, taking hands, footed it merrily to the tune of "Green Sleeves."

Long before this, Jocelyn and his attendant had come up, and both were so much interested that they felt no disposition to depart. Gillian's attractions had already fired the inflammable heart of the apprentice, who could not withdraw his gaze from her; and so ardent were his looks, and so expressive his gestures of admiration, that ere long he succeeded, to his no small delight, in attracting her notice in return.

Gillian Greenford was a bright-eyed, fair-haired young creature; light, laughing, radiant; with cheeks soft as peach bloom, and beautifully tinged with red, lips carnation-hued, and teeth white as pearls. Her parti-coloured, linsey-woolsey petticoats looped up on one side disclosed limbs with no sort of rustic clumsiness about them; but, on the contrary, a particularly neat formation both of foot and ankle. Her scarlet bodice, which, like the lower part of her dress, was decorated with spangles, bugles, and tinsel ornaments of various kinds,—very resplendent in the eyes of the surrounding swains, as well as in those of Dick Taverner,—her bodice, we say, spanning a slender waist, was laced across, while the snowy kerchief beneath it did not totally conceal a very comely bust. A wreath of natural flowers was twined very gracefully within her waving and almost lint-white locks, and in her hand she held a shepherdess's crook. Such was the Beauty of Tottenham, and the present Queen of the May. Dick Taverner thought her little less than angelic, and there were many besides who shared in his opinion.

If Dick had been thus captivated on the sudden, Jocelyn had not escaped similar fascination from another quarter. It befel in this way:

At an open oriel window, in one of the ancient and picturesque habitations before described as facing the green, stood a young maiden, whose beauty was of so high an order, and so peculiar a character, that it at once attracted and fixed attention. Such, at least, was the effect produced by it on Jocelyn. Shrinking from the public gaze, and, perhaps, from some motive connected with religious scruples, scarcely deeming it right to be a spectator of the passing scene, this fair maiden was so placed as to be almost screened from general view. Yet it chanced that Jocelyn, from the circumstance of being on horseback, and from his position, was able to command a portion of the room in which she stood; and he watched her for some minutes before she became aware she was the object of his regards.

When, at length, she perceived that his gaze was steadily fixed upon her, a deep blush suffused her cheeks, and she would have instantly retired, if the young man had not at once lowered his looks. Still, he ever and anon ventured a glance towards the oriel window, and was delighted to find the maiden still there, — nay, he fancied she must have advanced a step or two, for he could unquestionably distinguish her features more plainly. And lovely they were — most lovely! pensive in expression, and perhaps a thought too pale, until the crimsoning tide had mounted to her cheek. Thus mantled with blushes, her countenance might gain something in beauty, but it lost much of the peculiar charm which it derived from extreme transparency and whiteness of skin — a tint which set off to perfection the splendour of her magnificent black eyes, with their darkly-fringed lids and brows, while it also relieved, in an equal degree, the jetty lustre of her hair. Her features were exquisitely chiselled, delicate and classical in mould, and stamped with refinement and intelligence. Perfect simplicity, combined with a total absence of personal ornament, distinguished her attire; and her raven hair was plainly, but by no means unbecomingly, braided over her snowy forehead. Something in this simplicity of costume and in her manner inclined Jocelyn to think the fair maiden must belong to some family professing Puritanical opinions; and he found, upon inquiry from one of his neighbours in the throng — an old farmer — that this was actually the case.

The young lady was Mistress Aveline Calveley, his informant said, only child of Master Hugh Calveley, who had but lately come to dwell in Tottenham, and of whom little was known, save that he was understood to have fought at the battle of Langside, and served with great bravery, under Essex, both in Spain and in Ireland, in the times of good Queen Bess — such times as England would never see again, the old farmer parenthetically remarked, with a shake of the head. Master Hugh Calveley, he went on to say, was a strict Puritan, austere in his life, and morose in manner; an open railer against the licence of the times, and the profligacy of the court minions, — in consequence of which he had more than once got himself into trouble. He abhorred all such sports as were now going forward; and had successfully interfered with the parish priest, Sir Onesimus, who was somewhat of a precisian himself, to prevent the setting up the May-pole on the past Sunday, — for which, the farmer added, some of the young folks

owe him a grudge; and he expressed a hope, at the same time, that the day might pass by without any exhibition being made of their ill-will towards him.

"These Puritans are not in favour with our youth," the old man said; "and no great marvel they be not; for they check them in their pleasures, and reprove them for harmless mirth. Now, as to Mistress Aveline herself, she is devout and good; but she takes no part in the enjoyments proper to her years, and leads a life more like a nun in a convent, or a recluse in a cell, than a marriageable young lady. She never stirs forth without her father, and, as you may suppose, goes more frequently to lecture, or to church, or to some conventicle, than anywhere else. Such a life would not suit my grandchild, Gillian, at all. Nevertheless, Mistress Aveline is a sweet young lady, much beloved for her kindness and goodness; and her gentle words have healed many a wound occasioned by the harsh speech and severe reproofs of her father. There, Sir, — you may behold her fair and saintly countenance now. She seems pleased with the scene, and I am sure she well may be; for it is always a pleasant and a heart-cheering sight to see folks happy and enjoying themselves; and I cannot think that the beneficent Power above ever intended we should make ourselves miserable on earth, in order to win a place in heaven. I am an old man, Sir; and feeling this to be true, I have ever inculcated my opinions upon my children and grandchildren. Yet I confess I am surprised — knowing what I do of her father's character — that Mistress Aveline should indulge herself with beholding this profane spectacle, which ought, by rights, to be odious in her eyes."

The latter part of this speech was uttered with a sly chuckle on the part of the old farmer, not altogether agreeable to Jocelyn. The growing interest he felt in the fair Puritan rendered him susceptible. The eyes of the two young persons had met again more than once, and were not quite so quickly withdrawn on either side as before; perhaps, because Aveline was less alarmed by the young man's appearance, or more attracted by it; and perhaps, on his part, because he had grown a little bolder. We know not how this might be; but we do know that the fair Puritan had gradually advanced towards the front of the window, and was now leaning slightly out of it, so that her charms of face and figure were more fully revealed.

Meanwhile, the May-pole had been planted, and the first dance round it concluded. At its close, Gillian, quitting her post of honour near the tree, and leaving the morrice-dancers and mummers to resume their merry rounds, unsanctioned by her sovereign presence, took a tambourine from one of the minstrels, and proceeded to collect gratuities within it intended for the hired performers in the ceremony. She was very successful in her efforts, as the number of coins, soon visible within the tambourine, showed. Not without blushing and some hesitation did the May Queen approach Dick Taverner. The 'prentice made a pretence of fumbling in his pouch in order to prolong the interview, which chance had thus procured him; and after uttering all the complimentary phrases he could muster, and looking a great deal more than he said, he wound up his speech by declaring he would bestow a mark (and that was no slight sum, for the highest coin yet given was a silver groat) upon the minstrels, if they would play a lively dance for him, and she, the May Queen, would grace him with her hand in it. Encouraged by the laughter of the bystanders, and doubtless entertaining no great dislike to the proposal, Gillian, with a little affected coyness, consented; and the mark was immediately deposited in the tambourine by Dick, who, transported by his success, sprang from his saddle, and committing his steed to the care of a youth near him, whom he promised to reward for his trouble, followed close after the May Queen, as she proceeded with her collection. Ere long she came to Jocelyn, and held out the tambourine towards him. An idea just then occurred to the young man.

"You have a pretty nosegay there, fair maiden," he said, pointing to a bunch of pinks and other fragrant flowers in her breast. "I will buy it from you, if you list."

"You shall have it and welcome, fair Sir," Gillian replied, detaching the bouquet from her dress, and offering it to him.

"Well done, Gillian," the old farmer cried approvingly.

"Ah! are you there, grandsire!" the May Queen exclaimed. "Come! your gift for the minstrels and mummers — quick! quick!"

And while old Greenford searched for a small coin, Jocelyn placed a piece of silver in the tambourine.

"Will you do me a favour, my pretty maiden?" he said courteously.

"That I will, right willingly, fair Sir," she replied; "provided I may do it honestly."

"You shall not do it else," old Greenford observed.

"Come, your gift, grandsire — you are slow in finding it."

"Have patience, wench, have patience. Young folks are always in a hurry. Here 'tis!"

"Only a silver groat!" she exclaimed, tossing her head. "Why, this young man behind me gave a mark; and so did this gallant gentleman on horseback."

"Poh! poh! go along, wench. They will take better care of their money when they grow older."

"Stay, my pretty maiden," Jocelyn cried; "you have promised to do me a favour."

"What is it?" she inquired.

"Present this nosegay on my part to the young lady in yonder window."

"What! offer this to Mistress Aveline Calveley?" Gillian exclaimed in surprise. "Are you sure she will accept it, Sir?"

"Tut! do his bidding, child, without more ado," old Greenford interposed. "I shall like to see what will come of it — ha! ha!"

Gillian could not help smiling too, and proceeded on her mission. Jocelyn put his horse into motion, and slowly followed her, almost expecting Aveline to withdraw. But he was agreeably disappointed by finding her maintain her place at the window. She must have remarked what was going forward, and therefore her tarrying emboldened him, and buoyed up his hopes.

Arrived beneath the window, Gillian committed the tambourine to Dick Taverner, who still hovered behind her like her shadow, and fastening the bouquet to the end of her shepherdess's crook held it up towards Aveline, crying out, in a playful tone, and with an arch look, "'Tis a love gift to Mistress Aveline Calveley on the part of that young cavalier."

Whether the offering, thus presented, would have been accepted may be questioned; but it was never destined to reach her for whom it was intended. Scarcely was the flower-laden crook uplifted, than a man of singularly stern aspect, with gray hair cut close to the head, grizzled beard, and military habiliments of ancient make, suddenly appeared behind Aveline, and seizing the nosegay, cast it angrily and contemptuously forth; so that it fell at Jocelyn's feet.

CHAPTER XV.
HUGH CALVELEY.

Jocelyn at once comprehended that the person who had thus dashed the nosegay to the ground could be no other than Hugh Calveley. But all doubt on the point was removed by Aveline herself who exclaimed in a reproachful tone—"O father! what have you done?"

"What have I done?" the Puritan rejoined, speaking in a loud voice, as if desirous that his words should reach the assemblage outside. "I have done that which thou thyself should'st have done, Aveline. I have signified my abhorrence of this vain ceremonial. But wherefore do I find you here? This is no fitting sight for any discreet maiden to witness; and little did I think that daughter of mine would encourage such profane displays by her presence. Little did I think that you, Aveline, would look on and smile while these ignorant and benighted folk set up their idol, piping, dancing, and singing around it as the Gentiles did at the dedications of their deities. For it is an idol they have set up, and they have become like the heathens, worshippers of stocks and stones. Are we not expressly forbidden by the Holy Scriptures to make unto ourselves idols and graven images? The sins of idolatry and superstition will assuredly provoke the Divine displeasure, and kindle the fire of its wrath, as they did in the days of Moses, after the worshipping of the Golden Calf by the Israelites. Thus spake offended Heaven:—'Let me alone that my wrath may wax hot against them, and that I may consume them.' Grievously will the Lord punish such as are guilty of these sins, for hath He not declared, as we read in Leviticus, 'I will make your cities waste, and bring your sanctuaries to desolation?' And be assured, O daughter, that heavy judgments will descend upon the land, if warning be not taken in time."

"Nay, dear father, I cannot view the matter in the same serious light that you do," Aveline rejoined, "neither do I think evil can be derived from pastimes like the present, unless by the evil disposed. I must frankly own that it is pleasant to me to witness such innocent enjoyment as is here exhibited; while as to yon May-pole, with its pretty floral decorations, I can never be brought to regard it as an emblem of superstition and idolatry. Nevertheless, had you commanded me to refrain from the sight, I would unhesitatingly have obeyed you. But I thought I was free to follow my own inclinations."

"Why so you were, child," the Puritan rejoined, "because I had full reliance on you, and did not conceive you could have been so easily beguiled by Satan. I lament to find you cannot discern the superstition and wickedness lurking within this false, though fair-seeming spectacle. Do you not perceive that in setting up this wooden idol, and worshipping it, these people are returning to the dark and sinful practices of Paganism of which it is an undoubted remnant? If you cannot discern this, I will make it manifest to you anon. But I tell you now briefly," he continued in a voice of thunder, calculated to reach those at a distance, "that the ceremony is impious; that those who take part in it are idolaters; and that those who look on and approve are participators in the sin; yea, are equal in sin to the actors themselves."

Hereupon some murmurs of displeasure arose among the crowd, but they were instantly checked by the curiosity generally felt to hear Aveline's reply, which was delivered in clear and gentle, but distinct tones.

"Far be it from me to dispute with you, dear father," she said; "and it is with reluctance that I offer an opinion at all adverse to your own. But it seems to me impossible to connect these pastimes with heathenish and superstitious rites; for though they may bear some resemblance to ceremonials performed in honour of the goddesses Maia and Flora, yet, such creeds being utterly forgotten, and their spirit extinct, it cannot revive in sports that have merely reference to harmless enjoyment. Not one, I am sure, of these worthy folk has the slightest thought of impiety."

"You know not what you say, girl," the Puritan rejoined sharply. "The evil spirit is not extinct, and these growing abominations prove it to be again raising its baleful crest to pollute and destroy. Listen

to my words, ye vain and foolish ones!" he continued, advancing to the front of the window, and stretching forth his arms towards the assemblage. "Repent! and amend your ways ere it be too late! Hew down the offensive idol, which you term your May-pole, and cast it into the flames! Cease your wanton sports, your noisy pipings, your profane dances, your filthy tipplings. Hear what the prophet Isaiah saith: — 'Wo to them that rise up early in the morning, that they may follow strong drink.' And again: — 'Wo to the drunkards of Ephraim.' And I say Wo unto you also, for you are like unto those drunkards. 'O do not this abominable thing that my soul hateth.' Be not guilty of the brutish sin of drunkenness. Reflect on the words of holy Job, — 'They take the timbrel and harp, and rejoice at the sound of the organ. They spend their days in mirth, and in a moment go down, to the grave.' Hew down your idol I say again. Consume it utterly, and scatter its ashes to the winds. Strip off the gaudes and tinsel in which you have decked your foolish May Queen. Have done with your senseless and profane mummeries; and dismiss your Robin Hoods, your Friar Tucks, and your Hobby-horses. Silence your pestilent minstrels, and depart peaceably to your own homes. Abandon your sinful courses, or assuredly 'the Lord will come upon you unawares, and cut you in sunder, and appoint your portion among unbelievers.'"

So sonorous was the voice of the Puritan, so impressive were his looks and gestures, that his address commanded general attention. While he continued to speak, the sports were wholly stopped. The minstrels left off playing to listen to him, and the mummers suspended their merry evolutions round the May-pole. The poor denounced May Queen, who on the rejection of her nosegay had flown back to Jocelyn, now looked doubly disconcerted at this direct attack upon her and her finery, and pouted her pretty lips in vexation. Dick Taverner, who stood by her side, seemed disposed to resent the affront, and shook his fist menacingly at the Puritan. Jocelyn himself was perplexed and annoyed, for though inclined to take part with the assemblage, the growing interest he felt in Aveline forbade all interference with her father.

CHAPTER XVI.
OF THE SIGN GIVEN BY THE PURITAN TO THE ASSEMBLAGE.

Meanwhile, a great crowd had collected beneath the window, and though no interruption was offered to the speaker, it was easy to discern from the angry countenances of his hearers what was the effect of the address upon them. When he had done, Hugh Calveley folded his arms upon his breast, and sternly regarded the assemblage.

He was well-stricken in years, as his grizzled hair and beard denoted, but neither was his strength impaired, nor the fire of his eye dimmed. Squarely built, with hard and somewhat massive features, strongly stamped with austerity, he was distinguished by a soldier-like deportment and manner, while his bronzed countenance, which bore upon it more than one cicatrice, showed he must have been exposed to foreign suns, and seen much service. There was great determination about the mouth, and about the physiognomy generally, while at the same time there was something of the wildness of fanaticism in his looks. He was habited in a buff jerkin, with a brown, lackered, breast-plate over it, thigh-pieces of a similar colour and similar material, and stout leathern boots. A broad belt with a heavy sword attached to, it crossed his breast, and round his neck was a plain falling band. You could not regard Hugh Calveley without feeling he was a man to die a martyr in any cause he had espoused.

A deep groan was now directed against him. But it moved not a muscle of his rigid countenance.

Jocelyn began to fear from the menacing looks of the crowd that some violence might be attempted, and he endeavoured to check it.

"Bear with him, worthy friends," he cried, "he means you well, though he may reprove you somewhat too sharply."

"Beshrew him for an envious railer," cried a miller, "he mars all our pleasures with his peevish humours. He would have us all as discontented with the world as himself—but we know better. He will not let us have our lawful sports as enjoined by the King himself on Sundays, and he now tries to interfere with our recreations on holidays. A pest upon him for a cankerbitten churl!"

"His sullen looks are enough to turn all the cream in the village sour," observed an old dame.

"Why doth he not betake himself to the conventicle and preach there?" old Greenford cried. "Why should we have all these bitter texts of scripture thrown at our heads? Why should we be likened to the drunkards of Ephraim because we drink our Whitsun-ales? I have tasted nothing more than my morning cup as yet."

"Why should our May-pole be termed an idol? Answer me that, good grandsire?" Gillian demanded.

"Nay, let him who called it so answer thee, child, for I cannot," the old farmer rejoined. "I can see naught idolatrous in it."

"Why should our pretty May Queen be despoiled of her ornaments because they please not his fanatical taste?" Dick Taverner demanded. "For my part I can discern no difference between a Puritan and a knave, and I would hang both."

This sally met with a favourable reception from the crowd, and a voice exclaimed—"Ay, hang all knavish Puritans."

Again Hugh Calveley lifted up his voice. "Think not to make me afraid," he cried; "I have confronted armed hosts with boldness when engaged in a worse cause than this, and I am not likely to give way before a base rabble, now that I have become a soldier of Christ and fight his battles. I repeat my warnings to you, and will not hold my peace till you give heed to them. Continue not in the sins of the Gentiles lest their punishment come upon you. These are fearful times we live in. London is become another Nineveh, and will be devoured by flames like that great city. It is full of corruption and debauchery, of oppressions, thefts, and deceits. With the prophet Nahum I exclaim—'Wo to the city, it is full of lies and robbery! What griping usury, what extortion are practised within it! What fraud, what injustice, what misrule! But the Lord's anger will be awakened against it. Palaces of kings are of no more account in His eyes than cottages of peasants.—

He cutteth off the spirits of Princes: he is terrible to the Kings of the earth.' He knoweth no difference between them that sit on thrones, and those that go from door to door. For what saith the prophet Isaiah?—'I will punish the stout heart of the King of Assyria, and the glory of his high looks.' Let the Great Ones of the land be warned as well as the meanest, or judgment will come upon them."

"Methinks that smacks of treason," cried Dick Taverner. "Our Puritan has quitted us poor fowl to fly at higher game. Hark ye, Sir!" he added to Hugh Calveley. "You would not dare utter such words as those in the King's presence."

"Thou art mistaken, friend," the other rejoined. "It is my purpose to warn him in terms strong as those I have just used. Why should I hold my peace when I have a mission from on high? I shall speak to the King as Nathan spoke to David."

"He speaks like a prophet," cried the miller; "I begin to have faith in him. No doubt the iniquities of London are fearful."

"If he preach against extortioners and usurers only, I am with him," Dick Taverner said. "If he rid London of Sir Giles Mompesson and his peers he will do good service—still better, if he will put down corruption and injustice as exhibited in the Court of Star-Chamber—eh, Master Jocelyn Mounchensey?"

At the mention of this name the Puritan appeared greatly surprised, and looked round inquiringly, till his eye alighted upon the young man.

After regarding him for a moment fixedly, he demanded—"Art thou Jocelyn Mounchensey?"

The young man, equally surprised, replied in the affirmative.

"The son of Sir Ferdinando Mounchensey, of Massingham, in Norfolk?" inquired the Puritan.

"The same," Jocelyn answered.

"Thy father was my nearest and dearest friend, young man," Hugh Calveley said; "and thy father's son shall be welcome to my dwelling. Enter, I pray of you. Yet pause for a moment. I have a word more to declare to these people. Ye heed not my words, and make a

mock of me," he continued, addressing the assemblage: "but I will give you a sign that I have spoken the truth."

"He will bring the devil among us, I trow," cried Dick Taverner.

"'Tis to be hoped he will not split the May-pole with a thunderbolt," said the miller.

"Nor spoil our Whitsun-ales," cried old Greenford.

"Nor lame our Hobby-horse," said one of the mummers.

"Nor rob me of my wreath and garlands," said Gillian.

"That he shall not, I promise you, fair May Queen!" Dick Tavernor rejoined, gallantly.

"I will do none of these things. I would not harm you, even if I had the power," the Puritan said. "But I will discharge a bolt against the head of yon idol," he added, pointing towards the flower-crowned summit of the May-pole; "and if I break its neck and cast it down, ye will own that a higher hand than mine directs the blow, and that the superstitious symbol ought not to be left standing."

"As to what we may do, or what we may acknowledge, we will give no promise, Master Hugh Calveley," rejoined old Greenford. "But e'en let fly thy bolt, if thou wilt."

Some dissent was offered to this singular proposition, but the majority of voices overruled it; and withdrawing for a moment, Hugh Calveley returned with an arbalist, which he proceeded deliberately to arm in view of the crowd, and then placed a quarrel within it.

"In the name of the Lord, who cast down the golden idol made by Aaron and the Israelites, I launch this bolt," he cried, as he took aim, and liberated the cord.

The short, iron-headed, square-pointed arrow whizzed through the air, and, by the mischief it did as it hit its mark, seemed to confirm the Puritan's denunciation. Striking the May-pole precisely at the summit, it shattered the wood, and brought down the floral crown surmounting it, as well as the topmost streamers.

The spectators stared aghast.

"Be warned by this," thundered Hugh Calveley, with gloomy triumph. "Your idol is smitten—not by my hand, but by His who will chastise your wickedness."

Whereupon he closed the window, and departed. Presently afterwards, the door was opened by an old, grave-looking, decently-clad serving-man. Addressing Jocelyn, who had already dismounted and given his horse in charge to the youth engaged for a similar purpose by Dick Taverner, this personage invited him, in his master's name, to enter; and, with a heart throbbing with emotion, the young man complied. Chance seemed to befriend him in a way he could never have anticipated; and he now hoped to obtain an interview with Aveline.

His conductor led him through a passage to a large chamber at the back of the house, with windows looking upon a garden. The room was panelled with dark shining oak, had a polished floor, an immense chimney-piece, and a moulded ceiling. Within it were a few high-backed chairs, and some other cumbrous furniture, while on an oak table at the side, was spread the simple morning repast of the Puritan and his daughter. But all these things were lost upon Jocelyn, who had eyes only for one object. She was there, and how lovely she appeared! How exquisite in figure — how faultless in feature! Some little embarrassment was discoverable in her manner as the young man entered; but it quickly disappeared. Her father was with her; and advancing towards Jocelyn, he took him kindly by the hand, and bade him welcome. Then, without relinquishing his grasp, he presented the young man to his daughter, saying—

"This is Jocelyn, the son of my dear departed friend, Sir Ferdinando Mounchensey. Some inscrutable design of Providence has brought him hither, and right glad I am to behold him. Years ago, his father rendered me a signal service, which I requited as I best could; and there is nothing I would not gladly do for the son of such a friend. You will esteem him accordingly, Aveline."

"I will not fail in my duty, father," she replied, blushing slightly.

And Jocelyn thought these words were the sweetest he had ever heard pronounced.

"I would pray you to break your fast with us, if our simple fare will content you," said Hugh Calveley, pointing to the table.

"I am not over-dainty, and shall do ample justice to whatever is set before me," Jocelyn replied, smiling.

"It is well," said the Puritan. "I am glad to find the son of my old friend is not a slave to his appetites, as are most of the young men of this generation."

With this they approached the board; and, a lengthy grace being pronounced by Hugh Calveley, Jocelyn sat down by the side of Aveline, scarcely able to believe in the reality of his own happiness — so like a dream it seemed.

CHAPTER XVII.
A RASH PROMISE.

During the slender repast, Jocelyn, in reply to the inquiries of the Puritan, explained the two-fold motive of his coming to London; namely, the desire of taking vengeance on his father's enemies, and the hope of obtaining some honourable employment, such as a gentleman might accept.

"My chances in the latter respect are not very great," he said, "seeing I have no powerful friends to aid me in my endeavours, and I must consequently trust to fortune. But as regards my enemies, if I can only win an audience of the King, and plead my cause before him, I do not think he will deny me justice."

"Justice!" exclaimed the Puritan with deep scorn. "James Stuart knows it not. An archhypocrite, and perfidious as hypocritical, he holdeth as a maxim that Dissimulation is necessary to a Ruler. He has the cowardice and the ferocity of the hyaena. He will promise fairly, but his deeds will falsify his words. Recollect how his Judas kiss betrayed Somerset. Recollect his conduct towards the Gowries. But imagine not, because you have been evil intreated and oppressed, that the King will redress your wrongs, and reinstate you in your fallen position. Rather will he take part with the usurers and extortioners who have deprived you of your inheritance. How many poor wretches doth he daily condemn to the same lingering agonies and certain destruction that he doomed your father. Lamentable as is the good Sir Ferdinando's case, it stands not alone. It is one of many. And many, many more will be added to the list, if this tyrannical Herodias be suffered to govern."

And as if goaded by some stinging thought, that drove him nigh distracted, Hugh Calveley arose, and paced to and fro within the chamber. His brow became gloomier and his visage sterner.

"Bear with him, good Master Jocelyn," Aveline said in a low tone. "He hath been unjustly treated by the King, and as you see can ill brook the usage. Bear with him, I pray of you."

Jocelyn had no time to make reply. Suddenly checking himself, and fixing his earnest gaze upon the young man, the Puritan said—

"Give ear to me, my son. If I desired to inflame your breast with rage against this tyrant, I should need only to relate one instance of his cruelty and injustice. I had a friend—a very dear friend," he continued, in a tone of deep pathos—"confined within the Fleet Prison by a decree of the Star-Chamber. He was to me as a brother, and to see him gradually pining away cut me to the soul. Proud by nature, he refused to abase himself to his oppressor, and could not be brought to acknowledge wrongs he had never committed. Pardon, therefore, was denied him—not pardon merely, but all mitigation of suffering. My friend had been wealthy; but heavy fines and penalties had stripped him of his possessions, and brought him to destitution. Lord of an ancient hall, with woods and lands around it, wherein he could ride for hours without quitting his own domains, his territories were now narrowed to a few yards; while one dark, dreary chamber was alone accorded him. Finding he must necessarily perish, if left to rot there, I prevailed upon him (not without much reluctance on his part) to petition the King for liberation; and was myself the bearer of his prayer. Earnestly pleading the cause of the unfortunate man, and representing his forlorn condition, I besought his Majesty's gracious intercession. But when I had wearied the royal ear with entreaties, the sharp reply was—'Doth he make submission? Will he confess his offence?' And as I could only affirm, that as he was guilty of no crime, so he could confess none, the King returned me the petition, coldly observing—'The dignity of our Court of Star-Chamber must be maintained before all things. He hath been guilty of contempt towards it, and must purge him of the offence.' 'But the man will die, Sire,' I urged, 'if he be not removed from the Fleet. His prison-lodging is near a foul ditch, and he is sick with fever. Neither can he have such aid of medicine or of nursing as his case demands.' 'The greater reason he should relieve himself by speedy acknowledgment of the justice of his sentence,' said the King. 'The matter rests not with us, but with himself.' 'But he is a gentleman, Sire,' I persisted, 'to whom truth is dearer than life, and who would rather languish in misery

for thrice the term he is likely to last, than forfeit his own self-esteem by admitting falsehood and injustice.' 'Then let him perish in his pride and obstinacy,' cried the King impatiently. And thereupon he dismissed me."

"O Sir!" exclaimed Jocelyn, rising and throwing, his arms round the Puritan's neck; "you, then, were the friend who tended my poor father in his last moments. Heaven bless you for it!"

"Yes, Jocelyn, it was I who heard your father's latest sigh," the Puritan replied, returning his embrace, "and your own name was breathed with it. His thoughts were of his son far away—too young to share his distresses, or to comprehend them."

"Alas! alas!" cried Jocelyn mournfully.

"Lament not for your father, Jocelyn," said the Puritan, solemnly; "he is reaping the reward of his earthly troubles in heaven! Be comforted, I say. The tyrant can no longer oppress him. He is beyond the reach of his malice. He can be arraigned at no more unjust tribunals. He is where no cruel and perfidious princes, no iniquitous judges, no griping extortioners shall ever enter."

Jocelyn endeavoured to speak, but his emotion overpowered him.

"I have already told you that your father rendered me a service impossible to be adequately requited," pursued the Puritan. "What that service was I will one day inform you. Suffice it now, that it bound me to him in chains firmer than brass. Willingly would I have laid down my life for him, if he had desired it. Gladly would I have taken his place in the Fleet prison, if that could have procured him liberation. Unable to do either, I watched over him while he lived—and buried him when dead."

"O Sir, you have bound me to you as strongly as you were bound to my father," cried Jocelyn. "For the devotion shown to him, I hold myself eternally your debtor."

The Puritan regarded him steadfastly for a moment.

"What if I were to put these professions to the test?" he asked.

"Do so," Jocelyn replied earnestly. "My life is yours!"

"Your life!" exclaimed Hugh Calveley, grasping his arm almost fiercely, while his eye blazed. "Consider what you offer."

"I need not consider," Jocelyn rejoined. "I repeat my life is yours, if you demand it."

"Perhaps I shall demand it," cried Hugh Calveley. "Ere long, perhaps."

"Demand it when you will," Jocelyn said.

"Father!" Aveline interposed, "do not let the young man bind himself by this promise. Release him, I pray of you."

"The promise cannot be recalled, my child," the Puritan replied. "But I shall never claim its fulfilment save for some high and holy purpose."

"Are you sure your purpose is holy, father?" Aveline said in a low tone.

"What mean you, child?" cried Hugh Calveley, knitting his brows. "I am but an instrument in the hands of Heaven, appointed to do its work; and as directed, so I must act. Heaven may make me the scourge of the oppressor and evil-doer, or the sword to slay the tyrant. I may die a martyr for my faith, or do battle for it with carnal weapons. For all these I am ready; resigning myself to the will of God. Is it for nothing, think'st thou, that this young man — the son of my dear departed friend — has been brought hither at this particular conjuncture? Is it for nothing that, wholly unsolicited, he has placed his life at my disposal, and in doing so has devoted himself to a great cause? Like myself he hath wrongs to avenge, and the Lord of Hosts will give him satisfaction."

"But not in the way you propose, father," Aveline rejoined. "Heaven will assuredly give you both satisfaction for the wrongs you have endured; but it must choose its own means of doing so, and its own time."

"It hath chosen the means, and the time is coming quickly," cried the Puritan, his eye again kindling with fanatical light. "'The Lord will cut off from Israel head and tail.'"

"These things are riddles to me," observed Jocelyn, who had listened to what was passing with great uneasiness. "I would solicit an explanation?"

"You shall have it, my son," Hugh Calveley replied. "But not now. My hour for solitary prayer and self-communion is come, and I must withdraw to my chamber. Go forth into the garden, Jocelyn — and do thou attend him, Aveline. I will join you when my devotions are ended."

So saying he quitted the room, while the youthful pair went forth as enjoined.

CHAPTER XVIII.
HOW THE PROMISE WAS CANCELLED.

It was a large garden, once fairly laid out and planted, but now sadly neglected. The broad terrace walk was overgrown with weeds; the stone steps and the carved balusters were broken in places, and covered with moss; the once smooth lawn was unconscious of the scythe; the parterres had lost their quaint devices; and the knots of flowers — tre-foil, cinque-foil, diamond, and cross-bow — were no longer distinguishable in their original shapes. The labyrinths of the maze were inextricably tangled, and the long green alleys wanted clearing out.

But all this neglect passed unnoticed by Jocelyn, so completely was he engrossed by the fair creature at his side. Even the noise of the May Games, which, temporarily interrupted by Hugh Calveley, had recommenced with greater vigour than ever — the ringing of the church bells, the shouts of the crowd, and the sounds of the merry minstrelsy, scarcely reached his ear. For the first time he experienced those delicious sensations which new-born love excites within the breast; and the enchantment operated upon him so rapidly and so strongly, that he was overpowered by its spell almost before aware of it. It seemed that he had never really lived till this moment; never, at least, comprehended the bliss afforded by existence in the companionship of a being able to awaken the transports he now experienced. A new world seemed suddenly opened to him, full of love, hope, sunshine, of which he and Aveline were the sole inhabitants. Hitherto his life had been devoid of any great emotion. The one feeling latterly pervading it had been a sense of deep wrong, coupled with the thirst of vengeance. No tenderer influence had softened his almost rugged nature; and his breast continued arid as the desert. Now the rock had been stricken, and the living waters gushed forth abundantly.

Not that in Norfolk, and even in the remote part of the county where his life had been passed, female beauty was rare. Nowhere, indeed, is the flower of loveliness more thickly sown than in that favoured part of our isle. But all such young damsels as he had beheld had failed to move him; and if any shaft had been aimed at his breast it had fallen wide of the mark. Jocelyn Mounchensey was not one of those highly susceptible natures—quick to receive an impression, quicker to lose it. Neither would he have been readily caught by the lures spread for youth by the designing of the sex. Imbued with something of the antique spirit of chivalry, which yet, though but slightly, influenced the age in which he lived, he was ready and able to pay fervent homage to his mistress's sovereign beauty (supposing he had one), and maintain its supremacy against all questioners, but utterly incapable of worshipping at any meaner shrine. Heart-whole, therefore, when he encountered the Puritan's daughter, he felt that in her he had found an object he had long sought, to whom he could devote himself heart and soul; a maiden whose beauty was without peer, and whose mental qualities corresponded with her personal attractions.

Nor was it a delusion under which he laboured. Aveline Calveley was all his imagination painted her. Purity of heart, gentleness of disposition, intellectual endowments, were as clearly revealed by her speaking countenance as the innermost depths of a fountain are by the pellucid medium through which they are viewed. Hers was a virgin heart, which, like his own, had received no previous impression. Love for her father alone had swayed her; though all strong demonstrations of filial affection had been checked by that father's habitually stern manner. Brought up by a female relative in Cheshire, who had taken charge of her on her mother's death, which had occurred during her infancy, she had known little of her father till late years, when she had come to reside with him, and, though devout by nature, she could ill reconcile herself to the gloomy notions of religion he entertained, or to the ascetic mode of life he practised. With no desire to share in the pomps and vanities of life, she could not be persuaded that cheerfulness was incompatible with righteousness; nor could all the railings she heard against them make her hate those who differed from her in religious opinions. Still she made no complaint. Entirely obedient to her father's will, she accommodated herself, as far as she

could, to the rule of life prescribed by him. Aware of his pertinacity of opinion, she seldom or ever argued a point with him, even if she thought right might be on her side; holding it better to maintain peace by submission, than to hazard wrath by disputation. The discussion on the May Games was an exception to her ordinary conduct, and formed one of the few instances in which she had ventured to assert her own opinion in opposition to that of her father.

Of late, indeed, she had felt great uneasiness about him. Much changed, he seemed occupied by some dark, dread thought, which partially revealed itself in wrathful exclamations and muttered menaces. He seemed to believe himself chosen by Heaven as an instrument of vengeance against oppression; and her fears were excited lest he might commit some terrible act under this fatal impression. She was the more confirmed in the idea from the eagerness with which he had grasped at Jocelyn's rash promise, and she determined to put the young man upon his guard.

If, in order to satisfy the reader's curiosity, we are obliged to examine the state of Aveline's heart, in reference to Jocelyn, we must state candidly that no such ardent flame was kindled within it as burnt in the breast of the young man. That such a flame might arise was very possible, nay even probable, seeing that the sparks of love were there; and material for combustion was by no means wanting. All that was required was, that those sparks should be gently fanned—not heedlessly extinguished.

Little was said by the two young persons, as they slowly paced the terrace. Both felt embarrassed: Jocelyn longing to give utterance to his feelings, but restrained by timidity—Aveline trembling lest more might be said than she ought to hear, or if obliged to hear, than she could rightly answer. Thus they walked on in silence. But it was a silence more eloquent than words, since each comprehended what the other felt. How much they would have said was proclaimed by the impossibility they found of saying anything!

At length, Jocelyn stopped, and plucking a flower, observed, as he proffered it for her acceptance, "My first offering to you was rejected. May this be more fortunate."

"Make me a promise, and I will accept it," she replied.

"Willingly,", cried Jocelyn, venturing to take her hand, and gazing at her tenderly. "Most willingly."

"You are far too ready to promise," she rejoined with a sad, sweet smile. "What I desire is this. Recall your hasty pledge to my father, and aid me in dissuading him from the enterprise in which he would engage you."

As the words were uttered the Puritan stepped from behind the alley which had enabled him to approach them unperceived, and overhear their brief converse.

"Hold!" he exclaimed in a solemn tone, and regarding Jocelyn with great earnestness. "That promise is sacred. It was made in a father's name, and must be fulfilled. As to my purpose it is unchangeable."

The enthusiast's influence over Jocelyn would have proved irresistible but for the interposition of Aveline.

"Be not controlled by him," she said in a low tone to the young man; adding to her father, "For my sake, let the promise be cancelled."

"Let him ask it, and it shall be," rejoined the Puritan, gazing steadily at the young man, as if he would penetrate his soul. "Do you hesitate?" he cried in accents of deep disappointment, perceiving Jocelyn waver.

"You cannot misunderstand his wishes, father," said Aveline.

"Let him speak for himself," Hugh Calveley exclaimed angrily. "Jocelyn Mounchensey!" he continued, folding his arms upon his breast, and regarding the young man fixedly as before, "son of my old friend! son of him who died in my arms! son of him whom I committed to the earth! if thou hast aught of thy father's true spirit, thou wilt rigidly adhere to a pledge voluntarily given, and which, uttered as it was uttered by thee, has all the sanctity, all the binding force of a vow before Heaven, where it is registered, and approved by him who is gone before us."

Greatly moved by this appeal, Jocelyn might have complied with it, but Aveline again interposed.

"Not so, father," she cried. "The spirits of the just made perfect—and of such is the friend you mention—would never approve of the design with which you would link this young man, in consequence of a promise rashly made. Discharge him from it, I entreat you."

Her energy shook even the Puritan's firmness.

"Be it as thou wilt, daughter," he said, after the pause of a few moments, during which he waited for Jocelyn to speak; but, as the young man said nothing, he rightly interpreted his silence, — "be it as thou wilt, since he, too, wills it so. I give him back his promise. But let me see him no more."

"Sir, I beseech you —" cried Jocelyn.

But he was cut short by the Puritan, who, turning from him contemptuously, said to his daughter — "Let him depart immediately."

Aveline signed to the young man to go; but finding him remain motionless, she took him by the hand, and led him some way along the terrace. Then, releasing her hold, she bade him farewell!

"Wherefore have you done this?" inquired Jocelyn reproachfully.

"Question me not; but be satisfied I have acted for the best," she replied. "O Jocelyn!" she continued anxiously, "if an opportunity should occur to you of serving my father, do not neglect it."

"Be assured I will not," the young man replied. "Shall we not meet again?" he asked, in a tone of deepest anxiety.

"Perhaps," she answered. "But you must go. My father will become impatient. Again farewell!"

On this they separated: the young man sorrowfully departing, while her footsteps retreated in the opposite direction.

Meanwhile the May games went forward on the green with increased spirit and merriment, and without the slightest hinderance. More than once the mummers had wheeled their mazy rounds, with Gillian and Dick Taverner footing it merrily in the midst of them. More than once the audacious 'prentice, now become desperately enamoured of his pretty partner, had ventured to steal a kiss from her lips. More than once he had whispered words of love in her ear; though, as yet, he had obtained no tender response. Once — and once only — had he taken her hand; but then he had never quitted it afterwards. In vain other swains claimed her for a dance. Dick refused to surrender his prize. They breakfasted together in a little bower made of green boughs, the most delightful and lover-like retreat imaginable.

Dick's appetite, furious an hour ago, was now clean gone. He could eat nothing. He subsisted on love alone. But as she was prevailed upon to sip from a foaming tankard of Whitsun ale, he quaffed the remainder of the liquid with rapture. This done, they resumed their merry sports, and began to dance, again. The bells continued to ring blithely, the assemblage to shout, and the minstrels to play. A strange contrast to what was passing in the Puritan's garden.

CHAPTER XIX.
THEOBALDS' PALACE.

The magnificent palace of Theobalds, situated near Cheshunt, in Hertfordshire, originally the residence of the great Lord Treasurer Burleigh, and the scene of his frequent and sumptuous entertainments to Queen Elizabeth and the ambassadors to her Court, when she "was seen," says Stow, "in as great royalty, and served as bountifully and magnificently as at any other time or place, all at his lordship's charge; with rich shows, pleasant devices, and all manner of sports, to the great delight of her Majesty and her whole train, with great thanks from all who partook of it, and as great commendations from all that heard of it abroad:"—this famous and delightful palace, with its stately gardens, wherein Elizabeth had so often walked and held converse with her faithful counsellor; and its noble parks and chases, well stocked with deer, wherein she had so often hunted; came into possession of James the First, in the manner we shall proceed to relate, some years before the date of this history.

James first made acquaintance with Theobalds during his progress from Scotland to assume the English crown, and it was the last point at which he halted before entering the capital of his new dominions. Here, for four days, he and his crowd of noble attendants were guests of Sir Robert Cecil, afterwards Earl of Salisbury, who proved himself the worthy son of his illustrious and hospitable sire by entertaining the monarch and his numerous train in the same princely style that the Lord Treasurer had ever displayed towards Queen Elizabeth. An eyewitness has described the King's arrival at Theobalds on this occasion. "Thus, then," says John Savile, "for his Majesty's coming up the walk, there came before him some of the nobility, barons, knights, esquires, gentlemen, and others, amongst whom was the sheriff of Essex, and most of his men, the trumpets sounding next before his

highness, sometimes one, sometimes another; his Majesty riding not continually betwixt the same two, but sometimes one, sometimes another, as seemed best to his highness; the whole nobility of our land and Scotland round about him observing no place of superiority, all bare-headed, all of whom alighted from their horses at their entrance into the first court, save only his Majesty alone, who rid along still, four noblemen laying their hands upon his steed, two before and two behind. In this manner he came to the court door, where I myself stood. At the entrance into that court stood many noblemen, amongst whom was Sir Robert Cecil, who there meeting his Majesty conducted him into his house, all which was practised with as great applause of the people as could be, hearty prayer, and throwing up of hats. His Majesty had not stayed above an hour in his chamber, but hearing the multitude throng so fast into the uppermost court to see his highness, he showed himself openly out of his chamber window by the space of half an hour together; after which time he went into the labyrinth-like garden to walk, where he secreted himself in the Meander's compact of bays, rosemary, and the like overshadowing his walk, to defend him from the heat of the sun till supper time, at which was such plenty of provision for all sorts of men in their due places as struck me with admiration. And first, to begin with the ragged regiments, and such as were debarred the privilege of any court, these were so sufficiently rewarded with beef, veal, mutton, bread, and beer, that they sung holiday every day, and kept a continual feast. As for poor maimed and distressed soldiers, which repaired thither for maintenance, the wine, money, and meat which they had in very bounteous sort, hath become a sufficient spur to them to blaze it abroad since their coming to London." The reader will marvel at the extraordinary and unstinting hospitality practised in those days, which, as we have shown, was exhibited to all comers, irrespective of rank, even to the "ragged regiments," and which extended its bounties in the shape of alms to the wounded and disabled veteran. We find no parallel to it in modern times.

Theobalds produced a highly favourable impression upon James, who, passionately attached to the chase, saw in its well-stocked parks the means of gratifying his tastes to the fullest extent. Its contiguity to Enfield Chase was also a great recommendation; and its situation, beautiful in itself, was retired, and yet within easy distance of the

metropolis. It appeared to him to combine all the advantages of a royal hunting-seat with all the splendours of a palace; and his predilections were confirmed by a second visit paid by him to it in 1606, when he was accompanied by his brother-in-law, Christianus, King of Denmark, and when the two monarchs were gloriously entertained by the Earl of Salisbury. The Danish king drank inordinately; so did the whole of his suite: and they soon inoculated the English Court with their sottish tastes. Bonnie King Jamie himself got fou twice a-day; and, melancholy to relate, the ladies of the Court followed the royal example, and, "abandoning their sobriety, were seen to roll about in intoxication." So says Sir John Harington, who has given a very diverting account of the orgies at Theobalds, and the inebriate extravagances of Christianus. "One day," writes Sir John, "a great feast was held; and after dinner the representation of Solomon's Temple and the coming of the Queen of Sheba was made, or (as I may better say) was meant to have been made before their Majesties, by device of the Earl of Salisbury and others. But alas! as all earthly things do fail to poor mortals in enjoyment, so did prove our presentment thereof. The lady that did play the Queen's part did carry most precious gifts to both their Majesties, but forgetting the steps arising to the canopy, overset her casket into his Danish Majesty's lap, and fell at his feet, though I rather think it was into his face. Much was the hurry and confusion. Cloths and napkins were at hand to make all clean. His Majesty then got up, and would dance with the Queen of Sheba; but he fell down and humbled himself before her, and was carried to an inner chamber, and laid on a bed of state. The entertainment and show went forward, and most of the presenters went backward, or fell down; wine did so occupy their upper chambers." Worthy Sir John seems to have been greatly scandalized, as he well might be, at these shameless proceedings, and he exclaims pathetically, "The Danes have again conquered the Britons; for I see no man, or woman either, that can command himself or herself." Nor does he fail to contrast these "strange pageantries" with what occurred of the same sort, in the same place, in Queen Elizabeth's time, observing, "I never did see such lack of good order, discretion, and sobriety as I have now done."

Having set his heart upon Theobalds, James offered the Earl of Salisbury, in exchange for it, the palace and domains of Hatfield; and the proposal being accepted (it could not very well be refused), the

delivery of the much-coveted place was made on the 22nd May, 1607; the Prince Joinville, brother to the Duke de Guise, being present on the occasion, where fresh festivities were held, accompanied by an indifferent Masque from Ben Jonson. Whether the King or the Earl had the best of the bargain, we are not prepared to decide.

Enchanted with his acquisition, James commenced the work of improvement and embellishment by enlarging the park, appropriating a good slice of Enfield Chace, with parts of Northaw and Cheshunt Commons, and surrounding the whole with a high brick wall ten miles in circumference. Within this ring he found ample scope for the indulgence of his hunting propensities, since it contained an almost inexhaustible stock of the finest deer in the kingdom; and within it might be heard the sound of his merry horn, and the baying of his favourite stag-hounds, whenever he could escape from the cares of state, or the toils of the council-chamber. His escapes from these demands upon his time were so frequent, and the attraction of the woods of Theobalds so irresistible, that remonstrances were made to him on the subject; but they proved entirely ineffectual. He declared he would rather return to Scotland than forego his amusements.

Theobalds, in the time of its grandeur, might be styled the Fontainebleau of England. Though not to be compared with Windsor Castle in grandeur of situation, or magnificence of forest scenery, still it was a stately residence, and worthy of the monarch of a mighty country. Crowned with four square towers of considerable height and magnitude, each with a lion and vane on the top; it had besides, a large, lantern-shaped central turret, proudly domineering over the others, and "made with timber of excellent workmanship, curiously wrought with divers pinnacles at each corner, wherein were hung twelve bells for chimage, and a clock with chimes of sundry work." The whole structure was built, says the survey, "of excellent brick, with coigns, jambs, and cornices of stone." Approached from the south by a noble avenue of trees, planted in double rows, and a mile in length, it presented a striking and most picturesque appearance, with its lofty towers, its great gilded vanes, supported, as we have said, by lions, its crowd of twisted chimneys, its leaded and arched walks, its balconies, and its immense bay windows. Nor did it lose its majestic and beautiful aspect as you advanced nearer, and its vast proportions became more fully developed. Then you perceived

its grand though irregular facades, its enormous gates, its cloistered walks, and its superb gardens; and comprehended that with its five courts and the countless apartments they contained, to say nothing of the world of offices, that the huge edifice comprised a town within itself—and a well-peopled town too. The members of the household, and the various retainers connected with it, were multitudinous as the rooms themselves.

One charm and peculiarity of the palace, visible from without, consisted in the arched walks before referred to, placed high up on the building, on every side. Screened from the weather, these walks looked upon the different courts and gardens, and commanded extensive views of the lovely sylvan scenery around. Hence Cheshunt and Waltham Abbey, Enfield, and other surrounding villages, could be distinguished through the green vistas of the park.

On the south, facing the grand avenue, was "a large open cloister, built upon several large fair pillars of stone, arched over with seven arches, with a fair rail, and balusters, well painted with the Kings and Queens of England, and the pedigree of the old Lord Burleigh, and divers other ancient families."

The body of the palace consisted of two large quadrangles: one of which, eighty-six feet square, was denominated the Fountain Court, from the circumstance of a fountain of black and white marble standing within it. The other quadrangle, somewhat larger, being one hundred and ten feet square, was called the Middle Court. In addition to these, there were three other smaller courts, respectively entitled the Dial Court, the Buttery Court, and the Dove-house Court, wherein the offices were situated.

On the east side of the Fountain Court stood an arched cloister; and on the ground-floor there was a spacious hall, paved with marble, and embellished with a curiously-carved ceiling. Adjoining it were the apartments assigned to the Earl of Salisbury as Keeper of Theobalds, the council-chamber, and the chambers of Sir Lewis Lewkener, Master of the Ceremonies, and Sir John Finett. Above was the presence-chamber, wainscotted with oak, painted in liver-colour and gilded, having rich pendents from the ceiling, and vast windows resplendent with armorial bearings. Near this were the privy-chamber and the King's bed-chamber, together with a wide gallery, one hundred and twenty-three feet in length, wainscotted and roofed like the presence-

chamber, but yet more gorgeously fretted and painted. Its walls were ornamented with stags' heads with branching antlers. On the upper floor were the rooms assigned to the Duke of Lennox, as Lord Chamberlain, and close to them was one of the external leaded walks before alluded to, sixty-two feet long-and eleven wide, which, from its eminent position, carried the gaze to Ware.

In the Middle-court were the Queen's apartments, comprising her chapel, presence-chamber, and other rooms, and over them a gallery nearly equal in length to that reserved for the King. In this quadrangle, also, were Prince Charles's lodgings. Over the latter was the Green Gallery, one hundred and nine feet in length, and proportionately wide. And above the gallery was another external covered walk, wherein were two "lofty arches of brick, of no small ornament to the house, and rendering it comely and pleasant to all that passed by."

The gardens were enchanting, and in perfect keeping with the palace. Occupying several acres. They seemed infinitely larger than they were, since they abounded in intricate alleys, labyrinths, and mazes; so that you were easily lost within them, and sometimes wanted a clue to come forth. They contained some fine canals, fountains, and statues. In addition to the great gardens were the priory-gardens, with other inclosures for pheasants, aviaries, and menageries; for James was very fond of wild beasts, and had a collection of them worthy of a zoological garden. In one of his letters to Buckingham when the latter was at Madrid, we find him inquiring about the elephant, camels, and wild asses. He had always a camel-house at Theobalds. To close our description, we may add that the tennis-court, manége stable kennels, and falconry were on a scale of magnitude proportionate to the palace.

Beneath the wide-spreading branches of a noble elm, forming part of the great avenue, and standing at a short distance from the principal, entrance to the palace, were collected together, one pleasant afternoon in May, a small group of persons, consisting almost entirely of the reader's acquaintances. Chief amongst them was Jocelyn Mounchensey, who, having dismounted and fastened his horse to the branch, was leaning against the large trunk of the tree, contemplating the magnificent structure we have attempted to describe. Unacquainted as yet with its internal splendours, he had no difficulty in comprehending them from what he beheld from without.

The entrance gates were open, and a wide archway beyond leading to the great quadrangle, gave him a view of its beautiful marble fountain in the midst, ornamented with exquisite statues of Venus and Cupid. Numerous officers of the household, pages, ushers, and serving-men in the royal liveries, with now and then some personage of distinction, were continually passing across the Fountain Court. Gaily attired courtiers, in doublets of satin and mantles of velvet, were lounging in the balconies of the presence-chamber, staring at Jocelyn and his companions for, want of better occupation. Other young nobles, accompanied by richly-habited dames—some of them the highest-born and loveliest in the land—were promenading to and fro upon the garden terrace on the right, chattering and laughing loudly. There was plenty of life and movement everywhere. Even in the Lord Chamberlain's walk, which, as we have said, was contrived in the upper part of the structure, and formed a sort of external gallery, three persons might be discerned; and to save the reader any speculation, we will tell him that these persons were the Duke of Lennox (Lord Chamberlain), the Conde de Gondomar (the Spanish lieger-ambassador), and the Lord Roos. In front of the great gates were stationed four warders with the royal badge woven in gold on the front and back of their crimson doublets, with roses in their velvet hats, roses in their buskins, and halberts over their shoulders. Just within the gates stood a gigantic porter, a full head and shoulders taller than the burly warders themselves. From the summit of the lofty central tower of the palace floated the royal banner, discernible by all the country round.

On the other side of the tree against which Jocelyn was leaning, and looking down the long avenue, rather than towards the palace, stood Dick Taverner, who however bestowed little attention upon his master, being fully occupied by a more attractive object close at hand. Dickon, it appeared, had succeeded in inducing Gillian Greenford to accompany him in the expedition to Theobalds, and as the fair damsel could not of course go alone, she had cajoled her good-natured old grandsire into conveying her thither; and she was now seated behind him upon a pillion placed on the back of a strong, rough-coated, horse. Dick was in raptures at his success. The ride from Tottenham had been delightful. They had tarried for a short time to drink a cup of ale at the Bell at Edmonton, where Dick meant to have breakfasted,

though chance had so agreeably prevented him, and where the liquor was highly approved by the old farmer, who became thenceforth exceedingly chatty, and talked of nothing else but good Queen Bess and her frequent visits to Theobalds in the old Lord Burleigh's time, during the rest of the journey. Little heed was paid to his garrulity by the young couple. They let him talk on, feigning to listen, but in reality noting scarce a word he said. As they entered the park of Theobalds, however, they found their tongues, and Gillian became loud in her admiration of the beautiful glades that opened before them, and of the dappled denizens of the wood that tripped lightsomely across the sward, or hurried towards the thickets. The park, indeed, looked beautiful with its fine oaks in their freshly-opened foliage of the tenderest green, its numerous spreading beeches, its scattered thorns white with blossom, and the young fern just springing from the seed in the brakes. No wonder Gillian was delighted. Dick was equally enchanted, and regretted he was not like King James, master of a great park, that he might hunt within it at his pleasure. Of course, if he had been king, Gillian would naturally have been his queen, and have hunted with him. Old Greenford, too, admired the scene, and could not but admit that the park was improved, though he uttered something like a groan as he thought that Queen Elizabeth and the Lord Treasurer could be seen in it no longer.

After riding for a couple of miles along a road which led them over beautifully undulating ground, affording glimpses of every variety of forest scenery — sometimes plunging them into the depths of groves, where the path was covered by over-arching trees — sometimes crossing the open chace, studded by single aged oaks of the largest size — sometimes, skirting the margin of a pool, fringed with flags, reeds, and bulrushes for the protection of the water-fowl — now passing the large heronry, to the strict preservation of which James attached the utmost importance; they at length approached the long avenue leading to the palace. At its entrance they found Jocelyn waiting for them.

The young man, who cared not for their company, had ridden on in advance. The strange events of the morning gave him plenty of material for reflection, and he longed to commune with himself. Accordingly, when the others stopped at Edmonton, he quitted them, promising to halt till they came up, before entering the precincts of

the palace. If his ride was not so agreeable as their's, it at least enabled him to regain, in some degree, his composure of mind, which had been greatly disturbed by his abrupt parting with Aveline. Her image was constantly before him, and refusing to be dismissed, connected itself with every object he beheld. At first he despaired of meeting her again; but as he gradually grew calmer, his hopes revived, and difficulties which seemed insuperable began to disperse. By the time Dick Taverner and his companions came up, he felt some disposition to talk, and Gillian's hearty merriment and high spirits helped to enliven him. Having ascertained, from one of the royal keepers whom he had encountered, that the King, with a large company, was out hawking on the banks of the New River, which was cut through the park, and that he would in all probability return through the great avenue to the palace, he proposed that they should station themselves somewhere within it, in order to see him pass. This arrangement pleased all parties, so proceeding slowly up the avenue, they took up a position as described.

More than an hour, however, elapsed, and still James, who no doubt was pleased with his sport, came not.

Without being aware of their high quality, or having the slightest notion that the Conde Gondomar was one of them, Jocelyn had remarked the three personages in the Lord Chamberlain's Walk. He had seen them pause, and apparently look towards the little group of which he himself formed part. Shortly after this, two of the party retired, leaving the third alone in the gallery. By-and-by these two individuals were seen to cross the Fountain Court, and passing through the great gates, to direct their steps towards the avenue.

As they approached, Jocelyn recognised one of them as Lord Roos, whom he had seen play so singular a part at Madame Bonaventure's ordinary. The other was wholly unknown to him. But that he was a person of the utmost distinction he felt convinced, as well from his haughty bearing and sumptuous attire, as from the evident respect paid him by his companion. In stature he was rather short, being somewhat under the ordinary standard; but his figure was admirably proportioned, and was displayed to the greatest advantage by his rich habiliments. His doublet was of sea-green satin, embroidered with silver and black, with rich open sleeves, and his Spanish cloak was of velvet of the same colour and similarly embroidered. His hose were

of tawny silk, and the plumes in his bonnet black, striped with white. He was decorated with the order of the Golden Fleece, and bore at his side a genuine blade of Toledo, with a handle of rarest workmanship. Bound his throat he wore a large, triple ruff, edged with pointed lace. His face was oval in shape, his complexion of a rich olive hue, his eyes large, dark, and keen, his features singularly handsome, and his looks penetrating. His hair was raven-black, cut short, and removed from the forehead.

Lord Roos and his companion passed close to Jocelyn without appearing to notice him; but they halted before Gillian, regarding her with insolent admiration. Evidently she was the object that had brought them forth. The poor damsel was terribly confused by their ardent glances and libertine scrutiny, and blushed to her very temples. As to Dick Taverner, he trembled with rage and jealousy, and began to repent having brought his treasure into such a dangerous neighbourhood.

The person who seemed to be most struck with Gillian's charms was the wearer of the Spanish mantle.

"En verdad!" he exclaimed, "that is the loveliest piece of rusticity I have seen since I came to England. I thought mine eyes did not deceive me, as to her beauty, when I caught sight of her from the Lord Chamberlain's gallery."

"The Conde de Gondomar hath ever an eagle's eye for a pretty woman," Lord Roos replied, laughing.

"The Conde de Gondomar!" mentally ejaculated Jocelyn, who had overheard what he said. "Why, this is he to whom the ring must be shown. The opportunity must not be lost."

Accordingly, regardless of the impropriety of the proceeding, he uncovered his head, and advancing towards the Spaniard said—

"I believe I have the honour of addressing the Conde de Gondomar?"

"What means this intrusion, Sir?" Lord Roos demanded insolently. "What have you to say to his Excellency?"

"I bring him a token, my lord," the young man replied, exhibiting the ring, given him by the masked horseman, to the ambassador.

"Ha!" exclaimed De Gondomar, glancing at the ring, and then regarding Jocelyn steadfastly, "I must speak with this young man, my lord."

"And abandon the damsel?" demanded Lord Roos.

"No—no—you must take care of her," De Gondomar replied in a low tone. "Can you not induce Lady Exeter to take her into her service?"

"I will try," Lord Roos replied. "And see!" he added, pointing down the avenue, "the royal party is returning, so I can at once ascertain whether her ladyship will second your Excellency's designs."

"Do so," said De Gondomar, "and I shall be for ever indebted to you. This girl has quite taken my fancy, and I must not lose her. And now, Sir," he added, stepping aside with Jocelyn, "you have brought me the token from my assured agent, and I understand from it that you are a person upon whom I may rely."

"In all that beseems a gentleman and a man of honour and loyalty your Excellency may rely on me," Jocelyn replied.

"I shall require nothing inconsistent with those principles," the Spanish Ambassador said. "This point disposed of, let me know how I can serve you, for I presume you have some request to prefer?"

"Your Excellency can very materially serve me," Jocelyn returned. "I am in danger."

"I thought as much," De Gondomar observed with a smile. "Since you have placed yourself under my protection, I will do my best to hold you harmless. But who is your enemy?"

"I have two deadly enemies, Sir Giles Mompesson and Sir Francis Mitchell," Jocelyn rejoined.

"I know them well—instruments of Buckingham," said De Gondomar. "They are indeed dangerous enemies."

"I have another yet more dangerous," returned Jocelyn. "I have reason to fear that, by boldness of speech I have incurred the enmity of the Marquis of Buckingham himself."

"Ah! this, indeed, is serious," said De Gondomar.

"I am threatened with arrest by the Star-Chamber," pursued Jocelyn; "so your Excellency will perceive that my position is fraught with extreme peril. Still I persuade myself, if I could obtain a hearing

of the King, I should be able to set my enemies at defiance and obtain my right."

De Gondomar smiled somewhat scornfully.

"You will obtain little in that way," he said, "and your enemies will crush you effectually. But you must explain to me precisely how you are circumstanced, and I will then consider what can be done for you. And begin by acquainting me with your name and condition, for as yet I am entirely ignorant whom I am addressing."

Upon this Jocelyn succinctly related to the Ambassador all such particulars of his history as have been laid before the reader. De Gondomar listened to him with attention, and put some questions to him as he proceeded. At its close his countenance brightened.

"You are in an awkward dilemma, it must be owned, Master Jocelyn Mounchensey," he said. "But I think I can protect you in spite of them all—in spite of Buckingham himself. Luckily, he is not at Theobalds at present—so the coast is clear for action. The first blow is half the battle. I must present you to the King without delay. And see, his Majesty approaches. Stand close behind me, and act as I advise you by a sign."

CHAPTER XX.
KING JAMES THE FIRST.

Meantime the royal cavalcade came slowly up the avenue. It was very numerous, and all the more brilliant in appearance, since it comprised nearly as many high-born dames as nobles. Amongst the distinguished foreigners who with their attendants swelled the party were the Venetian lieger-ambassador Giustiniano, and the Marquis de Tremouille, of the family des Ursins, ambassador from France.

These exalted personages rode close behind the King, and one or the other of them was constantly engaged in conversation with him. Giustiniano had one of those dark, grave, handsome countenances familiarized to us by the portraits of Titian and Tintoretto, and even the King's jests failed in making him smile. He was apparelled entirely in black velvet, with a cloak bordered with the costly fur of the black fox. All his followers were similarly attired. The sombre Venetian presented a striking contrast to his vivacious companion, the gay and graceful De Tremouille, who glittered in white satin, embroidered with leaves of silver, while the same colour and the same ornaments were adopted by his retinue.

No order of precedence was observed by the court nobles. Each rode as he listed. Prince Charles was absent, and so was the supreme favourite Buckingham; but their places were supplied by some of the chief personages of the realm, including the Earls of Arundel, Pembroke, and Montgomery, the Marquis of Hamilton, and the Lords Haddington, Fenton, and Doncaster. Intermingled with the nobles, the courtiers of lesser rank, and the ambassadors' followers, were the ladies, most of whom claimed attention from personal charms, rich attire, and the grace and skill with which they managed their horses.

Perhaps the most beautiful amongst them was the young Countess of Exeter, whose magnificent black eyes did great execution. The

lovely Countess was mounted on a fiery Spanish barb, given to her by De Gondomar. Forced into a union with a gouty and decrepit old husband, the Countess of Exeter might have pleaded this circumstance in extenuation of some of her follies. It was undoubtedly an argument employed by her admirers, who, in endeavouring to shake her fidelity to her lord, told her it was an infamy that she should be sacrificed to such an old dotard as he. Whether these arguments prevailed in more cases than one we shall not inquire too nicely; but, if court-scandal may be relied on, they did—Buckingham and De Gondomar being both reputed to have been her lovers.

The last, however, in the list, and the one who appeared to be most passionately enamoured of the beautiful Countess, and to receive the largest share of her regard, was Lord Roos; and as this culpable attachment and its consequences connect themselves intimately with our history we have been obliged to advert to them thus particularly. Lord Roos was a near relative of the Earl of Exeter; and although the infirm and gouty old peer had been excessively jealous of his lovely young wife on former occasions, when she had appeared to trifle with his honour, he seemed perfectly easy and unsuspicious now, though there was infinitely more cause for distrust. Possibly he had too much reliance on Lord Roos's good feelings and principles to suspect him.

Very different was Lady Roos's conduct. This unhappy lady, whom we have already mentioned as the daughter of Sir Thomas Lake, Secretary of State, had the misfortune to be sincerely attached to her handsome but profligate husband, whose neglect and frequent irregularities she had pardoned, until the utter estrangement, occasioned by his passion for the Countess of Exeter, filled her with such trouble, that, overpowered at length by anguish, she complained to her mother Lady Lake,—an ambitious and imperious woman, whose vanity had prompted her to bring about this unfortunate match. Expressing the greatest indignation at the treatment her daughter had experienced, Lady Lake counselled her to resent it, undertaking herself to open the eyes of the injured Earl of Exeter to his wife's infidelity; but she was dissuaded from her purpose by Sir Thomas Lake. Though generally governed by his wife, Sir Thomas succeeded, in this instance, in over-ruling her design of proceeding at once to extremities with the guilty pair, recommending that, in the first instance, Lord Roos should be strongly remonstrated with

by Lady Lake and her daughter, when perhaps his fears might be aroused, if his sense of duty could not be awakened.

This final appeal had not yet been made; but an interview had taken place between Lady Roos and her husband, at which, with many passionate entreaties, she had implored him to shake off the thraldom in which he had bound himself, and to return to her, when all should be forgiven and forgotten, — but without effect.

Thus matters stood at present.

As we have seen, though the Countess of Exeter formed one of the chief ornaments of the hawking party, Lord Roos had not joined it; his absence being occasioned by a summons from the Conde de Gondomar, with some of whose political intrigues he was secretly mixed up. Whether the Countess missed him or not, we pretend not to say. All we are able to declare is, she was in high spirits, and seemed in no mood to check the advances of other aspirants to her favour. Her beautiful and expressive features beamed with constant smiles, and her lustrous black eyes seemed to create a flame wherever their beams alighted.

But we must quit this enchantress and her spells, and proceed with the description of the royal party. In the rear of those on horseback walked the falconers, in liveries of green cloth, with bugles hanging from the shoulder; each man having a hawk upon his fist, completely 'tired in its hood, bells, varvels, and jesses. At the heels of the falconers, and accompanied by a throng of varlets, in russet jerkins, carrying staves, came two packs of hounds, — one used for what was termed, in the language of falconry, the Flight at the River, — these were all water-spaniels; and the other, for the Flight at the Field. Nice music they made, in spite of the efforts of the varlets in russet to keep them quiet.

Hawking, in those days, was what shooting is in the present; fowling-pieces being scarcely used, if at all. Thus the varieties of the hawk-tribe were not merely employed in the capture of pheasants, partridges, grouse, rails, quails, and other game, besides water-fowl, but in the chase of hares; and in all of these pursuits the falconers were assisted by dogs. Game, of course, could only be killed at particular seasons of the year; and wild-geese, wild-ducks, woodcocks, and snipes in the winter; but spring and summer pastime was afforded by

the crane, the bustard, the heron, the rook, and the kite; while, at the same periods, some of the smaller description of water-fowl offered excellent sport on lake or river.

A striking and picturesque sight that cavalcade presented, with its nodding plumes of many colours, its glittering silks and velvets, its proud array of horsemen, and its still prouder array of lovely women, whose personal graces and charms baffle description, while they invite it. Pleasant were the sounds that accompanied the progress of the train: the jocund laugh, the musical voices of women, the jingling of bridles, the snorting and trampling of steeds, the baying of hounds, the shouts of the varlets, and the winding of horns.

But having, as yet, omitted the principal figure, we must hasten to describe him by whom the party was headed. The King, then, was mounted on a superb milk-white steed, with wide-flowing mane and tail, and of the easiest and gentlest pace. Its colour was set off by its red chanfrein, its nodding crest of red feathers, its broad poitrinal with red tassels, and its saddle with red housings. Though devoted to the chase, as we have shown, James was but an indifferent horseman; and his safety in the saddle was assured by such high-bolstered bows in front and at the back, that it seemed next to impossible he could be shaken out of them. Yet, in spite of all these precautions, accidents had befallen him. On one occasion, Sir Symonds D'Ewes relates that he was thrown headlong into a pond; and on another, we learn from a different source that he was cast over his horse's head into the New River, and narrowly escaped drowning, his boots alone being visible above the ice covering the stream. Moreover the monarch's attire was excessively stiff and cumbrous, and this, while it added to the natural ungainliness of his person, prevented all freedom of movement, especially on horseback. His doublet, which on the present occasion was of green velvet, considerably frayed,—for he was by no means particular about the newness of his apparel,—was padded and quilted so as to be dagger-proof; and his hose were stuffed in the same manner, and preposterously large about the hips. Then his ruff was triple-banded, and so stiffly starched, that the head was fixed immovably amidst its plaits.

Though not handsome, James's features were thoughtful and intelligent, with a gleam of cunning in the eye, and an expression of sarcasm about the mouth, and they contained the type of the peculiar

physiognomy that distinguished all his unfortunate line. His beard was of a yellowish brown, and scantily covered his chin, and his thin moustaches were of a yet lighter hue. His hair was beginning to turn gray, but his complexion was ruddy and hale, proving that, but for his constant ebriety and indulgence in the pleasures of the table, he might have attained a good old age — if, indeed, his life was not unfairly abridged. His large eyes were for ever rolling about, and his tongue was too big for his mouth, causing him to splutter in utterance, besides giving him a disagreeable appearance when eating; while his legs were so weak, that he required support in walking. Notwithstanding these defects, and his general coarseness of manner, James was not without dignity, and could, when he chose, assume a right royal air and deportment. But these occasions were rare. As is well known, his pedantry and his pretensions to superior wisdom and discrimination, procured him the title of the "Scottish Solomon." His general character will be more fully developed as we proceed; and we shall show the perfidy and dissimulation which he practised in carrying out his schemes, and tried to soften down under the plausible appellation of "King-craft."

James was never seen to greater advantage than on occasions like the present. His hearty enjoyment of the sport he was engaged in; his familiarity with all around him, even with the meanest varlets by whom he was attended, and for whom he had generally some droll nickname; his complete abandonment of all the etiquette which either he or his master of the ceremonies observed elsewhere; his good-tempered vanity and boasting about his skill as a woodsman, — all these things created an impression in his favour, which was not diminished in those who were not brought much into contact with him in other ways. When hunting or hawking, James was nothing more than a hearty country gentleman engaged in the like sports.

The cavalcade came leisurely on, for the King proceeded no faster than would allow the falconers to keep easily up with those on horseback. He was in high good humour, and laughed and jested sometimes with one ambassador, sometimes with the other, and having finished a learned discussion on the manner of fleeing a hawk at the river and on the field, as taught by the great French authorities, Martin, Malopin, and Aimé Cassian, with the Marquis de Tremouille, had just begun a similar conversation with Giustiniano

as to the Italian mode of manning, hooding, and reclaiming a falcon, as practised by Messer Francesco Sforzino Vicentino, when he caught sight of the Conde de Gondomar, standing where we left him at the side of the avenue, on which he came to a sudden halt, and the whole cavalcade stopped at the same time.

"Salud! Conde magnifico!" exclaimed King James, as the Spaniard advanced to make his obeisance to him; "how is it that we find you standing under the shade of the tree friendly to the vine,— amictoe vitibus ulmi as Ovid hath it? Is it that yon blooming Chloe," he continued, leering significantly at Gillian, "hath more attraction for you than our court dames? Troth! the quean is not ill-favoured; but ye ha' lost a gude day's sport, Count, forbye ither losses which we sall na particularize. We hae had a noble flight at the heron, and anither just as guid after the bustard. God's santy! the run the lang-leggit loon gave us. Lady Exeter, on her braw Spanish barb—we ken whose gift it is—was the only one able to keep with us; and it was her leddyship's ain peregrine falcon that checked the fleeing carle at last. By our faith the Countess understands the gentle science weel. She cared not to soil her dainty gloves by rewarding her hawk with a soppa, as his Excellency Giustiniano would term it, of the bustard's heart, bluid, and brains. But wha hae ye gotten wi' ye?" he added, for the first time noticing Jocelyn.

"A young gentleman in whom I am much interested, and whom I would crave permission to present to your Majesty," replied De Gondomar.

"Saul of our body, Count, the permission is readily granted," replied James, evidently much pleased with the young man's appearance. "Ye shall bring him to us in the privy-chamber before we gang to supper, and moreover ye shall hae full licence to advance what you please in his behoof. He is a weel-grown, weel-favoured laddie, almost as much sae as our ain dear dog Steenie; but we wad say to him, in the words of the Roman bard,

'O formose puer, nimium ne crede colori!'

Gude pairts are better than gude looks; not that the latter are to be undervalued, but baith should exist in the same person. We shall soon discover whether the young man hath been weel nurtured, and if all correspond we shall not refuse him the light of our countenance."

"I tender your Majesty thanks for the favour you have conferred upon him," replied De Gondomar.

"But ye have not yet tauld us the youth's name, Count?" said the King.

"Your Majesty, I trust, will not think I make a mystery where none is needed, if I say that my protegé claims your gracious permission to preserve, for the moment, his incognito," De Gondomar replied. "When I present him of course his name will be declared."

"Be it as you will, Count," James replied. "We ken fu' weel ye hae gude reason for a' ye do. Fail not in your attendance on us at the time appointed."

As De Gondomar with a profound obeisance drew back, the King put his steed in motion. General attention having been thus called to Jocelyn, all eyes were turned towards him, his appearance and attire were criticised, and much speculation ensued as to what could be the Spanish Ambassador's motive for undertaking the presentation.

Meanwhile, Lord Roos had taken advantage of the brief halt of the hunting party to approach the Countess of Exeter, and pointing out Gillian to her, inquired in a low tone, and in a few words, to which, however, his looks imparted significance, whether she would take the pretty damsel into her service as tire-woman or handmaiden. The Countess seemed surprised at the request, and, after glancing at the Beauty of Tottenham, was about to refuse it, when Lord Roos urged in a whisper, "'T is for De Gondomar I ask the favour."

"In that case I readily assent," the Countess replied. "I will go speak to the damsel at once, if you desire it. How pretty she is! No wonder his inflammable Excellency should be smitten by her." And detaching her barb, as she spoke, from the cavalcade, she moved towards Gillian, accompanied by Lord Roos. The pretty damsel was covered with fresh confusion at the great lady's approach; and was, indeed, so greatly alarmed, that she might have taken to her heels, if she had been on the ground, and not on the pillion behind her grandsire.

"Be not abashed, my pretty maiden," the Countess said, in a kind and encouraging tone; "there is nothing to be afraid of. Aware that I am in want of a damsel like yourself, to tire my hair and attend upon me, Lord Roos has drawn my attention to you; and if I may trust to

appearances—as I think I may," she added, with a very flattering and persuasive smile, "in your case—you are the very person to suit me, provided you are willing to enter my service. I am the Countess of Exeter."

"A Countess!" exclaimed Gillian. "Do you hear that, grandsire? The beautiful lady is a countess. What an honour it would be to serve her!"

"It might be," the old man replied, with hesitation, and in a whisper; "yet I do not exactly like the manner of it."

"Don't accept the offer, Gillian. Don't go," said Dick Taverner, whose breast was full of uneasiness.

"Your answer, my pretty maiden?" the Countess said, with a winning smile.

"I am much beholden to you, my lady," Gillian replied, "and it will delight me to serve you as you propose—that is, if I have my grandsire's consent to it."

"And the good man, I am sure, has your welfare too much at heart to withhold it," the Countess replied. "But follow me to the palace, and we will confer further upon the matter. Inquire for the Countess of Exeter's apartments." And with another gracious smile, she rejoined the cavalcade, leaving Lord Roos behind. He thanked her with a look for her complaisance.

"O Gillian, I am sure ill will come of this," Dick Taverner exclaimed.

"Wherefore should it?" she rejoined, almost beside herself with delight at the brilliant prospect suddenly opened before her. "My fortune is made."

"You are right, my pretty damsel, it is," Lord Roos remarked. "Fail not to do as the Countess has directed you, and I will answer for the rest."

"You hear what the kind young nobleman says, grandsire?" Gillian whispered in his ear. "You cannot doubt his assurance?"

"I hear it all," old Greenford replied; "but I know not what to think. I suppose we must go to the palace."

"To be sure we must," Gillian cried; "I will go there alone, if you will not go with me."

Satisfied with what he had heard, Lord Roos moved away, nodding approval at Gillian.

The cavalcade, as we have said, was once more in motion, but before it had proceeded far, it was again, most unexpectedly, brought to a halt.

Suddenly stepping from behind a large tree which had concealed him from view, a man in military habiliments, with grizzled hair and beard, and an exceedingly resolute and stern cast of countenance, planted himself directly in the monarch's path, and extending his hand towards him, exclaimed, in a loud voice, "Stand! O King!"

"Who art thou, fellow? and what wouldst thou?" demanded James, who had checked his horse with such suddenness as almost to throw himself out of his high-holstered saddle.

"I have a message to deliver to thee from Heaven," replied Hugh Calveley.

"Aha!" exclaimed James, recovering in some degree, for he thought he had a madman to deal with. "What may thy message be?"

And willing to gain a character for courage, though it was wholly foreign to his nature, he motioned those around him to keep back. "Thy message, fellow!" he repeated.

"Hear, then, what Heaven saith to thee," the Puritan replied. "Have I not brought thee out of a land of famine into a land of plenty? Thou oughtest, therefore, to have judged my people righteously! But thou hast perverted justice, and not relieved the oppressed. Therefore, unless thou repent, I will rend thy kingdom from thee, and from thy posterity after thee! Thus saith the Lord, whose messenger I am."

CHAPTER XXI.
CONSEQUENCES OF THE PURITAN'S WARNING.

Coupling Hugh Calveley's present strange appearance and solemn warning with his previous denunciations uttered in secret, and his intimations of some dread design, with which he had sought to connect the young man himself, intimating that its execution would jeopardize his life; putting these things together, we say, Jocelyn could not for an instant doubt that the King was in imminent danger, and he felt called upon to interfere, even though he should be compelled to act against his father's friend, and the father of Aveline. No alternative, in fact, was allowed him. As a loyal subject, his duty imperiously required him to defend his sovereign; and perceiving that no one (in consequence of the King's injunctions) advanced towards the Puritan, Jocelyn hastily quitted the Conde de Gondomar, and rushing forward stationed himself between the monarch and his bold admonisher; and so near to the latter, that he could easily prevent any attack being made by him upon James.

Evidently disconcerted by the movement, Hugh Calveley signed to the young man to stand aside, but Jocelyn refused compliance; the rather that he suspected from the manner in which the other placed his hand in his breast that he had some weapon concealed about his person. Casting a look of bitterest reproach at him, which plainly as words said—"Ungrateful boy, thou hast prevented my purpose," the Puritan folded his hands upon his breast with an air of deep disappointment.

"Fly!" cried Jocelyn, in a tone calculated only to reach his ears. "I will defend you with my life. Waste not another moment—fly!"

But Hugh Calveley regarded him with cold disdain, and though he moved not his lips, he seemed to say, "You have destroyed me; and I will not remove the guilt of my destruction from your head."

The Puritan's language and manner had filled James with astonishment and fresh alarm; but feeling secure in the propinquity of Jocelyn to the object of his uneasiness, and being closely environed by his retinue, the foremost of whom had drawn their swords and held themselves in readiness to defend him from the slightest hostile attempt, it was not unnatural that even so timorous a person as he, should regain his confidence. Once more, therefore, he restrained by his gestures the angry impetuosity of the nobles around him, who were burning to chastise the rash intruder, and signified his intention of questioning him before any measures were adopted against him.

"Let him be," he cried. "He is some puir demented creature fitter for Bedlam than anywhere else; and we will see that he be sent thither; but molest him not till we hae spoken wi' him, and certified his condition more fully. Quit not the position ye hae sae judiciously occupied, young Sir, albeit against our orders," he cried to Jocelyn. "Dinna draw your blade unless the fellow seeks to come till us. Not that we are under ony apprehension; but there are bluidthirsty traitors even in our pacific territories, and as this may be ane of them, it is weel not to neglect due precaution. And now, man," he added, raising his voice, and addressing the Puritan, who still maintained a steadfast and unmoved demeanour, with his eye constantly fixed upon his interrogator. "Ye say ye are a messenger frae heaven. An it be sae,—whilk we take leave to doubt, rather conceiving ye to be an envoy from the Prince of Darkness than an ambassador from above,—an ill choice hath been made in ye. Unto what order of prophets do ye conceive yourself to belong?"

To this interrogation, propounded in a jeering tone, the Puritan deigned no reply; but an answer was given for him by Archee, the court jester, who had managed in the confusion to creep up to his royal master's side.

"He belongs to the order of Melchisedec," said Archee. A reply that occasioned some laughter among the nobles, in which the King joined heartily.

"Tut, fule! ye are as daft as the puir body before us," cried James. "Ken ye not that Melchisedec was a priest and not a prophet; while to judge frae yon fellow's abulyiements, if he belongs to any church at all, it maun be to the church militant. And yet, aiblins, ye are na sae far out after a'. Like aneuch, he may be infected with the heresy of the Melchisedecians,—a pestilent sect, who plagued the early Christian Church sairly, placing their master aboon our Blessed Lord himself, and holding him to be identical wi' the Holy Ghaist. Are ye a Melchisedecian, sirrah?"

"I am a believer in the Gospel," the Puritan replied. "And am willing to seal my faith in it with my blood. I am sent hither to warn thee, O King, and thou wilt do well not to despise my words. Repent ere it be too late. Wonderfully hath thy life been preserved. Dedicate the remainder of thy days to the service of the Most High. Persecute not His people, and revile them not. Purge thy City of its uncleanness and idolatry, and thy Court of its corruption. Profane not the Sabbath"—

"I see how it is," interrupted Archee with a scream; "the man hath been driven stark wud by your Majesty's Book of Sports."

"A book devised by the devil," cried Hugh Calveley, catching at the suggestion; "and which ought to be publicly burnt by the hangman, instead of being read in the churches. How much, mischief hath that book done! How many abominations hath it occasioned! And, alas! how much persecution hath it caused; for have not many just men, and sincere preachers of the Word, been prosecuted in thy Court, misnamed of justice, and known, O King! as the Star-Chamber; suffering stripes and imprisonment for refusing to read thy mischievous proclamation to their flocks."

"I knew it!—I knew it!" screamed Archee, delighted with the effect he had produced. "Take heed, sirrah," he cried to the Puritan, "that ye make not acquaintance wi' 'that Court misnamed of justice' yer ain sell."

"He is liker to be arraigned at our court styled the King's Bench, and hanged, drawn, and quartered afterwards," roared James, far more enraged at the disrespectful mention made of his manifesto, than by anything that had previously occurred. "The man is not sae doited as we supposed him."

"He is not sane enough to keep his neck from the halter," rejoined Archee. "Your Majesty should spare him, since you are indirectly the cause of his malady."

"Intercede not for me," cried Hugh Calveley. "I would not accept any grace at the tyrant's hands. Let him hew me in pieces, and my blood shall cry out for vengeance upon his head."

"By our halidame! a dangerous traitor!" exclaimed James.

"Hear me, O King!" thundered the Puritan. "For the third and last time I lift up my voice to warn thee. Visions have appeared to me in the night, and mysterious voices have whispered in mine ear. They have revealed to me strange and terrible things—but not more strange and terrible than true. They have told me how thy posterity shall suffer for the injustice thou doest to thy people. They have shown me a scaffold which a King shall mount—and a block whereon a royal head shall be laid. But it shall be better for that unfortunate monarch, though he be brought to judgment by his people, than for him who shall be brought to judgment by his God. Yet more. I have seen in my visions two Kings in exile: one of whom shall be recalled, but the other shall die in a foreign land. As to thee, thou mayst live on yet awhile in fancied security. But destruction shall suddenly overtake thee. Thou shalt be stung to death by the serpent thou nourishest in thy bosom."

Whatever credit might be attached to them, the Puritan's prophetic forebodings produced, from the manner in which they were delivered, a strong impression upon all his auditors. Unquestionably the man was in earnest, and spoke like one who believed that a mission had been entrusted to him. No interruption was offered to his speech, even by the King, though the latter turned pale as these terrible coming events were shadowed forth before him.

"His words are awsome," he muttered, "and gar the flesh creep on our banes. Will nane o' ye stap his tongue?"

"Better hae stapt it afore this," said Archee; "he has said ower meikle, or not aneuch, The Deil's malison on thee, fellow, for a prophet of ill! Hast thou aught to allege why his Majesty should not tuck thee up with a halter?"

"I have spoken," responded the Puritan; "let the King do with me what he lists."

"Seize him! arrest him! ye are nearest to him, Sir," shouted the king to Jocelyn.

The command could not be disobeyed. As Jocelyn drew near, and laid his hand upon Hugh Calveley, the latter looked reproachfully at him, saying, "Thou doest well, son of my old friend."

Jocelyn was unable to reply, for a crowd now pressed forward on all sides, completely surrounding the prisoner. Some of the nobles threatened him with their swords, and the warders, who had come up from the gateway, thrust at him with their partizans. Jocelyn had great difficulty in shielding him from the infuriated throng.

"Touch him not!" he cried, clearing a space around them with the point of his sword. "His Majesty has committed him to my custody, and I am responsible for him. Pardon me if I disarm you, Sir," he added in an undertone to the prisoner.

"Here is my sword," replied Hugh Calveley, unbuckling his belt and delivering up the weapon it sustained to Jocelyn; "it hath never been dishonoured, and," he added, lowering his voice, "it hath been twice drawn in thy father's defence."

The reproach cut Jocelyn to the heart.

At this moment the crowd drew aside to allow the King's approach.

"Hath he been searched to see whether any deadly or offensive weapon is concealed about him?" demanded James.

"He cannot have any more offensive weapon than his tongue," cried Archee, who accompanied his royal master. "I counsel your Majesty to deprive him of that."

"There is something hidden in his breast," cried one of the warders, searching in his jerkin, and at length drawing forth a short, clumsy pistol, or dag, as the weapon was then called. "It is loaded, an please your Majesty," the man continued, after examining it.

Exclamations of horror arose from those around, and Jocelyn had again some difficulty in protecting the prisoner from their fury.

"A dag!" ejaculated James, "a loaded dag, crammed to the muzzle wi' bullets, nae doubt. Haud it down, man! haud it down! it may fire off of itsel', and accomplish the villain's murtherous and sacrilegious design. And sae this was to be the instrument of our destruction! Dost

thou confess thy guilt, thou bluid-thirsty traitor, or shall the torture force the truth from thee?"

"The torture will force nothing from me," replied Hugh Calveley. "But I tell thee, tyrant, that I would have slain thee, had not my hand been stayed."

"Heard ye ever the like o' that?" exclaimed James, his ruddy cheek blanched with fright, and his voice quavering. "Why, he exceedeth in audacity the arch-traitor Fawkes himsel'. And what stayed thy hand, villain?" he demanded, — "what stayed thy hand, thou blood-thirsty traitor?"

"The presence of this youth, Jocelyn Mounchensey," rejoined Hugh Calveley. "Had he not come between us when he did, and checked my purpose, I had delivered my country from oppression. I told thee, tyrant, thou hadst been marvellously preserved. Thy preserver stands before thee."

"Heaven defend us!" exclaimed James, trembling. "What an escape we hae had. There hath been a special interposition o' Providence in our behoof. Our gratitude is due to Him who watcheth ower us."

"And in some degree to him who hath been made the instrument of your Majesty's preservation," observed the Conde de Gondomar, who formed one of the group near the King. "Since the foul traitor hath proclaimed the name of my young protegé, there can be no need for further concealment. Master Jocelyn Mounchensey hath been singularly fortunate in rendering your Majesty a service, and may for ever congratulate himself on his share — accidental though it be — in this affair."

"By my halidame! he shall have reason for congratulation," cried James, graciously regarding the young man.

"Ay, let him rise by my fall. 'Tis meet he should," cried the Puritan, bitterly. "Shower thy honours upon him, tyrant. Give him wealth and titles. I could not wish him worse misfortune than thy favour."

"Hold thy scurril tongue, villain, or it shall be torn out by the roots," said James. "Thou shalt see that I can as promptly reward those that serve me, as thou shalt presently feel I can severely punish those that seek to injure me. Hark ye, Count!" he added to the Spanish

Ambassador, while those around drew back a little, seeing it was his Majesty's pleasure to confer with him in private, "this youth—this Jocelyn Mounchensey, hath gentle bluid in his veins?—he comes of a good stock, ha?"

"He is the representative of an old Norfolk family," De Gondomar replied.

"What! the son of Sir Ferdinando?" demanded James, a shade crossing his countenance, which did not escape the wily ambassador's notice.

"You have guessed right, Sire," he said. "This is Sir Ferdinando's son; and, if I may be permitted to say so, your Majesty owes him some reparation for the wrongs done his father."

"How! Count!" exclaimed James, with a look of slight displeasure. "Do you venture to question our judgments on hearsay—for ye can know naething o' your ain knowledge?"

"I know enough to be satisfied that misrepresentations were made to your Majesty respecting this young man's father," De Gondomar replied; "for I am well assured that if you ever erred at all, it must have been through ignorance, and want of due information. This was what I designed to explain more fully than I can well do now, when I availed myself of your Majesty's gracious permission to bring the young man into your presence; and I should then have taken leave to express how much he merited your Majesty's favour and protection. Fortune, however, has outrun my wishes, and given him a stronger claim upon you than any I could urge."

"Ye are right, Count," rejoined James cautiously. "He hath the strongest claim upon us, and he shall not find us ungrateful. We will confer wi' Steenie—wi' Buckingham, we mean—about him."

"Pardon me, Sire," said De Gondomar, "if I venture to suggest that your Majesty hath an admirable opportunity, which I should be sorry to see neglected, of showing your goodness and clemency, and silencing for ever the voice of calumny, which will sometimes be raised against you."

"What mean ye, Count?" cried James. "Ye wad na hae me pardon yon traitor?"

"Most assuredly not, Sire," De Gondomar rejoined. "But I would urge some present mark of favour for him who hath saved you from

the traitor's fell designs. And I am emboldened to ask this, because I feel assured it must be consonant to your Majesty's own inclinations to grant the request."

"It is sae, Count," rejoined James. "We only desired to consult wi' Buckingham to ascertain whether he had ony objections; but as this is altogether unlikely, we will follow our ain inclinations and do as your Excellency suggests."

De Gondomar could scarcely conceal his satisfaction.

At this moment Lord Roos pressed towards the King.

"I have something to say in reference to this young man, my liege," he cried.

"In his favour?" demanded the King.

"Yes, yes; in his favour, Sire," said De Gondomar, looking hard at the young nobleman. "You need not trouble his Majesty further, my lord. He is graciously pleased to accede to our wishes."

"Ay, ay; nae mair need be said," cried James. "Let the young man stand forward."

And as Jocelyn obeyed the injunction which was immediately communicated to him by De Gondomar, the King bade him kneel down, and taking Lord Roos's sword, touched him with it upon the shoulder, exclaiming, "Arise! Sir Jocelyn."

"You are safe now," whispered De Gondomar. "This is the first blow, and it has been well struck."

So confused was the new-made knight by the honour thus unexpectedly conferred upon him, that when he rose to his feet he could scarcely command himself sufficiently to make the needful obeisance, and tender thanks to the King. For a moment, his brow was flushed with pride, and his breast beat high; but the emotions were instantly checked, as he thought how the title had been purchased. Looking towards the prisoner, he beheld him in the hands of the warders, to whose custody he had been committed, with his arms bound behind him by thongs. His gaze had never quitted the young man during the ceremony which had just taken place, and he still regarded him sternly and reproachfully.

"Let the prisoner be removed, and kept in a place of safety till our pleasure respecting him be made known," cried James. "And now, my lords and ladies, let us forward to the palace."

And the cavalcade was once more put in motion, and passing through the great gateway entered the Fountain Court, where the nobility of both sexes dismounted, while their attendants and the falconers and varlets passed off to the offices.

The prisoner was conveyed to the porter's lodge, and strictly guarded, till some secure chamber could be prepared for him. On the way thither Jocelyn contrived to approach him, and to say in a low tone—"Can I do aught for Aveline?"

"Concern not yourself about her, Sir Jocelyn," rejoined Hugh Calveley, with stern contempt. "She is in a place of safety. You will never behold her more."

CHAPTER XXII.
WIFE AND MOTHER-IN-LAW.

Quick steps descended the narrow staircase—steps so light and cautious that they made no sound. Before drawing aside the arras that covered the secret entrance to the chamber, the lady paused to listen; and hearing nothing to alarm her, she softly raised a corner of the woof and looked in.

What did she behold? A young man seated beside a carved oak table, with his back towards her. He was reading a letter, the contents of which seemed greatly to disturb him, for he more than once dashed it aside, and then compelled himself to resume its perusal. No one else was in the room, which was spacious and lofty, though somewhat sombre, being wholly furnished with dark oak; while the walls were hung with ancient tapestry. Heavy curtains were drawn before the deep bay windows, increasing the gloom. The chamber was lighted by a brass lamp suspended from the moulded ceiling, the ribs of which were painted, and the bosses, at the intersections, gilded. Near the concealed entrance where the lady stood was placed a large curiously-carved ebony cabinet, against which leaned a suit of tilting armour and a lance; while on its summit were laid a morion, a brigandine, greaves, gauntlets, and other pieces of armour. On the right of the cabinet the tapestry was looped aside, disclosing a short flight of steps, terminated by the door of an anti-chamber.

Almost as the lady set foot within the room, which she did after a brief deliberation, dropping the arras noiselessly behind her, the young man arose. Her entrance had not been perceived, so violently was he agitated. Crushing the letter which had excited him so much between his fingers, and casting it furiously from him, he gave vent to an incoherent expression of rage. Though naturally extremely handsome, his features at this moment were so distorted by passion

that they looked almost hideous. In person he was slight and finely-formed; and the richness of his attire proclaimed him of rank.

The lady who, unperceived, had witnessed his violent emotion was remarkably beautiful. Her figure was superb; and she had the whitest neck and arms imaginable, and the smallest and most delicately-formed hands. Her features derived something of haughtiness from a slightly aquiline nose and a short curled upper lip. Her eyes were magnificent — large, dark, and almost Oriental in shape and splendour. Jetty brows, and thick, lustrous, raven hair, completed the catalogue of her charms. Her dress was of white brocade, over which she wore a loose robe of violet-coloured velvet, with open hanging sleeves, well calculated to display the polished beauty of her arms. Her ruff was of point lace, and round her throat she wore a carcanet of pearls, while other precious stones glistened in her dusky tresses.

This beautiful dame, whose proud lips were now more compressed than usual, and whose dark eyes emitted fierce rays — very different from their customary tender and voluptuous glances — was the Countess of Exeter. He whom she looked upon was Lord Roos, and the chamber she had just entered was the one assigned to the young nobleman in the Palace of Theobalds.

She watched him for some time with curiosity. At length his rage found vent in words.

"Perdition seize them both!" he exclaimed, smiting his forehead with his clenched hand. "Was ever man cursed with wife and mother-in-law like mine! They will, perforce, drive me to desperate measures, which I would willingly avoid; but if nothing else will keep them quiet, the grave must. Ay, the grave," he repeated in a hollow voice; "it is not my fault if I am compelled to send them thither. Fools to torment me thus!"

Feeling she had heard more than she ought, the Countess would have retired; but as retreat might have betrayed her, she deemed it better to announce her presence by saying, "You are not alone, my Lord."

Startled by her voice, Lord Roos instantly turned, and regarded her with haggard looks.

"You here, Frances?" he exclaimed; "I did not expect you so soon."

"I came before the hour, because—but you seem greatly agitated. Has anything happened?"

"Little more than what happens daily," he replied. "And yet it is more; for the crisis has arrived, and a fearful crisis it is. O, Frances!" he continued vehemently, "how dear you are to me. To preserve your love I would dare everything, even my soul's welfare. I would hesitate at no crime to keep you ever near me. Let those beware who would force you from me."

"What means this passion, my Lord?" inquired the Countess.

"It means that since there are those who will mar our happiness; who, jealous of our loves, will utterly blight and destroy them; who will tear us forcibly asunder, recking little of the anguish they occasion: since we have enemies who will do this; who will mortally wound us—let us no longer hesitate, but strike the first blow. We must rid ourselves of them at any cost, and in any way."

"I will not affect to misunderstand you, my Lord," the Countess replied, her beautiful features beginning to exhibit traces of terror. "But has it arrived at this point? Is the danger imminent and inevitable?"

"Imminent, but not inevitable," Lord Roos rejoined. "It can be avoided, as I have hinted, in one way, and in one way only. There is a letter I have just received from my wife; wherein, after her usual upbraidings, remonstrances, and entreaties, she concludes by saying, that if I continue deaf to her prayers, and refuse to break off entirely with you, and return to her, our 'criminal attachment,'—for so she terms our love—should be divulged to the deluded Earl of Exeter, who will know how to redress her wrongs, and avenge his own injured honour. What answer, save one, can be returned to that letter, Frances? If we set her at defiance, as we have hitherto done, she will act, for she is goaded on by that fury, her mother. We must gain a little time, in order that the difficulties now besetting us may be effectually removed."

"I shudder to think of it, William," said the Countess, trembling and turning deathly pale. "No; it must not be. Rather than such a crime should be committed, I will comply with their demand."

"And leave me?" cried Lord Roos, bitterly. "Frances, your affection is not equal to mine, or you could not entertain such a thought for a moment. You almost make me suspect," he added, sternly, "that you

have transferred your love to another. Ah! beware! beware! I am not to be trifled with, like your husband."

"I forgive you the doubt, my Lord—unjust though it be—because your mind is disturbed; but were you calm enough to view the matter as it really is, you would perceive that my resolution has nothing in it inconsistent with affection for you; but rather that my very love for you compels me to the step. What I propose is best for both of us. The remedy you suggest would work our ruin here and hereafter; would drive us from society, and render us hateful to each other. My soul revolts at it. And though I myself have received a mortal affront from your wife's mother, Lady Lake; though she has poured forth all the malice of which she is capable upon my devoted head; yet I would rather forgive her—rather sue for pity from her than go the fearful length you propose. No, William. The pang of parting from you will indeed be terrible, but it must be endured. Fate wills it so, and it is therefore useless to struggle against it."

"O, recall those words, Frances!" cried the young nobleman, throwing himself at her feet, and clasping her hands passionately. "Recall them, I implore' of you. In uttering them you pronounce my doom—a doom more dreadful than death, which would be light in comparison with losing you. Plunge this sword to my heart," he exclaimed, plucking the shining weapon from his side, and presenting it to her. "Free me from my misery at once, but do not condemn me to lingering agony."

"Rise, William! rise, I pray of you," ejaculated the Countess, overcome by the intensity of his emotion, "and put up your sword. The love you display for me deserves an adequate return, and it shall meet it. Come what will, I will not leave you. But, O! let us not plunge deeper in guilt if it can be avoided."

"But how can it be avoided?" cried Lord Roos. "Will they listen to our prayers? Will they pity us? Will they hesitate at our destruction?"

"I know not—I know not," replied the Countess, bewildered; "but I stand appalled before the magnitude of the offence."

"They will not spare us," pursued Lord Roos; "and therefore we cannot spare them."

"In my turn I bend to you, William," said the Countess, sinking on her knee before him, and taking his hand. "By the love you bear

me, I beseech you not to harm your wife! We have wronged her deeply—let us not have her death to answer for. If the blow must fall, let it be upon the mother's head. I have less compassion for her."

"Lady Lake deserves no compassion," replied Lord Roos, raising the Countess, and embracing her tenderly, "for she is the cause of all this mischief. It is to her agency we owe the storm which threatens us with ruin. But things have gone too far now to show compunction for either of them. Our security demands that both should be removed."

"I may now say as you have just said, William, and with, far greater reason," cried the Countess, "that you love me not, or you would not refuse my request."

"How can I comply with it?" he rejoined. "Nothing were done, if only partly done. Know you the charge that Lady Roos means to bring against you? Though alike false and improbable, it is one to find easy credence with the King; and it has been framed with that view. You will understand this, when I tell you what it is. In this letter," he added, picking up the paper he had thrown down, and unfolding it, "she accuses you of practising sorcery to enslave my affections. She declares you have bewitched me; and that she has proof of the manner in which it was done, and of the sinful compact you have entered into for the purpose."

"O William! this is false—utterly false!" exclaimed the Countess, in despair.

"I know it," he rejoined. "You have no need to practise other enchantments with me than those you possess by nature. But what I tell you will show you the extent of their malice, and steel your heart, as it hath already steeled mine, against them."

"But this accusation is too monstrous. It will not be believed," cried the Countess.

"Monstrous as it is, it is more likely to be believed—more certain to be maintained—than the other which they lay at our door. We may deny all their assertions; may intimidate or give the lie to the witnesses they may produce against us; may stamp as forgeries your letters which have unluckily fallen into their hands; but if this charge of witchcraft be once brought against you, it will not fall to the ground. The King will listen to it, because it flatters his prejudices;

and even my voice would fail to save you from condemnation—from the stake."

"Horrible!" exclaimed Lady Exeter spreading her hands before her eyes, as if to exclude some dreadful object. "O to live in an age when such enormities can be perpetrated! when such frightful weapons can be used against the innocent—for I am innocent, at least of this offence. All seems against me; all doors of escape—save one—closed. And whither does that door lead? To the Bottomless Pit, if there be truth in aught we are told by Heaven."

Lord Roos seemed unable or unwilling to reply; and a deep pause ensued for a few moments, during which the guilty pair shunned each other's regards. It was broken at length by Lady Exeter, who said, reproachfully, "You should have burnt my letters, William. Without them, they would have had no evidence against me. Imprudent that you were, you have destroyed me!"

"Reproach me not, Frances," he rejoined. "I admit my imprudence, and blame myself severely for it. But I could not part with a line I had received from you. I inclosed the letters in a little coffer, which I deposited in a secret drawer of that cabinet, as in a place of perfect safety. The coffer and its contents mysteriously disappeared. How it was purloined I cannot inform you."

"Do your suspicions alight on no one?" she inquired.

"They have fallen on several; but I have no certainty that I have been right in any instance," he replied. "That I have some spy near me, I am well aware; and if I detect him, he shall pay for his perfidy with his life."

"Hist!" cried Lady Exeter. "Did you not hear a noise?"

"No," he rejoined. "Where?"

She pointed to the little passage leading to the ante-chamber. He instantly went thither, and examined the place, but without discovering any listener.

"There is no one," he said, as he returned. "No one, in fact, could have obtained admittance without my knowledge, for my Spanish servant, Diego, in whom I can place full confidence, is stationed without."

"I distrust that man, William," she observed. "When I asked whom you thought had removed the letters, my own suspicions had attached to him."

"I do not think he would have done it," Lord Roos replied. "He has ever served me faithfully; and, besides, I have a guarantee for his fidelity in the possession of a secret on which his own life hangs. I can dispose of him as I please."

"Again that sound!" exclaimed the Countess. "I am sure some one is there."

"Your ears have deceived you," said the young nobleman, after examining the spot once more, and likewise the secret entrance by which the Countess had approached the chamber. "I heard nothing, and can find nothing. Your nerves are shaken, and make you fanciful."

"It may be so," she rejoined. But it was evident she was not convinced, for she lowered her tones almost to a whisper as she continued. It might be that the question she designed to put was one she dared not ask aloud. "What means do you purpose to employ in the execution of your design?"

"The same as those employed by Somerset and his Countess in the removal of Sir Thomas Overbury; but more expeditious and more certain," he replied under his breath.

"Dreadful!" she exclaimed, with a shudder. "But the same judgment that overtook the Somersets may overtake us. Such crimes are never hidden."

"Crimes fouler than theirs have never been brought to light, and never will. There was one in which Somerset himself was concerned, involving the destruction of a far higher personage than Overbury; and this dare not even be hinted at."

"Because the greatest person in the land was connected with it," returned the Countess, "I conclude you refer to the death of Prince Henry?"

"I do," answered Lord Roos. "Somerset would never have been questioned about Overbury, if his fall had not been resolved upon by the King."

"One other question, and I ask no more," said the Countess, scarcely able to syllable her words. "Who is to administer the deadly draught?"

"Luke Hatton, Lady Lake's apothecary. He is a creature of mine, and entirely devoted to me."

"Our lives will be in his hands ever afterwards," said the Countess, in a deep whisper.

"They will be in safe keeping," he rejoined, endeavouring to reassure her.

"O, William! I would I could prevail upon you to defer this project."

"To what end? The sooner it is done the better. It cannot, indeed, be deferred. I shall send for Luke Hatton to-night."

At this announcement, the Countess, who had gradually been growing fainter and becoming paler, lost all power of supporting herself, and, uttering a cry, fell into his outstretched arms in a state of complete insensibility.

While Lord Roos, half distracted, was considering what means he could adopt for her restoration, a man, with an almost tawny complexion, hair and eyes to match, and habited in the young nobleman's livery of crimson and white, suddenly entered from the ante-chamber.

"How dare you come in unsummoned, Diego?" cried Lord Roos, furiously. "Begone instantly, sirrah!".

"I crave your lordship's pardon," replied the Spanish servant; "but I was obliged to apprise you that your wife, the Baroness Roos, and Lady Lake are without, and will not be denied admission."

"Damnation!" exclaimed Lord Roos. "What brings them here at such an hour? But you must on no account admit them, Diego—at least, till I have had time to remove the Countess to her own chamber. What a cursed mischance!"

Diego instantly withdrew, apparently to obey his lord's command; but he had scarcely entered the little passage when two ladies pushed past him, and made their way into the room. They arrived just in time to intercept Lord Roos, who was conveying his insensible burthen towards the secret staircase.

The young nobleman was as much confounded by their appearance as if two spectres had risen before him. Both ladies were very richly attired, and the younger of the two was by no means destitute of beauty, though of a pale and pensive character. The elder had a full, noble figure, haughty features, now lighted up with a smile of triumph as she gazed on Lord Roos. Very different was the expression of the other, who seemed so much grieved and agitated by what she beheld, as to be almost ready to lapse into the same condition as the Countess.

If Lord Roos could have seen the grin upon Diego's swarthy visage, as he stood at the entrance of the passage leading to the antechamber, he would have had little doubt to whom he was indebted for this surprise.

It is needless to say that the ladies who had thus broken upon Lord Roos's privacy, and obtained full confirmation of their suspicions (if they had any doubts remaining) were his wife and mother-in-law.

CHAPTER XXIII.
THE TRESS OF HAIR.

How to extricate himself from the dilemma in which he was placed, Lord Roos scarcely knew. But he had a good deal of self-possession, and it did not desert him on the present trying occasion. After such consideration as circumstances permitted, he could discern only one chance of escape, and though well-nigh hopeless, he resolved to adopt it. If consummate audacity could carry him through—and it was required in the present emergency—he had no lack of it.

Hitherto, not a word had passed between him and the intruders on his privacy. Lady Lake seemed to enjoy his confusion too much to do anything to relieve it, and his wife was obliged to regulate her movements by those of her mother. Without breaking the silence, which by this time had become painfully oppressive, he proceeded to deposit the still inanimate person of the Countess of Exeter upon a couch, and, casting a handkerchief, as if undesignedly, over her face, he marched quickly up to the spot where Diego was standing, and said to him, in a deep, determined tone, but so low as not to be overheard by the others:

"You have betrayed me, villain; and unless you obey me unhesitatingly, and corroborate all my assertions, however startling they may appear, you shall pay for your treachery with your life."

This done, he turned towards the two ladies, and with more calmness than might have been expected, addressed himself to Lady Lake:

"You imagine you have made an important discovery, Madam," he said; "a discovery which will place me and a noble lady, whose reputation you and your daughter seek to injure, in great perplexity. And you conclude that, being completely (as you fancy) in your power, I shall consent to any terms you and Lady Roos may propose,

rather than suffer you to go forth from this chamber and reveal what you have seen in it. Is it not so, Madam?"

"Ay, my lord," Lady Lake replied, bitterly. "You have stated the matter correctly enough, except in one particular. We do not imagine we have made a discovery; because we are quite sure of it. We do not fancy you will agree to our terms; because we are certain you will only too gladly screen yourself and the partner of your guilt from exposure and disgrace, at any sacrifice. And allow me to observe, that the tone adopted by your lordship is neither befitting the circumstances in which you are placed, nor the presence in which you stand. Some sense of shame must at least be left you—some show of respect (if nothing more) ought to be observed towards your injured wife. Were I acting alone in this matter, I would show you and my lady of Exeter no consideration whatever; but I cannot resist the pleadings of my daughter; and for her sake—and hers alone—I am content to suspend the blow, unless forced to strike; in which case, nothing shall stay my hands."

"I thank your ladyship for your clemency," said Lord Roos, with mock humility.

"O, my dear lord! do not for ever close the door between us!" cried Lady Roos. "Return to me, and all shall be forgiven."

"Peace, Elizabeth!" exclaimed Lady Lake, impatiently. "Know you not, from sad experience, that your husband is inaccessible to all gentle entreaty? His heart is steeled to pity. Solicit not that which is your right, and which must be conceded, whether he like or not. Let him bend the knee to you. Let him promise amendment, and implore pardon, and it will then be for you to consider whether you will extend forgiveness to him."

Lady Roos looked as if she would fain interrupt her mother, but she was too much under her subjection to offer a remark.

"It is time to undeceive you, Madam," said Lord Roos, wholly unmoved by what was said. "I am not in the strait you suppose; and have not the slightest intention of soliciting Lady Roos's pardon, or making any promise to her."

"O mother! you see that even you fail to move him," said Lady Roos, tearfully. "What is to happen to me?"

"You will make me chide you, daughter, if you exhibit this weakness," cried Lady Lake, angrily. "Let me deal with him. In spite of your affected confidence, my lord, you cannot be blind to the position in which you stand. And though you yourself personally may be careless of the consequences of a refusal of our demands, you cannot, I conceive, be equally indifferent to the fate of the Countess of Exeter, which that refusal will decide."

"I am so little indifferent to the safety of the Countess, Madam, that I cannot sufficiently rejoice that she is out of the reach of your malice."

"How, my lord!" exclaimed Lady Lake, astounded at his assurance. "Out of reach, when she is here! You cannot mean," she added, with an undefinable expression of satisfaction, "that she is dead?"

"Dead!" ejaculated Lady Roos; "the Countess dead! I thought she was only in a swoon."

"What riddle is it you would have us read, my lord?" demanded Lady Lake.

"No riddle whatever, Madam," replied Lord Roos. "I only mean to assert that the person you behold upon that couch is not the Countess of Exeter."

"Not the Countess!" exclaimed Lady Roos. "Oh, if this were possible! But no, no! I cannot be deceived."

"I now see the reason why her face has been covered with a 'kerchief," cried Lady Lake. "But it shall not save her from our scrutiny."

So saying, she advanced towards the couch, with the intention of removing the covering, when Lord Roos barred her approach.

"Not a step nearer, Madam," he cried, in a peremptory tone. "I will not allow you to gratify your curiosity further. You and Lady Roos may make the most of what you have seen; and proclaim abroad any tale your imaginations may devise forth. You will only render yourselves ridiculous, and encounter derision in lieu of sympathy. No one will credit your assertions, because I shall be able to prove that, at this moment, Lady Exeter is in a different part of the palace."

"This bold falsehood will not serve your turn, my lord. Whoever she may be, the person on that couch shall be seized, and we shall then ascertain the truth."

And she would have moved towards the door, if Lord Roos had not caught hold of her arm, while at the same time he drew his sword. Thinking from his fierce looks and menacing gestures that her mother might be sacrificed to his fury, Lady Roos fell on her knees before him, imploring pity; and she continued in this supplicating posture till Lady Lake angrily bade her rise.

"You have come here without my permission, Madam," Lord Roos cried furiously to his mother-in-law, "and you shall not depart until I choose. Secure the door, Diego, and bring me the key. It is well," he continued, as the injunction was obeyed.

Lady Lake submitted without resistance to the constraint imposed upon her. She could not well do otherwise; for though her screams would have brought aid, it might have arrived too late. And, after all, she did not intend to settle matters in this way. But she betrayed no symptoms of fear, and, as we have stated, ordered her daughter to discontinue her supplications.

"And now, Madam," said Lord Roos, releasing Lady Lake, as he took the key from Diego, "I will tell you who that person is," pointing to the couch.

"Add not to the number of falsehoods you have already told, my lord," rejoined Lady Lake, contemptuously. "I am perfectly aware who she is."

"But I would fain hear his explanation, mother," said Lady Roos.

"What explanation can be offered?" cried Lady Lake. "Do you doubt the evidence of your senses?"

"I know not what I doubt, or what I believe," exclaimed Lady Roos distractedly.

"Then believe what I tell you, Bess," said her husband. "This is the countess's handmaiden, Gillian Greenford."

"An impudent lie!" cried Lady Lake.

"A truth, my lady," interposed Diego. "A truth to which I am ready to swear."

"No doubt of it, thou false knave, and double traitor! thou art worthy of thy lord. There is no lie, however absurd and improbable, which he can invent, that thou wilt not support. Thou art ready now to perjure thyself for him; but let him place little reliance on thee, for thou wilt do the same thing for us to-morrow."

"I scarcely think it probable, my lady," Diego replied, bowing.

Lady Lake turned from him in supreme disgust.

"Admitting for a moment the possibility of your lordship's assertion being correct," said Lady Roos, "how comes Gillian Greenford (for so methinks you name her) in her mistress's attire?"

"'T is easily explained, chuck," Lord Roos rejoined. "Anxious, no doubt, to set herself off to advantage, she hath made free with the countess's wardrobe. Your own favourite attendant, Sarah Swarton, hath often arranged herself in your finest fardingales, kirtlets, and busk-points, as Diego will tell you. Is it not so, rascal?"

"'T is precisely as my lord hath stated, my lady," said the Spaniard to Lady Roos. "When Sarah Swarton hath been so habited, I have more than once mistaken her for your ladyship."

"Yet Sarah is very unlike me," said Lady Roos.

"That only shows how deceptive appearances are, chuck, and how little we ought to trust to them," observed Lord Roos.

"How can you suffer yourself to be thus duped, Elizabeth?" said Lady Lake.

"Because her ladyship would rather believe me than you, Madam," rejoined Lord Roos. "But she is not duped."

"Heaven forgive him!" exclaimed Diego, aside.

"And supposing it were Gillian, how would the case be mended, as far as you are concerned, Elizabeth?" said Lady Lake. "Are you not as much injured by one as by the other?"

"It may be," replied her daughter, "but I am jealous only of the Countess. I would kneel to any other woman, and thank her, who would tear my husband from her embraces!"

"Weak fool! I disown you," exclaimed Lady Lake, angrily.

"What a wife!" cried Diego, apart. "His lordship is quite unworthy of her. Now I should appreciate such devotion."

At this juncture there was a slight movement on the part of Lady Exeter, and something like a sigh escaped her.

"She revives!" whispered Lady Lake to her daughter. "We shall soon learn the truth. I will find a means to make her speak. Well, my lord," she added aloud, and speaking in a sarcastic tone, "if you will have it so, it is idle to dispute it. But what will the Countess say, when she discovers your infidelity?"

On this a brisker movement took place on the couch, and a hand was raised as if to snatch away the 'kerchief.

"We have her," whispered Lady Lake triumphantly to her daughter. "Surely," she proceeded aloud, "the Countess will deeply resent the transfer of your affections to her handmaiden."

Lord Roos saw the peril in which he stood. A moment more and Lady Lake had gained her point, and the Countess betrayed herself.

"Lady Exeter will place little reliance on any representations you may make, Madam," he said, giving particular significance to his words, "except so far as they concern herself, and then she will take care to refute them. As to the circumstance of Gillian Greenford visiting me, fainting in my arms (from excess of timidity, poor girl!) and being discovered by you and Lady Roos in that position, the Countess will laugh at it when it comes to her knowledge—as why should she do otherwise? But she will feel very differently when she finds that you and your daughter insist that it was she herself, and not her handmaiden, whom you beheld. Rely on it, Madam, Lady Exeter will contradict that assertion, and disprove it."

"Let it be disproved now. Let the person on that couch disclose her features, and we shall then see whether she be the Countess or Gillian."

"Ay, let her do that, my lord,—let her speak to us," urged Lady Roos.

"Diablo! how is this request to be complied with, I marvel?" said Diego apart.

But Lord Roos was too experienced a player to be defeated by this turn in the game.

"Gillian has already been sufficiently annoyed," he cried; "and shall not submit to this ordeal. Besides, she has relapsed into insensibility, as you see."

"She does what your lordship wills her, it is clear," said Lady Lake, contemptuously. "We know what construction to put upon your refusal."

"I care not what construction you put upon it," cried Lord Roos, losing patience. "You and Lady Roos may think what you please, and act as you please. Enough for me, you can prove nothing."

"Why, this is more like yourself, my lord," retorted Lady Lake, derisively. "Having thrown aside the mask, you will be spared the necessity of further subterfuge. The Countess, doubtless, will imitate your example, lay aside her feigned insensibility, and defy us. She need be under no apprehension; since she has your own warrant that we can prove nothing."

"Your purpose, I perceive, is to irritate me, Madam," cried Lord Roos, fiercely; "and so far you are likely to succeed, though you fail in all else. I have no mask to throw off; but if you will have me declare myself your enemy, I am ready to do so. Henceforth, let there be no terms kept between us—let it be open warfare."

"Be it so, my lord. And you will soon find who will be worsted in the struggle."

"Oh, do not proceed to these fearful extremities, dear mother, and dearest husband!" cried Lady Roos, turning from one to the other imploringly. "Cease these provocations, I pray of you. Be friends, and not enemies."

"As you please—peace or war; it is the same to me," said Lord Roos. "Meantime, I am wearied of this scene, and must put an end to it. Diego!" And beckoning his servant to him, he whispered some directions in his ear.

"My lord shall be obeyed," said Diego, as he received his commission. "Gillian shall be conveyed with all care to her chamber."

"We must have some proof that she has been here," thought Lady Lake. But how to obtain it? I have it. "Take these," she added in a whisper to her daughter, and giving a pair of scissors; "and contrive, if possible, to sever a lock of her hair before she be removed."

By a look Lady Roos promised compliance.

While this was passing, Diego had approached the couch; and fastening the kerchief securely round the Countess's face, he raised

her in his arms, and moved towards the secret staircase, the tapestried covering of which was held aside by Lord Roos to give him passage.

Rapidly as the Spaniard moved, he did not outstrip Lady Roos, whose design being favoured by the escape from its confinement of one of the Countess's long dark tresses, she had no difficulty of possessing, herself of it in the manner prescribed by her mother. Lady Exeter was aware of the loss she had sustained, and uttered a stifled cry; but this was attributed to the fright natural to the occasion by Lord Roos, who had not noticed what had taken place, and only caused him to hurry Diego's departure. But before the latter had wholly disappeared with his burthen, the perfumed and silken tress of hair was delivered to Lady Lake, who muttered triumphantly as she received it—"This will convict her. She cannot escape us now."

The prize was scarcely concealed when Lord Roos, sheathing the sword which he had hitherto held drawn, advanced towards his mother-in-law.

"Now that the object of your disquietude is removed, Madam, it will not be necessary to prolong this interview," he said.

"Have we then your lordship's permission to depart?" rejoined Lady Lake, coldly. "We are not, I presume, to avail ourselves of the private means of exit contrived for your amorous adventures, lest we should make other discoveries."

"Your ladyship will leave by the way you entered," rejoined Lord Roos. "I will attend you to the door—and unfasten it for you."

"Before we go, I would have a word with my husband—it may be my last," said Lady Roos to her mother. "I pray you withdraw a little, that we may be alone."

"Better not," rejoined Lady Lake. But unable to resist her daughter's imploring looks, she added, "Well, as you will. But it is useless."

With this she proceeded to the little passage, and remained there.

As Lady Roos turned to her husband, she saw, from the stern and inflexible look he had assumed, that any appeal made to him would be unavailing, and she attempted none. A moment elapsed before she could utter a word, and then it was only a murmur to heaven for guidance and support.

"What say you, Elizabeth?" demanded Lord Roos, thinking she had addressed him.

"I asked for support from on High, William, and it has been accorded to me," she replied in a low sweet voice. "I can now speak to you. It is not to weary you with supplications or reproaches that I thus detain you. I have something to impart to you, and I am sure you will eagerly listen to it. Come nearer, that we may not be overheard."

Lord Roos, whose curiosity was aroused by her manner, obeyed her.

"I am all attention," he said.

"I feel I am in your way, William," she rejoined, in a deep whisper; "and that you desire my death. Nay, interrupt me not; I am sure you desire it; and I am equally sure that the desire will be gratified, and that you will kill me."

"Kill you, Bess!" cried Lord Roos, startled. "How can you imagine aught so frightful?"

"There is a power granted to those who love deeply as I do, of seeing into the hearts of those they love, and reading their secrets. I have read yours, William. Nay, be not alarmed. I have kept it to myself hitherto, and will keep it to the end. You wish me dead, I say; and you shall have your wish—but not in the way you propose. Having lost your love, I am become indifferent to life—or, rather, life is grown intolerable to me. But though death may be a release, it must not come from your hand."

"You cannot mean to destroy yourself, Elizabeth?" cried Lord Roos, appalled.

"I mean to trouble you no longer. I mean to make the last and greatest sacrifice I can for you; and to save you from a crime—or, if you must share the crime, at least to screen you from punishment. Look, here!" she added, producing a small phial. "Bid me drink of this, and ere to-morrow you are free, and I am at rest. Shall I do it?"

"No—no," rejoined Lord Roos, snatching the phial from her. "Live, Bess, live!"

"Am I to live for you, William?" she cried, with inexpressible joy.

He made no answer, but averted his head.

"In mercy give me back the phial," she exclaimed, again plunged into the depths of despair.

"I must refuse your request," he replied.

"Have you done, Elizabeth?" demanded Lady Lake, coming forth from the passage.

"A moment more, mother," cried Lady Roos. "One word—one look!" she added to her husband.

But he neither spoke to her, nor regarded her.

"I am ready to accompany you now, mother," said the poor lady faintly.

"Nerve yourself, weak-hearted girl," said Lady Lake, in a low tone. "Revenge is ours."

"If I could only strike her without injuring him, I should not heed," thought Lady Roos. "But where he suffers, I must also suffer, and yet more acutely."

And scarcely able to support herself, she followed her mother to the door of the ante-chamber, which was unlocked, and thrown open for them by her husband. He did not bid her farewell!

As Lady Lake passed forth, she paused for a moment, and said—

"To-morrow, my Lord, we will ascertain whether the tress of hair we have obtained from the fair visitant to your chamber, matches with that of Gillian Greenford or with the raven locks of the Countess of Exeter."

And satisfied with the effect produced by this menace, she departed with her daughter, before Lord Roos could utter a reply.

CHAPTER XXIV.
THE FOUNTAIN COURT.

On the morning after the eventful passage in his life, previously related, our newly-created knight was standing, in a pensive attitude, beside the beautiful fountain, adorned with two fair statues, representing the Queen of Love and her son, heretofore described as placed in the centre of the great quadrangle of the Palace of Theobalds. Sir Jocelyn was listening to the plashing of the sparkling jets of water, as they rose into the air, and fell back into the broad marble basin, and appeared to be soothed by the pleasant sound. His breast had been agitated by various and conflicting emotions. In an incredibly short space of time events had occurred, some of which seemed likely to influence the whole of his future career; while one of them, though it had advanced him far beyond what he could have anticipated, appeared likely to mar 0altogether his prospects of happiness.

Though the difficulties, therefore, that surrounded him had been unexpectedly overcome; though, by the exertions of the Conde de Gondomar, who had followed up his first success with wonderful promptitude and perseverance, and had dexterously contrived, by all the insidious arts of which he was so perfect a master, to ingratiate his protegé still further with the King, without the protegé himself being aware of the manner in which he was served; though James himself appeared greatly pleased with him, at the banquet in the evening, to which, owing to the skilful management of the Spanish ambassador, he was invited, and bestowed such marked attention upon him, that the envy and jealousy of most of the courtiers were excited by it; though he seemed on the high-road to still greater favour, and was already looked upon as a rising favourite, who might speedily supplant others above him in this ever-changing sphere, if he did not receive a check; though his present position was thus comparatively

secure, and his prospects thus brilliant, he felt ill at ease, and deeply dissatisfied with himself. He could not acquit himself of blame for the part he had played, though involuntarily, in the arrest of Hugh Calveley. It was inexpressibly painful to him; and he felt it as a reproach from which he could not free himself, to have risen, however unexpectedly on his own part, by the unfortunate Puritan's fall. How could he ever face Aveline again! She must regard him with horror and detestation, as the involuntary cause of her father's destruction. A bar had been placed between them, which nothing could ever remove. And though, on the one hand, he was suddenly exalted far beyond his hopes; yet on the other he was as suddenly cast down, and threatened to be for ever deprived of the bliss he had in view, the possession of which he coveted far more than wealth or grandeur. Additional complexity had been given to his position from the circumstance that, at De Gondomar's secret instance, of which, like all the rest, he was unaware, he had been appointed as officer in custody of Hugh Calveley, until the latter, who was still detained a close prisoner in the porter's lodge, should be removed to the Tower, or the Fleet, as his Majesty might direct. This post he would have declined, had there been a possibility of doing so. Any plan he might have formed of aiding the prisoner's escape was thus effectually prevented, as he could not violate his duty; and it was probably with this view that the wily ambassador had obtained him the appointment. In fact, he had unconsciously become little more than a puppet in the hands of the plotting Spaniard, who pulled the strings that moved him at pleasure, regardless of the consequences. What De Gondomar's ulterior designs were with him had not yet become manifest.

These perplexing thoughts swept through Sir Jocelyn's breast, as he stood by the marble fountain, and listened to the sound of its falling waters.

While thus occupied, he perceived two persons issue from the arched entrance fronting the gate (adjoining the porter's lodge, in which the prisoner was still detained), and make their way slowly across the quadrangle, in the direction of the cloister on its eastern side, above which were apartments assigned to the Secretary of State, Sir Thomas Lake.

The foremost of the two was merely a yeoman of the guard, and would not for a moment have attracted Sir Jocelyn's attention, if it

had not been for a female who accompanied him, and whom he was evidently conducting to Sir Thomas Lake's rooms, as Sir Jocelyn not only saw the man point towards them, but heard him mention the Secretary of State's name.

Something whispered him that this closely-hooded female,—the lower part of whose face was shrouded in a muffler, so that the eyes alone were visible,—was Aveline. Little could be discerned of the features; but the exquisitely-proportioned figure, so simply yet so tastefully arrayed, could only be hers; and if he could have doubted that it was Aveline, the suddenness with which her looks were averted as she beheld him, and the quickness with which she stepped forward, so as even to outstrip her companion—these circumstances, coupled with the violent throbbing of his own heart, convinced him he was right. He would have flown after her, if he had dared; would have poured forth all his passionate feelings to her, had he been permitted; would have offered her his life, to deal with as she pleased; but his fears restrained him, and he remained riveted to the spot, gazing after her until she entered the great hall on the ground floor, beneath the Secretary of State's apartments. Why she sought Sir Thomas Lake he could easily understand. It was only from him that authority to visit her father could be obtained.

After remaining irresolute for a few minutes, during which the magnificent structure around him faded entirely from his view like a vision melting into air, and he heard no more the pleasant plashing of the fountain, he proceeded to the great hall near the cloister, resolved to wait there till her return.

CHAPTER XXV.
SIR THOMAS LAKE.

A grave-looking man, of a melancholy and severe aspect, and attired in a loose robe of black velvet, was seated alone in a chamber, the windows of which opened upon the Fountain Court, which we have just quitted. He wore a silken skull-cap, from beneath which a few gray hairs escaped; his brow was furrowed with innumerable wrinkles, occasioned as much by thought and care as by age; his pointed beard and moustaches were almost white, contrasting strikingly with his dark, jaundiced complexion, the result of an atrabilarious temperament; his person was extremely attenuated, and his hands thin and bony. He had once been tall, but latterly had lost much of his height, in consequence of a curvature of the spine, which bowed down his head almost upon his breast, and fixed it immoveably in that position. His features were good, but, as we have stated, were stamped with melancholy, and sharpened by severity.

This person was Sir Thomas Lake, Secretary of State.

The table at which he sat was strewn over with official documents and papers. He was not, however, examining any of them, but had just broken the seal of a private packet which he had received from his wife, when an usher entered, and intimated that a young maiden, who was without, solicited a moment's audience. The request would have been refused, if the man had not gone on to say that he believed the applicant was the daughter of the crazy Puritan, who had threatened the King's life on the previous day. On hearing this, Sir Thomas consented to see her, and she was admitted accordingly.

As soon as the usher had retired, Aveline unmuffled herself, and, cold and apathetic as he was, Sir Thomas could not help being struck by her surpassing beauty, unimpaired even by the affliction under

which she laboured; and he consequently softened in some degree the customary asperity of his tones in addressing her.

"Who are you, maiden, and what seek you?" he demanded, eyeing her with curiosity.

"I am daughter to the unfortunate Hugh Calveley, now a prisoner in the palace," she replied.

"I am sorry to hear it," rejoined Sir Thomas, resuming his habitually severe expression; "for you are the daughter of a very heinous offender. The enormity of Hugh Calveley's crime, which is worse than parricide, deprives him of all human sympathy and compassion. In coming to me you do not, I presume, intend to weary me with prayers for mercy; for none is deserved, and none will be shown. For my own part, I shall not utter a word in mitigation of the dreadful sentence certain to be pronounced upon him; nor shall I advise the slightest clemency to be shown him on the part of his Majesty. Such an offender cannot be too severely punished. I do not say this," he continued, somewhat softening his harshness, "to aggravate the distress and shame you naturally feel; but I wish to check at once any hopes you may have formed. Yet though I have no pity for him, I have much for you, since, doubtless, you are innocent of all knowledge of your father's atrocious design—happily prevented. And I would therefore say to you, shut out all feelings for him from your heart. The man who raises his hand against his sovereign cuts off by the act all ties of kindred and love. Affection is changed to abhorrence; and such detestation does his horrible offence inspire, that those of his own blood are bound to shun him, lest he derive comfort and consolation from their presence. Thus considered, you are no longer his daughter, for he has himself severed the links between you. You no longer owe him filial duty and regard, for to such he is no more entitled. Leave him to his fate; and, if possible, for ever obliterate his memory from your breast."

"You counsel what I can never perform, honourable Sir," replied Aveline; "and were he even branded like Cain, I could not shut my heart towards him. Nothing can make me forget that I am his daughter. That his offence will be dreadfully expiated, I do not doubt; but if I can alleviate his sufferings in any way, I will do so; and I will never cease to plead for mercy for him. And O, honourable Sir! you regard his offence in a darker light than it deserves. You treat him as

if he had actually accomplished the direful purpose attributed to him; whereas, nothing has been proven against him beyond the possession of a weapon, which he might keep about his person for self-defence."

"The plea you urge is futile, maiden," rejoined Sir Thomas; "he is judged out of his own mouth, for his own lips have avowed his criminal intention."

"Still, it was but the intention, honourable Sir!"

"In such cases, the intention is equal to the crime—at least in the eyes of law and justice. No plea will save Hugh Calveley. Of that rest assured."

"One plea may be urged for him, which, whether it avail or not, is the truth, and shall be made. It is painful to speak of my father as I must now do; but there is no help for it. Of late years he has been subject to strange mental hallucinations, which have bordered close upon madness, if they have not reached that terrible point. Nocturnal vigils, fastings, and prayers have affected his health. He has denied himself sufficient rest, and has only partaken of food barely sufficient to sustain nature, and no more. The consequence has been that strange fancies have troubled his brain; that at dead of night, when alone in his chamber, he has imagined that visions have appeared to him; that voices have spoken—awful voices—talking of prophecies, lamentations, and judgments, and charging him with a mighty and terrible mission. All these things I have heard from his own lips, and I have heard and seen much more, which has satisfied me that his intellects are disordered, and that he cannot be held accountable for his actions."

"If such be the case, he should have been kept under restraint, and not suffered to go abroad," said Sir Thomas. "Such madmen are highly mischievous and dangerous. Much blame rests with you, maiden."

"The whole blame is mine!" she exclaimed. "I confess my error—my crime—and will atone for it willingly with my life, provided he be spared. If a sacrifice must be made, let me be the victim."

"There is no sacrifice, and no victim," returned Sir Thomas gravely, though he was not unmoved by her filial devotion. "There is an offender, and there will be justice; and justice must be satisfied. Inexorable as fate, her dread sentences cannot be averted."

"O, honourable Sir! you may one day recall those words; for which of us can hold himself free from offence? My father is not guilty in the eyes of Heaven; or if he be, I am equally culpable, since I ought to have prevented the commission of the crime. O, I shall never forgive myself that I did not follow him when he parted from me yesterday!"

"Let me hear how that occurred, maiden?" asked Sir Thomas.

"It chanced in this way, Sir. I have already described my father's state of mind, and the distempered view he has been accustomed to take of all things. Yesterday, May-day sports were held in the village of Tottenham, where we dwelt; and as such things are an abomination in his sight, he took upon him to reprove the actors in the pastimes. They who witnessed his conduct on that occasion would hardly hold him to be under the due control of reason. Amongst the spectators was the son of an old friend, whose name having accidentally reached my father, he invited him into the house, and a misunderstanding having arisen between them, the latter suddenly left—dismissed almost with rudeness. On his departure, my father was greatly disturbed—more so than I have ever seen him. After awhile, he withdrew to his own chamber, as was his habit, to pray, and I hoped would become tranquillized; but the very reverse happened, for when he reappeared, I saw at once that a fearful change had taken place in him. His eye blazed with preternatural light, his gestures were wild and alarming, and his language full of menace and denunciation. He again spoke of his mission from Heaven, and said that its execution could no longer be delayed."

"This should have been a warning to you," observed Sir Thomas, knitting his brows.

"It should, honourable Sir. But I did not profit by it. I knew and felt that he was no longer under the dominion of reason—that he was labouring under some terrible delusion that approached its crisis; but I did not check him. I yielded passive obedience to his injunction, that I should depart instantly with an old servant to London; and I agreed to tarry at a house, which he mentioned, till I heard from him. I had sad forebodings that I should never hear from him again—or if I did, that the tidings would be worse than none at all; but I obeyed. I could not, indeed, resist his will. I set forth with my attendant, and my father parted with us at the door. He placed money in my hand, and bade me farewell! but in such a tone, and with such a look, that I felt

his senses were gone, and I would have stayed him, but it was then too late. Breaking from my embrace, he sprang upon his horse, which was ready saddled, and rode off, taking the direction of Edmonton; while I, with a heart full of distress and misgiving, pursued my way to London. Ere midnight, my sad presentiments were verified. A messenger traced me out, bringing intelligence of the direful event that had happened, and informing me that my father was a prisoner at Theobalds. As soon as I could procure means of reaching the palace, I set forth, and arrived here about an hour ago, when, failing in my efforts to obtain an interview with my father, who is closely confined, and none suffered to come near him save with authority from the Secretary of State, I sought an audience of you, honourable Sir, in the hope that you would grant me permission to see him."

"If I do grant it, the interview must take place in the presence of the officer to whom his custody has been committed," replied Sir Thomas. "With this restriction, I am willing to sign an order for you."

"Be it as you please, honourable Sir; and take my heartfelt gratitude for the grace."

Sir Thomas struck a small bell upon the table, and the usher appeared at the summons.

"Bid the officer in charge of Hugh Calveley attend me," he said.

The man bowed, and departed.

Sir Thomas Lake then turned to the paper which he had just opened before Aveline's appearance, and was soon so much engrossed by it that he seemed quite unconscious of her presence. His countenance became gloomier and more austere as he read on, and an expression of pain—almost a groan—escaped him. He appeared then to feel sensible that he had committed an indiscretion, for he laid down the paper, and, as if forcibly diverting himself from its contents, addressed Aveline.

"What you have said respecting your father's condition of mind," he observed, "by no means convinces me that it is so unsound as to render him irresponsible for his actions. It were to put a charitable construction upon his conduct to say that no one but a madman could be capable of it; but there was too much consistency in what he has said and done to admit of such an inference. But for the interposition of another person he owned that he would have killed the King; and the

disappointment he exhibited, and the language he used, prove such to have been his fixed intention. His mind may have been disturbed; but what of that? All who meditate great crimes, it is to be hoped, are not entirely masters of themselves. Yet for that reason they are not to be exempt from punishment. He who is sane enough to conceive an act of wickedness, to plan its execution, and to attempt to perpetrate it, although he may be in other respects of unsettled mind, is equally amenable to the law, and ought equally to suffer for his criminality with him who has a wiser and sounder head upon his shoulders."

Aveline attempted no reply, but the tears sprang to her eyes.

At this moment the door was thrown open by the usher to admit Sir Jocelyn Mounchensey.

The emotion displayed by the young couple when thus brought together passed unnoticed by the Secretary of State, as he was occupied at the moment in writing the authority for Aveline, and did not raise his eyes towards them.

"Are you the officer to whom my father's custody has been entrusted?" exclaimed Aveline, as soon as she could give utterance to her surprise.

"Why do you ask that question, mistress?" demanded Sir Thomas, looking up. "What can it signify to you who hath custody of your father, provided good care be taken of him? There is a Latin maxim which his Majesty cited at the banquet last night—Etiam aconito inest remedium—and which may be freely rendered by our homely saying, that 'It is an ill wind that bloweth nobody good luck;' and this hath proved true with Sir Jocelyn Mounchensey—for the gust that hath wrecked your father hath driven him into port, where he now rides securely in the sunshine of the King's favour. Nor is this to be wondered at, since it was by Sir Jocelyn that his Majesty's life was preserved."

"The King preserved by him!" exclaimed Aveline, in bewilderment.

"Ay, marry and indeed, young mistress," rejoined Sir Thomas. "He arrested the fell traitor; was knighted on the spot for the service, by the King; was invited afterwards to the grand banquet in the evening, and received with more distinction than any other guest; and he is now, as you find, entrusted with the custody of the prisoner.

Thus, if your father has done little good to himself, he hath done much to Sir Jocelyn."

Aveline could not repress an exclamation of anguish.

"No more of this, I entreat, Sir Thomas," cried Sir Jocelyn.

"It is right she should hear the truth," replied the Secretary of State. "Here is her authority for admittance to her father," he continued, giving it to him. "It must take place in your presence, Sir Jocelyn. And you will pay strict attention to what they say," he added in a low tone, "for you will have to report all that passes between them to the council. Something may arise to implicate the girl herself, so let naught escape you. Be vigilant in your office, as is needful. I mention this as you are new to it. If the prisoner continues obstinate, as he hath hitherto shown himself, threaten him with the torture. The rack will certainly be applied when he reaches the Tower. I need not give you further instructions I think, Sir Jocelyn. Be pleased to return to me when the interview is over."

Upon this, he bowed gravely, and sounded the bell for the usher. Unable to offer any remonstrance, Sir Jocelyn approached Aveline, who could scarcely support herself, with the intention of offering her assistance; but she shrank from him, and again muffling her face, went forth, while he slowly followed her.

CHAPTER XXVI.
THE FORGED CONFESSION.

Some little time had elapsed since Aveline's departure on her sorrowful errand, and Sir Thomas Lake was still alone, and once more deeply engrossed in the consideration of the document, which, it will be recollected, had occasioned him so much disquietude; and the feeling by no means diminished when the usher entered and announced Lady Lake. Severe and inflexible as we have described him, the Secretary of State was generally yielding enough towards his lady, of whom he stood in great awe, and whom he treated with the utmost deference; but on this occasion, contrary to habitude, he received her very coldly, and without rising motioned her to a seat beside him. Disregarding the want of attention, which, under other circumstances, she would have resented, Lady Lake took the seat indicated without remark, and continued silent till the usher had retired. Then turning quickly towards her husband, and fixing an inquiring look upon him, she said in a low voice—

"What think you of this document, Sir Thomas?"

"This forgery?" he rejoined in the same tone, but without raising his eyes towards her.

"Ay, this forgery, if you choose to call it so," she returned. "Let me have your opinion upon it? Is it as it should be? Are its expressions such as would be used by a guilty woman, like the Countess, imploring pity, and seeking to shield herself from disgrace? Do you find fault with it? Can it be amended in any particular?"

"I find such grave fault with it," replied the Secretary of State, still without looking up, "that I would amend it by casting it into the flames. Lady Lake, it is my duty to warn you. This is a fearful crime you would commit, and severely punishable by the law. You may excuse it to yourself, because you have an end in view which seems to

justify the means; but the excuse will not avail you with others. You have said that in a conflict with one so cunning and unscrupulous as our noble son-in-law, you are compelled to fight him with his own weapons—to meet trick with trick, manoevre with manoeuvre; but take my word for it, you would more easily defeat him by straight-forward means. Be ruled by me in this one instance. Abandon a scheme which must inevitably lead to consequences I shudder to contemplate; and let this fabricated confession be destroyed."

"Give it me," she cried, snatching the paper from him. "You were ever timid, Sir Thomas; and if you had not lacked courage, this expedient would not have been necessary. Odious and dangerous as it is, the measure is forced upon me, and I shall not shrink from it. But you shall not be called upon to play any part in the transaction. I alone will do it. I alone will be responsible for all that may ensue."

"We shall all be responsible!" he rejoined. "You will not only ruin yourself, but all your family, if this fearful step be taken. Hitherto we have had right on our side, but henceforth we shall be more culpable than the others."

"I am resolved upon the course," cried Lady Lake; "and all your arguments—all your warnings will not dissuade me from it, so you may spare your breath, Sir Thomas. As you see, I have omitted the charge of witchcraft, and have only made the Countess confess her criminality with Lord Roos, and of this we have had abundant proofs; nay, we should have them still, if those condemnatory letters of hers, which had come into our possession, had not been stolen. That mischance necessitates the present measure. Having managed to deprive us of our weapons, Lord Roos thinks himself secure. But he will find his mistake when this document is produced to confound him."

"I tremble at the thought," groaned the Secretary of State.

"These fears are worse than womanish," exclaimed his lady. "Shake them off, and be yourself. Who is to prove that the confession proceeds not from the Countess? Not she herself; since no one will believe her. Not Lord Roos; for he will be equally discredited. Not Diego; for his testimony would be valueless. The Countess's hand-writing has been so skilfully imitated, that the falsification cannot be detected. Compare it with this note written by herself to Lady Roos,

and which, though it proves nothing, has so far answered my purpose. Compare, I say, the writing of the confession and the signature with this note, and declare if you can discern any difference between them. As to the signatures of Lord Roos and Diego affixed to the document, they are equally well simulated."

"That the forgery is skilfully executed, I do not deny," replied the Secretary of State; "and that circumstance, though it does not lessen the crime, may lessen the chance of detection. Since nothing I can urge will turn you from your design, and you are determined to employ this dangerous instrument, at least be cautious in its use. Terrify Lord Roos with it, if you choose. Threaten to lay it before the Earl of Exeter — before the King himself — in case of our son-in-law's non-compliance with your demands. But beware how you proceed further. Do not part with it for a moment; so that, if need be, you may destroy it. Do you heed me, my lady?"

"I do, Sir Thomas," she replied. "Be assured I will act with due caution. — I am glad to find you are coming round to my views, and are disposed to countenance the measure."

"I countenance it!" exclaimed the Secretary of State, in alarm. "No such thing. I disapprove of it entirely, and cannot sufficiently reprehend it. But, as I well know, when you have once made up your mind, the fiend himself cannot turn you from your purpose, I give you the best counsel I can under the circumstances. I wash my hands of it altogether. Would to Heaven I had never been consulted upon it — never even been made acquainted with the project. However, as you have gone so far with me you may go a step further, and let me know what story you mean to attach to this confession? How will you feign to have obtained it?"

"The statement I shall make will be this, and it will be borne out by so many corroborative circumstances that it will be impossible to contradict it. You observe that the document is dated on the 10th of April last. It is not without reason that it is so dated. On that day I and our daughter, Lady Roos, attended by her maid, Sarah Swarton, proceeded to the Earl of Exeter's residence at Wimbledon, for the purpose of having an interview with the Countess, and we then saw her in the presence of Lord Roos and his servant Diego."

"But you gained nothing by the journey?" remarked her husband.

"Your pardon, Sir Thomas," she rejoined; "I gained this confession. On the way back I reflected upon what had occurred, and I thought how flushed with triumph I should have been if, instead of meeting with discomfiture, I had gained my point—if I had brought the haughty Countess to her knees—had compelled her to write out and sign a full avowal of her guilt, coupled with supplications for forgiveness from my injured daughter and myself—and as a refinement of revenge, had forced Lord Roos and his servant to attest by their signatures the truth of the confession! I thought of this—and incensed that I had not done it, resolved it should be done."

"An ill resolve!" muttered her husband.

"In Luke Hatton, our apothecary, I had the man for my purpose," pursued Lady Lake. "Aware of his marvellous talent for imitating any writing he pleased—aware, also, that I could entirely rely upon him, I resolved to call in his aid."

"Imprudent woman! You have placed yourself wholly in his power," groaned Sir Thomas. "Suppose he should betray the terrible trust you have reposed in him?"

"He will not betray it," replied Lady Lake. "He is too deeply implicated in the matter not to keep silence for his own sake. But to proceed. The document, such as you see it, was drawn out by myself and transcribed by Luke Hatton, and the writing so admirably counterfeited that Lady Exeter herself may well doubt if it be not her own. Then, as to the circumstances, they will all bear me out. We were known to have been at Wimbledon on the day in question. We were known to have had an interview with Lady Exeter, at which Lord Roos and Diego were present. The interview was private, and therefore no one can tell what took place at it; but the probabilities are that what I shall assert really did occur."

Sir Thomas signified his assent, and she went on.

"The plot is well contrived, and, with prudent management, cannot fail of success. We have the time of the supposed occurrence—the actors in it—and the scene—for I shall describe the particular room in which the interview really did take place, and I shall further bring forward Sarah Swarton, who will declare that she was concealed behind the hangings, and heard the Countess read over the confession before she signed it."

"Another party to the affair—and a woman!" ejaculated Sir Thomas. "The dangers of discovery are multiplied a hundredfold."

"The danger exists only in your imagination," said his Lady. "Come, admit, Sir Thomas, that the scheme is well contrived, and that they must be cunning indeed if they escape from the meshes I have woven for them."

"You have displayed ingenuity enough, I am free to own, if it had been directed to a better end; but in the best contrived scheme some flaw is ever found, which is sure to mar it."

"You can detect no flaw in this I am persuaded, Sir Thomas. If you can, let me know it?"

"Nay, it is only when too late that such things are found out. The supposed armour of proof is then found wanting at some vital point. However, I will say no more," he observed, perceiving her impatience. "What is done cannot be undone. Have you prepared our daughter? Will she consent to aid you?"

"She will," replied Lady Lake. "I had some difficulty with her at first, but I found means to overrule her scruples, and she consented at last to act as I desired, provided all other means failed of accomplishing the object in view. And they have failed since we have lost those letters, for though I have one other proof left which might perhaps be adduced, I do not attach much importance to it."

"What is it?" inquired Sir Thomas, quickly.

"You shall know anon," she answered. "Suffice it, I have done all I could to avoid having recourse to the present measure; and have delayed—its execution to the last moment."

"But that proof of which you were speaking?" cried Sir Thomas. "Let me hear it? Perhaps it may obviate the necessity of this dangerous proceeding?"

"I do not think so. But you shall judge. Last night, our daughter and myself obtained secret admittance to Lord Roos's chamber, and we found the Countess there, and fainting in his arms."

"Why that is enough to convict them. You want nothing more."

"Hear me to an end, and you will change your opinion. Placing the inanimate Countess on a couch, and covering her face with a handkerchief, Lord Roos had the effrontery to assert that we were

mistaken; insisting that it was not Lady Exeter we beheld—but her hand-maiden, Gillian Greenford; and he appealed to the perfidious knave, Diego, in confirmation of his assertion."

"But you did not leave without satisfying yourselves of the truth?" demanded Sir Thomas.

"His lordship took care we should have no means of doing so," she answered. "He caused Diego to convey her away by a secret staircase."

"'Sdeath! that was unlucky. You have no proof then that it was the Countess you beheld?"

"Nothing beyond a lock of her hair, which was secured by Lady Roos as the man was removing her."

"That may be enough," cried the Secretary of State; "and prevent the necessity of resorting to this frightful expedient. We must see the girl, and interrogate her. Gillian Greenford you say she is called. She shall be brought hither at once."

"It is possible she may be without," returned Lady Lake. "Before I came here, I summoned her in your name."

"We will see," cried Sir Thomas, striking upon the bell. And the usher, appearing to the summons, informed him that in effect the damsel in question was in attendance. "She seems much alarmed, Sir Thomas," said the usher, "and has with her a young man, who appears to take a tender interest in her, and wishes to be present at the investigation."

"Let him come in with her," said the Secretary of State. And seeing the usher pause, he inquired if he had anything further to say.

"His Excellency the Spanish Ambassador and my Lord Roos are without, and desire admittance," replied the man.

Sir Thomas consulted his lady by a look; and as she made no objection, he signified his pleasure that they should be admitted, and accordingly the door was thrown open for the entrance of all the persons mentioned.

Gillian came first, and seemed much embarrassed by the situation in which she found herself. She had been well tutored for the part she had to play; but the instructions she had received entirely fled from her mind as she found herself in the presence of two such awful

personages as Sir Thomas Lake and his lady, both of whom fixed keen glances upon her. Feeling ready to drop with fright, she looked at Dick Taverner, as if imploring his support. But this Dick declined to afford. His jealousy having been roused by what he had heard, he determined to be governed in his conduct towards her by the result of the investigation. Accordingly, though it cost him an effort, he held back. As the Conde de Gondomar appeared, Sir Thomas Lake arose, and made him a profound salutation, which was returned with equal ceremony by the Spanish Ambassador. The latter, however, did not take a seat, but remained standing with Lord Roos, whose presence was acknowledged by a cold and distant bow from his father-in-law. The young nobleman did not appear in the slightest degree disconcerted by the reception he met with, or apprehensive of the result of the investigation. He jested apart with De Gondomar; and both he and the Spanish Ambassador appeared greatly amused by Gillian's embarrassment. Behind him stood his servant Diego.

"You are handmaiden to the Countess of Exeter, I presume?" demanded Lady Lake of the damsel.

"I am, my lady," she answered.

"The girl does not look as if the imputations cast upon her character can be true," observed Sir Thomas Lake.

As this was said, poor Gillian became suffused with blushes, and hung her head.

"Before I put any further questions to her," remarked Lady Lake, "I will ask Lord Roos if he still persists in affirming that it was this damsel who visited him last night?"

Dick Taverner looked as if his fate depended upon the response the young nobleman might make to the inquiry.

"I must decline to answer your ladyship's question," returned Lord Roos.

"Why cannot he speak out?" muttered Dick. "This uncertainty is worse than anything."

"What says the damsel herself," observed Sir Thomas Lake. "Does she admit the charge?"

"You cannot expect her to do that, Sir Thomas," interposed Lord Roos.

"I expect her to answer my question," rejoined the Secretary of State, sharply. "Were you in Lord Roos's room last night?" he added, to Gillian.

"Oh, dear! I am ready to faint," she exclaimed. "Catch me, Dick—catch me!"

"Answer 'yes' or 'no,' or I won't," he rejoined.

"Well, then, 'yes!' if I must say something," she replied.

Poor Dick fell back, as if struck by a shot.

"I don't believe it," cried Sir Thomas.

"Nor I either," said Dick, recovering himself. "I don't believe she could do such a wicked thing. Besides, it was the foreign ambassador, there," he added, pointing to De Gondomar, "who seemed most enamoured of her yesterday; and I shouldn't have been so much surprised if she had gone to see him. Perhaps she did," he continued, addressing the poor damsel, who again hung her head.

"I can take upon me to affirm that such was not the case," observed De Gondomar.

"Have you the lock of hair with you?" whispered Sir Thomas to his lady.

"I have," she replied, taking a small packet from her bosom.

The movement did not pass unnoticed by Lord Roos and the Spanish Ambassador, between whom an almost imperceptible smile passed.

"If you have put all the interrogations you desire to make to Gillian, Madam," said Lord Roos to his mother-in-law, "perhaps she may be permitted to depart? The situation cannot be agreeable to her."

"A moment more, my lord," cried Lady Lake. "If I detain her it is to clear her character. I know her to be perfectly innocent."

At this announcement, Dick Taverner's countenance brightened, and he extended his arms towards Gillian, who gladly availed herself of his support.

"I am quite sure she was not the person I surprised in your chamber last night," continued Lady Lake.

"Indeed, Madam! How do you arrive at that conviction?"

"Because that person's hair was jet black, whereas Gillian's, as we see, is of the exactly opposite colour."

Dick Taverner could not help pressing his lips against the back of the pretty damsel's neck as this was uttered.

"Your proof of this, Madam?" demanded Lord Roos.

"Behold it!" she cried. "This look of hair was cut off before your visitant escaped, and has remained in my possession ever since. Ha! how is this?" she exclaimed, as she unfolded the packet, and disclosed a tress of fair hair, evidently matching Gillian's lint-white locks. "What transformation has taken place! Witchcraft has been practised. This is the Countess's work."

"The minion must have been there, after all," cried Dick Taverner, thrusting Gillian from him.

"The charge of witchcraft will not serve your turn, Madam," said Lord Roos derisively. "The explanation is simple. Your eyes have deceived you."

"Most palpably," cried the Conde de Gondomar, who had caught Gillian in his arms, as the jealous apprentice cast her from him. "I am afraid her ladyship cannot see very clearly."

"I see clearly enough that a trick has been practised upon me," Lady Lake rejoined sharply. "But let Lord Roos look to himself. I will have my revenge, and a terrible one it shall be."

"Do not commit yourself," said Sir Thomas in a low tone.

"Your business here is at an end, fair maiden," said the Conde de Gondomar to Gillian; "and as your lover abandons you, I am ready to take charge of you."

So saying he led her forth, followed by Lord Roos, whose smile of triumph exasperated his mother-in-law almost beyond endurance.

For a moment Dick Taverner remained irresolute; but his mistress had no sooner disappeared, than he rushed after her, vowing he would have her back if it cost him his life.

CHAPTER XXVII.
THE PURITAN'S PRISON.

Hugh Calveley, it has already been intimated, was lodged in a vault beneath the gateway. The place was commonly used as a sort of black-hole for the imprisonment of any refractory member of the royal household, or soldier on guard guilty of neglect of duty. Circular in shape, it contained a large pillar, to which iron rings and chains were attached. The walls were of stone, the roof arched with ribs springing from the pillar that supported it, and the floor was paved. Window there was none; but air was admitted through a small grated aperture in the roof; and thus imperfectly ventilated, it will not be wondered at that the vault should be damp. Moisture constantly trickled down the walls, and collected in pools on the broken pavement; but unwholesome as it was, and altogether unfit for occupation, it was deemed good enough for those generally thrust into it, and far too good for its present tenant.

As the prisoner exhibited no violence, the thongs with which his hands were bound were removed on his entrance to the vault, and he was allowed the free use of his limbs. The breast-plate in which he was clad was taken from him, and his vesture was again closely searched, but no further discovery was made either of concealed weapon, or of any paper or letter tending to show that he had accomplices in his dread design. The only thing found upon him, indeed, was a small Bible, and this, after it had been examined, he was permitted to retain. To the interrogatories put to him by Master Dendy, the serjeant-at-arms, he returned the briefest answers; and when he had said as much as he thought fit, he obstinately refused to make further reply.

Incensed at his perversity, and determined to extort a full confession, in order that it might be laid before the King, the serjeant-at-arms ordered the manacles to be applied. But though the torture

was exquisite, he bore it with firmness, and without uttering a groan; maintaining the same determined silence as before. Had he dared, Master Dendy would have had recourse to severer measures; but having no warrant for any such proceeding, he was obliged to content himself with threats. To these Hugh Calveley replied by a grim smile of contempt; but as the serjeant-at-arms was departing to make his report to Sir Thomas Lake, he said, "I have something to disclose; but it is for the King's ear alone."

"Better reveal it to me," rejoined Dendy, halting. "I have it in my power to render your situation far more tolerable, or to inflict greater torment upon you. Make your choice."

"Deal with me as you please," returned Hugh Calveley sternly. "What I have to say is to the King, and to the King only; and though you break every bone in my body with your engines, and tear off my flesh with red-hot pincers, you shall not force the secret from me."

Master Dendy looked at him, and felt disposed to place him in the dreadful instrument of torture called Skeffington's irons, which was hanging against the wall; but the consideration that had hitherto restrained him—namely, that he was without authority for the step, and might be called to account for it—weighed with him still; wherefore he contented himself with ordering the prisoner to be chained to the pillar; and having seen the injunction obeyed, he left him.

In this miserable plight Hugh Calveley remained for some hours, without light and without food. How the time was passed none knew; but the two yeomen of the guard who entered the vault found him on his knees absorbed in prayer. They brought a lamp with them, and refreshments of a better kind than those usually afforded to a prisoner, and set them before him. But he refused to partake of them. The only favour he besought was permission to read his Bible; and the lamp placed within reach, he was soon deeply engrossed in the perusal of those pages from which, when earnestly sought, consolation has ever been derived under the most trying circumstances.

Sir Jocelyn had forborne to visit the prisoner from a fear that his presence might be painful; but the office imposed upon him by the King left him no alternative; and about midnight he descended to the vault, to ascertain from personal inspection that Hugh Calveley was

in safe custody. The door was unlocked by the halberdier stationed at it, and the young man found himself alone with the prisoner. He was inexpressibly shocked by the spectacle he beheld, as he had no idea how severely the unfortunate Puritan had been treated, nor of the sort of prison in which he was confined.

Hugh Calveley, who was still intently reading the Bible, which he had placed upon his knee while he held the lamp near it, to throw the light upon its leaves, did not appear to be disturbed by the opening of the door, nor did he raise his eyes. But, at last, a deep groan issuing from the breast of the young man aroused him, and he held up the lamp to ascertain who was near. On discovering that it was Sir Jocelyn, he knitted his brow, and, after sternly regarding him for a moment, returned to his Bible, without uttering a word; but finding the other maintained his post, he demanded, almost fiercely, why he was disturbed?

"Can I do aught for your relief?" rejoined the young man. "At least, I can have those chains taken off."

"Thou speakest as one in authority," cried Hugh Calveley, regarding him, fixedly. "Art thou appointed to be my jailer?"

Sir Jocelyn made no answer, but averted his head.

"This only was wanting to fill up the measure of my scorn for thee," pursued the Puritan. "Thou art worthy of thine office. But show me no favour, for I will receive none at thy hands. I would rather wear these fetters to my death, however much they may gall my limbs, than have them struck off by thee. I would rather rot in this dungeon—ay, though it were worse than it is—than owe my liberation to thee. The sole favour thou canst show me is to rid me of thy presence, which is hateful to me, and chases holy thoughts from my breast, putting evil in their place."

"Why should this be so, O friend of my father?" exclaimed Sir Jocelyn. "And why should my presence be hateful to you? There is no man living whom I would less willingly offend than yourself; and in all I have done, where you have been concerned, I have had no free agency. Judge me not then too harshly. I commiserate your situation from the depths of my heart, and would relieve it were it possible."

"Then wherefore persist in troubling me?" rejoined Hugh Calveley. "Have I not good cause for my dislike of you? You have

disappointed the expectations I had formed of you. You failed me when I put your professions to the test. You thwarted my design at the moment when its success was certain, and when the tyrant was completely in my power. But for you I should not be here, loaded with these fetters; or if I were, I should be consoled by the thought that I had liberated my country from oppression, instead of being crushed by the sense of failure. What seek you from me, miserable time-server? Have you not had your reward for the service you have rendered the King? Is he not grateful enough? I have served as your stepping-stone to promotion. What more can I do?"

"You can cease to do me injustice," returned Sir Jocelyn. "Honours, procured as mine have been, are valueless, and I would rather be without them. I sought them not. They have been forced upon me. Look at the matter fairly, and you will see that all these consequences, whether for good or ill, have sprung from your own desperate act."

"It may be so," rejoined the Puritan. "I will not dispute it. But though ill has accrued to me, and good to you, I would not change positions with you. You will wear the tyrant's fetters for ever. I shall soon be free from mine."

"Have you nothing to say concerning your daughter?" demanded the young man.

"Nothing," replied the Puritan, with an expression of deep pain, which, however, he checked by a mighty effort. "I have done with the world, and desire not to be brought back to it."

"And you refuse to be freed from your chains?"

"My sole desire, as I have said, is to be freed from you."

"That wish, at least, shall be granted," replied Sir Jocelyn, as, with a sad heart, he departed.

CHAPTER XXVIII.
THE SECRET.

Thrice was the guard relieved during that long night, and as often was the prisoner visited. On the first occasion, he was found to be still engaged with his Bible, and he so continued during the whole time the man remained in the vault.

The next who came discovered him on his knees, praying loudly and fervently, and, unwilling to disturb him, left him at his devotions.

But the third who entered was struck with terror at the prisoner's appearance. He had risen from the ground, and was standing as erect as the fetters would permit, with his hands outstretched, and his eyes fixed on vacancy. He was muttering something, but his words were unintelligible. He looked like one who beheld a vision; and this impression was produced upon the man, who half expected some awful shape to reveal itself to him. But whatever it might be, spirit of good or ill, it was visible to the Puritan alone.

After gazing at him for some minutes, in mixed wonderment and fright, the halberdier ventured to draw near him. As he touched him, the Puritan uttered a fearful cry, and attempted to spring forward, as if to grasp some vanishing object, but being checked in the effort by the chain, he fell heavily to the ground, and seemed to sustain severe injury; for when the man raised him, and set him against the pillar, though he made no complaint, it was evident he suffered excruciating pain. The halberdier poured out a cup of wine, and offered it to him; but, though well-nigh fainting, he peremptorily refused it.

From this moment a marked change was perceptible in his looks. The hue of his skin became cadaverous; his eyes grew dim and glassy; and his respiration was difficult. Everything betokened that his sufferings would be speedily over, and that, however he might deserve it, Hugh Calveley would be spared the disgrace of death by

the hands of the executioner. The halberdier was not unaware of his condition, and his first impulse was to summon assistance; but he was deterred from doing so by the earnest entreaty of the Puritan to be left alone; and thinking this the most merciful course he could pursue under the circumstances, he yielded to the request, scarcely expecting to behold him alive again.

It was by this same man that the door of the vault was opened to Sir Jocelyn and Aveline.

The shock experienced by the maiden at the sight of her father had well-nigh overcome her She thought him dead, and such was Sir Jocelyn's first impression. The unfortunate Puritan was still propped against the pillar, as the halberdier had left him, but his head had fallen to one side, and his arms hung listlessly down. With a piercing shriek his daughter flew towards him, and kneeling beside him, raised his head gently, and gazing eagerly into his face, perceived that he still lived, though the spirit seemed ready to wing its flight from its fleshly tabernacle.

The situation was one to call forth every latent energy in Aveline's character. Controlling her emotion, she uttered no further cry, but set herself, with calmness, to apply such restoratives as were at hand to her father. After bathing his temples and chafing his hands, she had the satisfaction, ere long, of seeing him open his eyes. At first, he seemed to have a difficulty in fixing his gaze upon her, but her voice reached his ears, and the feeble pressure of his hand told that he knew her.

The power of speech returned to him at length, and he faintly murmured, "My child, I am glad to see you once more. I thought all was over; but it has pleased Heaven to spare me for a few moments to give you my blessing. Bow down your head, O my daughter, and take it; and though given by a sinner like myself, it shall profit you! May the merciful God, who pardoneth all that repent, even at the last hour, and watcheth over the orphan, bless you, and protect you!"

"Amen!" exclaimed Jocelyn, fervently.

"Who was it spoke?" demanded the Puritan. And as no answer was returned, he repeated the inquiry.

"It was I—Jocelyn Mounchensey, the son of your old friend," replied the young man.

"Come nigh to me, Jocelyn," said the dying man. "I have done you wrong, and entreat your pardon."

"O, talk not thus!" cried Jocelyn, springing towards him. "I have nothing to forgive, but much to be forgiven."

"You have a noble heart, Jocelyn," rejoined Hugh Calveley; "and in that respect resemble your father. In his name, I conjure you to listen to me. You will not refuse my dying request. I have a sacred trust to commit to you."

"Name it!" cried the young man; "and rest assured it shall be fulfilled."

"Give me some wine," gasped the Puritan, faintly. "My strength is failing fast, and it may revive me."

And with, great effort he swallowed a few drops from the cup filled for him by Jocelyn. Still, his appearance was so alarming, that the young man could not help urging him not to delay.

"I understand," replied Hugh Calveley, slightly pressing his hand. "You think I have no time to lose; and you are right. My child, then, is the trust I would confide to you. Son, behold thy sister! Daughter, behold thy brother!"

"I will be more than a brother to her," cried Sir Jocelyn, earnestly.

"More thou canst not be," rejoined Hugh Calveley; "unless—"

"Unless what?" demanded Sir Jocelyn.

"I cannot explain," cried the Puritan, with an expression of agony; "there is not time. Suffice it, she is already promised in marriage."

"Father!" exclaimed Aveline, in surprise, and with something of reproach. "I never heard of such an engagement before. It has been made without my consent."

"I charge you to fulfil it, nevertheless, my child, if it be required," said Hugh Calveley, solemnly. "Promise me this, or I shall not die content. Speak! Let me hear you."

And she reluctantly gave the required promise.

Sir Jocelyn uttered an exclamation of anguish.

"What afflicts you, my son?" demanded the Puritan.

"To whom have you promised your daughter in marriage?" inquired the young man. "You have constituted me her brother, and I am therefore entitled to inquire."

"You will learn when the demand is made," said the Puritan. "You will then know why I have given the promise, and the nature of the obligation imposed upon my daughter to fulfil it."

"But is this obligation ever to remain binding?" demanded Sir Jocelyn.

"If the claim be not made within a year after my death, she is discharged from it," replied Hugh Calveley.

"O, thanks, father, thanks!" exclaimed Aveline

At this moment the door of the vault was thrown open, and two persons entered, the foremost of whom Sir Jocelyn instantly recognised as the King. The other was his Majesty's physician, Doctor Mayerne Turquet. A glance sufficed to explain to the latter the state of the Puritan.

"Ah! parbleu! the man is dying, your Majesty," he exclaimed.

"Deeing! is he?" cried James. "The mair reason he suld tell his secret, to us without procrastination. Harkye, prophet of ill!" he continued, as he strode forward. "The judgment of Heaven ye predicated for us, seems to have fallen on your ainsell, and to have laid you low, even afore our arm could touch you. Ye have gude reason to be thankful you have escaped the woodie; sae e'en make a clean breast of it, confess your enormities, and reveal to us the secret matter whilk we are tauld ye hae to communicate!"

"Let all else withdraw a few paces," said Hugh Calveley, "and do thou, O King, approach me. What I have to say is for thine ear alone."

"There will be no danger in granting his request?" inquired James of his physician.

"None whatever," replied Doctor Mayerne Turquet. "The only danger is in delay. Your Majesty should lose no time. The man is passing rapidly away. A few moments more, and he will have ceased to exist."

On a sign from the King, Sir Jocelyn then stepped aside, but Aveline refused to quit her father, even for a moment.

As James drew near, Hugh Calveley raised himself a little in order to address him. "I say unto thee, O King," he cried, "as Elijah said unto Ahab, 'Because thou hast sold thyself to work evil in the sight of the Lord—behold! I will bring evil upon thee, and will take away thy posterity. And I will make thine house like the house of Jeroboam the son of Nebat, and like the house of Baasha the son of Ahijah, for the provocation wherewith thou hast provoked me to anger, and made Israel to sin.'"

"Now the muckle Diel seize thee, villain!" exclaimed James furiously. "Is it to listen to thy texts that thou hast brought me hither?" And as Hugh Calveley, exhausted by the effort he had made, fell back with a groan, he bent his head towards him, crying, "The secret, man, the secret! or the tormenter shall wring it from thee?"

The Puritan essayed to speak, but his voice was so low that it did not reach the ears of the King.

"What sayest thou?" he demanded. "Speak louder. Saul of our body!" he exclaimed, after a moment's pause, during which the sudden alteration that took place in the prisoner's features made him suspect that all was over. "Our belief is he will never speak again. He hath escaped us, and ta'en his secret wi' him."

A loud shriek burst from Aveline, as she fell upon her father's lifeless body.

"Let us forth," cried the King, stopping his ears. "We carena to be present at scenes like this. We hae had a gude riddance o' this traitor, though we wad hae gladly heard what he had to tell. Sir Jocelyn Mounchensey, ye will see that this young woman be cared for; and when ye have caused her to be removed elsewhere, follow us to the tennis-court, to which we shall incontinently adjourn."

So saying, he quitted the vault with his physician.

CHAPTER XXIX.
LUKE HATTON.

Feigning sudden indisposition (and the excuse was not altogether without foundation), the Countess of Exeter quitted Theobalds Palace on the day after her unlucky visit to Lord Roos's chamber, and proceeded to her husband's residence at Wimbledon, where she was speedily joined by her lover, who brought her word of the advantage he had gained over their foe.

"I have fairly checkmated my gracious mother-in-law," he cried, with a laugh; "and it would have diverted you as much as it did me and De Gondomar, who was present on the occasion, if you could have witnessed her rage and mortification, when she discovered the change that had been effected; and that in place of your magnificent black ringlet (which I now wear next my heart, and shall ever keep as a love-token), she had only a sorry specimen of your hand-maiden's lint-white locks. As I live, it was truly laughable. The good lady would have annihilated me if she could; and threatened me with terrible reprisals. At first, she tried to attribute the transformation, which she could not otherwise account for, to witchcraft; and though I derided the charge, I must needs say, the trick was so cleverly performed, that it did look like magic. The packet containing the tress of hair had never been out of her own keeping. This she affirmed; and it was true. But there was a friendly hand to open it nevertheless; to purloin its priceless treasure; and to substitute something of a similar kind, though of comparatively little value in its place. That hand,— one not likely to be suspected, was no other than that of my lady's confidential attendant, Sarah Swarton. The juggle was played by her at the instance of Diego. Anticipating some such occurrence as the present, and desirous of having a spy upon the movements of our enemies, I some time since directed Diego to pay secret court to Sarah,

and my forethought has now been rewarded. The main difficulty lay with poor Gillian. She was greatly embarrassed by her situation; and her perplexity was increased by the presence of a jealous lover in the shape of an apprentice, who refused to leave her till his doubts should be satisfied. This was awkward, as the story could not be very well reconciled so as to suit all parties. Accordingly, when the discovery was made, which seemed to proclaim the poor girl's infidelity, the youth's rage and consternation were nearly equal to Lady Lake's; a circumstance that added considerable zest to the comedy. But I see it does not divert you so much as I expected, and therefore, to relieve your mind, I may tell you that the jealous varlet soon repented of his rash determination, and pursuing his mistress, whom Do Gondomar had considerately taken under his protection, prevailed upon her to give the amorous ambassador the slip, and return with him to her father's abode at Tottenham."

"I am right glad to hear it," said the Countess. "Though I have seen so little of Gillian, I cannot help taking an interest in her; she is so pretty, and so innocent in appearance, and her manners are so artless and engaging. I owe her some reparation for the mischief I have done her, and will not neglect to make it. I am sorry I ever was induced by you to take her into my service; and I am thankful to hear she has escaped De Gondomar's snares."

"You are wonderfully interested about her, methinks, Frances; and I hope she will be grateful for your consideration," rejoined Lord Roos, with a laugh. "But I should not be surprised if De Gondomar still gained his point. It is not his way to give up a pursuit he has once undertaken. However, to leave the pretty damsel to her fate, which will depend entirely on her own conduct, let us return to ourselves. We have good reason to be satisfied with the issue of this adventure of the lock of hair. Nevertheless, that recurrence to the charge of witchcraft on the part of my vindictive mother-in-law shows the extent of her malice, and I cannot doubt that in threatening me with reprisals she will be as good as her word. It behoves us, therefore, to be beforehand with her. What she may intend I cannot say, but I am satisfied she has a formidable scheme on foot, and that nothing but her husband's interposition prevented its disclosure when she was so violently incensed against me."

"You fill me with terror, William," exclaimed the Countess. "Will this woman's hostility towards me never cease?"

"Never," replied Lord Roos, with a sudden change of manner, and laying aside the levity he had hitherto exhibited. "There is but one way of ending the struggle. Luke Hatton can help us to it. Persuaded we should require him, I have brought him with me. He waits in the hall below with Diego. Shall I summon him to our conference?"

"On no account," exclaimed Lady Exeter hastily; "I will not see him. You have done wrong to bring that poisoner here, my lord. You will destroy me."

"Listen to me, Frances," replied Lord Roos. "The next step taken by Lady Lake will be fatal to us. There must be no delay, no irresolution on our part, or all is lost. I cannot depend upon myself, or I would not call in another's aid. You will comprehend how wanting in firmness I am, when I tell you what happened the other night. Incredible as it may sound, my wife, in order to prove her devotion to me and to free me from further annoyance on her part, offered to take poison; and but for my interference (fool that I was to stay her!) would have drained the phial containing the deadly potion. The weakness was momentary, and I reproached myself for it when too late. But it convinced me that a firmer hand than mine must be employed in the task."

"And can you, after what you have related, William,—can you seriously meditate the destruction of a fond woman, who has generosity enough to lay down her life for you? This is more incredible than the rest—more monstrously wicked."

"Wicked it may be; but the excuse—if I have any—lies in my overwhelming passion for you, Frances," replied Lord Roos in a frenzied tone. "And it seems decided by the relentless destiny that governs me, that the continued indulgence of the fatal passion shall only be purchased at the price of my soul. That penalty I am prepared to pay rather than lose you. I will become obdurate, will turn my heart to stone, so that it shall no more melt at the tears of this fond, foolish woman; and I will slay her without remorse. Any other obstacle between us shall be removed;—be it her mother, her father—your husband! I will immolate a hundred victims at the altar of our love. I will shrink from nothing to make you mine for ever. For I would

rather share eternal bale with you, Frances, than immortal bliss with another."

"You almost make me fancy some evil being has obtained possession of you, William," said the Countess, gazing at him with affright.

"It may be that the Fiend himself hath accepted my wild offer," he rejoined gloomily; "but if my wish be granted it matters not."

"I will not listen to such fearful impiety," said the Countess, shuddering. "Let us dismiss this subject for the present, and recur to it when you are calmer."

"It cannot be postponed, Frances. Time presses, and even now Lady Lake may have got the start of us. I shall be calm enough when this is over. Will you consent to see Luke Hatton?"

"Why need I see him?" inquired the Countess with increasing uneasiness. "Why will you force his hateful presence upon me? If the deed must be done, why can you not alone undertake it?"

"I will tell why I cannot," he replied in a sombre tone, and regarding her fixedly. "I must have a partner in the crime. It will bind us to each other in links not to be severed. I shall have no fear of losing you then, Countess. I go to bring Luke Hatton to you."

And without waiting for her reply he strode out of the room. Lady Exeter would have arrested him, but she had not the nerve to do so, and with an exclamation of anguish she fell back in her chair.

"What dominion sin has usurped over me!" she mentally ejaculated. "I have lost the power of resisting its further encroachment. I see the enormity of the offence I am about to commit, and though my soul revolts at it, I cannot hold back. I am as one on the brink of a precipice, who beholds the dreadful gulf before him, into which another step must plunge him, yet is too giddy to retreat, and must needs fall over. Pity me, kind Heaven! I am utterly helpless without thy aid."

While the unhappy lady thus unavailingly deplored the sad position in which her own misconduct had placed her, and from which she felt wholly incapable of extricating herself; while in this wretched frame of mind, she awaited her lover's return,—with, as we have shown, some remains of good struggling with the evil in her bosom,—we will cast a hasty glance round the chamber in which she

sat. And we are prompted to do this, not because it merits particular description, but because it was the room referred to by Lady Lake as the scene of the confession she had forged.

The apartment, then, was spacious and handsomely furnished in the heavy taste of the period, with but little to distinguish it from other rooms visited by us in the course of this story. Like most of them, it had a gloomy air, caused by the dark hue of its oaken panels, and the heavy folds of its antiquated and faded tapestry. The latter was chiefly hung against the lower end of the chamber, and served as a screen to one of the doors. At the opposite end, there was a wide and deep bay window, glowing with stained glass, amid the emblazonry of which might be discerned the proud escutcheon of the house of Exeter, with the two lions rampant forming its supporters. On the right of the enormous carved mantel-piece, which, with its pillars, statues, 'scutcheons, and massive cornice, mounted to the very ceiling, was hung a portrait of the Earl of Exeter—a grave, dignified personage, clad in the attire of Elizabeth's time; and on the left, was a likeness of the Countess herself, painted in all the pride of her unequalled beauty, and marvellous in resemblance then; but how different in expression from her features now!

In the recess of the window stood an oak table, covered with a piece of rich carpet fringed with gold, on which a massive silver inkstand and materials for writing were placed; and this table was seized upon by Lady Lake as a feature in her plot. Here she would have it the confession was signed by the Countess.

Another point in reference to this scheme must not be passed unnoticed. We have mentioned the heavy hangings at the lower end of the room. According to the plotter, it was behind these that Sarah Swarton—the intended witness of the imaginary scene—was concealed. The principal subjects represented on the arras were the Judgment of Solomon, and the Temptation of our first Parents in the Garden by the Serpent. The hangings had evidently not been removed for years, and did not reach within two feet of the ground—a circumstance that had escaped the attention of Lady Lake—proving the truth of her husband's observation, that in the best contrived plot some imperfection will exist certain to operate in its detection.

To return to the unhappy Countess. So lost was she in reflection, that she did not remark Lord Roos's return till made aware of it by a

slight touch on the shoulder. When she raised her eyes, they fell upon an object that inspired her with the dread and aversion that a noxious reptile might have produced. She had never seen Luke Hatton before; and if she had figured him to her mind at all, it was not as anything agreeable; but she was not prepared for so hideous and revolting a personage as he appeared to be. His face was like an ugly mask, on which a sardonic grin was stamped. His features were large and gaunt, and he had the long, hooked nose, and the sharp-pointed bestial ears of a satyr, with leering eyes—betokening at once sensuality and cunning. He had the chin and beard of a goat, and crisply-curled hair of a pale yellow colour. With all this, there was something sordid in his looks as well as his attire, which showed that to his other vices he added that of avarice. A mock humility, belied by the changeless sneer upon his countenance, distinguished his deportment. It could be seen at once that, however cringing he might be, he despised the person he addressed. Moreover, in spite of all his efforts to control it, there was something sarcastic in his speech. His doublet and hose, both of which had endured some service, and were well-nigh threadbare, were tawny-coloured; and he wore a short yellow cloak, a great ruff of the same colour, and carried a brown steeple-crowned hat in his hand.

"I await your ladyship's commands," said Luke Hatton, bowing obsequiously.

"I have none to give you," Lady Exeter rejoined with irrepressible disgust. "I have not sent for you. Go hence."

Not at all abashed by this reception, Luke Hatton maintained his place, and threw an inquiring glance at Lord Roos.

"My dear Countess," said the young nobleman, seating himself negligently upon a tabouret beside her, "I must pray you not to dismiss this worthy man so hastily. You will find him eminently serviceable; and as to his trustworthiness, I have the best reasons for feeling satisfied of it, because I hold in my hand a noose, which, whenever I please, I can tighten round his neck. Of this he is quite aware, and therefore he will serve us faithfully, as well from fear as from gratitude."

"Her ladyship may place entire confidence in me," remarked Luke Hatton, with a grin. "This is not the first affair of the kind in

which I have been engaged. I have prepared potions and powders which Mistress Turner (with whose reputation your ladyship must needs be acquainted) used to vend to her customers. My draughts have removed many a troublesome husband, and silenced many a jealous wife. I have helped many an heir to the speedy enjoyment of an inheritance, which, but for my assistance, would not have come to him for years. The lover with a rival in his way, who has come to me, has soon been freed from all anxiety on that score. The courtier, eager for a post which a superior held, has gained it by my aid. Yet none of those whom I have thus benefited have been suspected. Your ladyship, I repeat, need have no fears of me—and no scruples with me. State your wishes, and they shall be implicitly obeyed."

"I have no wish, except to be relieved of a presence which is disagreeable to me," replied the Countess.

Again Luke Hatton consulted Lord Roos with a regard.

"I find I must act for her ladyship," said the young nobleman. "You will take, therefore, the instructions I shall give you, as proceeding from her. What two names do you find upon that paper?"

"Those of your lordship's wife and mother-in-law," returned Luke Hatton.

"You comprehend what her ladyship would have done with those persons?" said Lord Roos, looking at him steadfastly.

"Perfectly," replied Luke Hatton.

"O, do not give this fatal order, my Lord!" cried Lady Exeter, trembling.

"How many days do you require to effect their removal?" demanded Lord Roos, without appearing to notice her remark.

"I do not require many hours," replied Luke Hatton; "but it will be well not to be too precipitate. Neither must they die at the same time. All precaution shall be taken. The names are placed in a particular order. Is it so the Countess would have them taken? In that case I must commence with Lady Roos."

"Wretch! dost thou dare to make such an appeal to me?" cried Lady Exeter rising. "Begone, instantly, I say. Thou hast no order whatever from me; or if thou fanciest so, I revoke it."

"The order cannot be revoked," cried Lord Roos, grasping her arm. "This is not a time for hesitation or repentance. Having

commenced the work, you must go through with it—whether you will or not."

"Whether I will or not!" exclaimed Lady Exeter, regarding him with angry surprise. "Have I heard you aright, my Lord? Am I to be forced into association in this foul deed? Have I sunk so low in your esteem that you venture to treat me thus?"

"Pardon me, Frances—pardon me!" he cried, imploringly. "I have said more than I intended. If I appear to exercise undue influence over you now, you will forgive me hereafter, because the situation is one that requires decision, and that quality I possess in a higher degree than yourself. Luke Hatton must obey the orders given him. And you must sanction them."

"Never!" she exclaimed, emphatically.

"Then we part for ever," cried Lord Roos. "No matter what the pang may be—nor what befals me—I will go. Farewell for ever, Countess!"

"Stay!" she cried. "We must not part thus."

"Then you consent?" he exclaimed. "Luke Hatton receives his orders from you?"

"Ask me not that question!" she cried, with a shudder.

"If her ladyship will but sign this," said Luke Hatton, holding towards her the paper on which the names were written, "it will suffice for me."

"You hear what he says, Frances. You will do it?" cried Lord Roos. "'Tis but a few strokes of a pen."

"Those few strokes will cost me my soul," she rejoined. "But if it must be so, it must. Give me the pen."

And as Lord Roos complied, she signed the paper.

"Now you may go," said Lord Roos to Luke Hatton, who received the paper with a diabolical grin. "You may count upon your reward."

"In a week's time, my lord," said Luke Hatton, still grinning, and shifting his glance from the half-fainting Countess to the young nobleman; "in a week's time," he repeated, "you will have to put on mourning for your wife—and in a month for your mother-in-law."

And with a cringing bow, and moving with a soft cat-like footstep, he quitted the room, leaving the guilty pair alone together.

END OF VOL. I.